BEAST

## Richard Van Camp titles

ALSO AVAILABLE FROM DOUGLAS & MCINTYRE

*The Lesser Blessed: A Novel*

*Moccasin Square Gardens: Short Stories*

RICHARD VAN CAMP

# BEAST

Douglas & McIntyre

1 2 3 4 5 — 28 27 26 25 24



Douglas and McIntyre (2013) Ltd.
P.O. Box 219, Madeira Park, BC, V0N 2H0
www.douglas-mcintyre.com

Edited by Barbara Pulling and Noel Hudson
Cover illustration by Chief Lady Bird
Cover design by DSGN Dept.
Text design by Libris Simas Ferraz / Onça Publishing
Printed and bound in Canada
Printed on 100% recycled, FSC®-certified paper

Canadä

Douglas and McIntyre acknowledges the support of the Canada Council for the Arts, the Government of Canada, and the Province of British Columbia through the BC Arts Council.

Library and Archives Canada Cataloguing in Publication

Title: Beast : a novel / Richard Van Camp.
Names: Van Camp, Richard, author
Identifiers: Canadiana (print) 20240421574 | Canadiana (ebook) 20240421612 | ISBN 9781771624145 (softcover) | ISBN 9781771624152 (EPUB)
Subjects: CSH: First Nations—Fiction. | LCGFT: Novels.
Classification: LCC PS8593.A5376 B43 2024 | DDC jC813/.54—dc23

*For my dear sweet brother Garth Prosper,*
*with love and respect and admiration.*

# Don't You (Forget About Me)

FOR AS LONG AS I CAN REMEMBER, MY LIFE HAS BEEN ABOUT the treaty: the supposed peace treaty between the Dogrib and the Chipewyan of the Northwest Territories. I grew up hearing about how our ancestors used to be warring tribes, and how it was our duty as Dogrib and Chipewyan families to defend that treaty and never let tribal warfare return.

But I was, like, *Hello, it's 1986, my favourite band is Platinum Blonde, and the new* Savage Sword of Conan *comes out this Wednesday, and I could be watching* The Outsiders *on the Movie Channel.*

Before we lost Mom, my dad, my adopted uncle and I used to—out of Yabati duty—chop wood, split it, stack it, cut kindling and fill the woodbox at the Craneses' house in Indian Village for Lester Cranes, the Chipewyan Elder who claimed that he was a descendant of Akaitcho, the most revered Chipewyan war chief ever. I also had to shovel the Craneses' front and back driveways at forty below with Dad and Uncle Sonny because I was a direct descendant of Edzo, our ancestral Dogrib leader, and so was Sonny. Kind of. I still don't understand how. Every time he'd try to explain it to me, my eyes would cross and my brain would try to leave my body. I remember cutting grass in the summer and being covered in a crawling sweater of mosquitoes and sandflies, but still doing it to show respect to the Cranes family. I was told we did all this to honour the peace treaty.

And there Lester Cranes would be, with his big, long willow stick that he always had with him, scowling at us. With him, sitting out on the porch and watching us work, would be his three sons: Stanley, Cody and Silver, who'd sit with his bent leg propped up. Stanley and Cody would look away in shame at how we were being treated. I could tell they wanted to help but were not allowed. Each time we'd go and take care of their yard, I'd say, "Why do we always go there when they don't even thank us? They don't even smile. Mr. Cranes and Silver just laugh at us. Where is the peace? What do they ever do for us?"

"We do it to honour the treaty," my uncle Sonny would explain each time. "That's who we are as Dogribs. We defend the treaty through acts of service."

Dad would sigh. "Let's just do our best, okay? We gotta honour it, son. You're a Yabati."

I'd roll my eyes. *Yeah, right. I'm free frickin' labour, more like it.* I'd give both Dad and Sonny the invisible stink eye because they were the ones who'd started it and now we were stuck doing it: doomed to repeat this forever times squared, frickin' amen.

I was always surprised that Dad held this peace treaty so high in his heart. He wasn't even Dogrib or Chipewyan, he was a Mountain Dene, but he did this to support Mom and me, who were both Dogrib and descendants of Edzo. I always felt better when Sonny joined because he worked fast and hard. He never said anything to the Craneses when we went there to work, and no words were needed. You could feel a hatred for Sonny rolling off Mr. Cranes, with a little bit left over for me. (Being Mountain Dene, Dad was not on Lester Cranes' enemy list—yet.) We worked hard for the Cranes family every season—on top of our own chores—and I despised every second of it. Dad would always wave goodbye when we were done, and Lester Cranes would look away, spit, and I swear he'd call us dog scum, and Silver would laugh. It was so dumb. I'd shake my head and look down as I returned to the truck with Dad and Sonny. Sonny would put his hand on my shoulder and give it a squeeze.

"What's the Yabati motto?" he'd ask.

"Protect, accept, respect," I'd say with a sigh, "and defend with honour."

"I wish you believed in what we're doing and why we're doing it," Sonny said one day, looking at me with concern in his eyes. "Nephew, why do you think we do this for our Chipewyan neighbours?"

I replied in my Mr. Roboto voice: "We have to honour the treaty to respect our ancestors on both sides that we all lost in our wars. We do this for future generations so tribal warfare will only be a memory."

Dad snorted and shook his head.

"He doesn't believe," Sonny said defeatedly. "I feel like saying the serenity prayer."

"Well, maybe you should, with all your damned drinking," said Dad. He turned his attention to me. "Lawson, trust me, all of this matters."

Dad gave Sonny a serious look, then said, "Tell him."

"A long time ago," Sonny explained, "war was bad. Dogrib and Chipewyan. Holy. 'You ran for your life,' Granny said. 'All the time running,' my ehtsı̨ told me. First they used clubs. Then the Chipewyan got rifles from the traders. A big hunting party, which included Akaitcho's son, went out and never returned. Akaitcho blamed the Dogrib and said it was time to kill every last one of us. They killed many of our people. Both sides had medicine. They used our skulls for fur."

"What?" *Did I hear him correctly?*

Sonny nodded. "The Chipewyan took our scalps and told the fur buyers they were from an animal that lived in the water."

I felt sick.

Dad added, "As brutal as the Chipewyan were to the Dogrib, you can bet the Dogrib were just as brutal in their retaliations. There was blood on everyone's hands. We must always honour the peace treaty between the tribes."

"Horrible," said Sonny. "Lester Cranes still preaches that Edzo used mind-control medicine to trick Akaitcho. Lester was the one who started calling the Dogrib the 'dog scum' people."

"So what happened between Edzo and Akaitcho?" I asked.

Sonny shrugged. "Edzo stole into the Chipewyan camp at Mesa Lake to make the treaty. He had to make peace. Akaitcho was about to declare all-out war on the Dogrib—every last woman, child, dog, man and Elder. He wanted all of us dead for the killing of his son, but Edzo spoke with him. Edzo had lost his son to war, too. And that is where they made peace. The tribes danced together for three days at Mesa Lake. They were so happy. They feasted. They talked."

"Nephew," Sonny said, "even if you don't believe you are a Yabati, we must show the Cranes respect. If we don't honour this treaty between the Dogrib and the Chipewyan, we disrespect everyone who was massacred. Our ancestors made a promise to never let things get that brutal ever again, and it's up to you and other defenders of the treaty to carry that promise forward."

"It's 1986," I said. "Come on. As if war will return!"

"Old hatreds die hard," he said. "Plus, our leaders made a promise, and it's the duty of every Dogrib and every Chipewyan to protect it."

"It'd sure be nice if Silver, Cody and Stanley came by and honoured our home and yours the next time it's forty below out," I replied.

"Yeah, right," said Sonny. "In the meantime, let's keep doing our part, okay?"

"Like I have a choice," I said glumly. I wanted to eat, go home, put on my headphones and listen to both sides of Platinum Blonde's *Standing in the Dark* on my Walkman. Enough with the treaty.

The only good thing about doing chores for the Craneses was that afterwards we'd go for cheeseburgers, fries with gravy, and strawberry milkshakes—Dad's treat. If Sonny was hungover or preparing to go on a bender, he'd ask me how school was and hand me a twenty-dollar bill, which he called a green queen, for school supplies. This always made me happy, as later I'd head to the drugstore and buy Doritos, a Coffee Crisp, a Jolt Cola, batteries for my Walkman and a new album on cassette. I loved music. It took me to anywhere other than Fort Simmer and the Northwest Territories. It took my imagination to a night out in the city, or to soaring over the Earth and making out with cool babes.

Burgers, fries, gravy, milkshakes and coffee arrived.

"Let's pray," said Sonny.

He looked to my dad and held his plate with both hands, lifting it off the table just a little. I never knew what any of the Dogrib that Sonny prayed with meant. I never learned Dogrib.

We had to learn French in school here. It didn't matter if you were Inuit, Métis, Slavey or Yellowknives Dene, we all had to *parlez français* or, we were told, we'd never get into any college or university.

Mom said she'd teach me Dogrib, but she was always busy working at the Friendship Centre—even on nights and weekends.

Sonny slid a green queen across the table as we ate.

"School good?"

"Yup," I said, putting the twenty in my pocket.

"Get yourself some school supplies," Sonny said while Dad looked away and rolled his eyes.

I said, "Mahsi cho," which meant "thank you" in our language.

Sonny was biding his time for a drink. His hands were a little shaky as he ate fry after fry and downed his coffee.

---

THE SAME SUMMER MOM PASSED, SHE TOOK A PILE OF US STUdents out to an island in Tsu Lake to meet and learn from respected Cree Elders Dave and Mary Prince. We all had to write essays saying why we wanted to be part of a back-to-the-land program. Cody came with us as part of his rehabilitation plan with Social Services and the RCMP. The hope, Mom told me, was that if we kept Cody away from his oldest brother, Silver, Cody would go his own way and be who he deserved to be. Next summer, she told me, she wanted to do the same for the middle brother, Stanley.

We all bunked in what they called hunter's tents. They were twelve-by-fourteen canvas tents, and each had a pot-bellied wood stove and two single beds on either side. We were responsible for cutting our own wood and kindling, and for keeping our tent clean. We had a Coleman lantern that we had to maintain as well. During the days, we learned gun safety, chainsaw safety, bush cooking, moosehide tanning, trapping, water safety, boat safety, plant identification and skeet shooting.

We also learned about paying the land—respectful ceremonies offering tobacco or fireweed to the land that you'd perform before going on road trip or boat ride, or when you hunted, especially after your hunt was a success. It was a way of showing respect to Mother Earth and honouring your ancestors and the spirits that guided you in a good way. Mary and Dave also taught us how to speak to the plants, trees, berries and anything we were about to hunt, to share with them the reasons we were taking what we were about to take. They taught us to take only what we needed, and if we were collecting a plant—like yarrow to make salve, for example—and we did not have tobacco for an offering, we could offer some of our own hair instead.

Originally, I was supposed to share Mom's tent, but when no one wanted to bunk with Cody, I offered. Although we weren't close, Cody and I had grown up together. As descendants of Akaitcho and Edzo, it was our duty to deliver food to the Elders at the old folks' home after every Terry Fox Run. We'd joke around and have fun together when we did this, and I was looking forward to catching up with him.

At first Cody didn't want to be there, but Mary took him under her wing from the start, and it didn't take him long to embrace the experience. The two of them would go for medicine walks. Cody had a gift when it came to finding rat root, mint, bear root, white spruce gum, fireweed and tree fungus. While the rest of us worked on the floating dock and sauna, and "spiffied the biffies," Cody and Mary would take their walks and come back with abandoned hornets' nests and plucked geese. Within days, Cody went from having a tough exterior to being funny and charming. Dave, who also acted as bush cook, gave him a homemade slingshot as a gift. Cody was a pretty good shot.

After a few days, Cody began opening up to me about his life. At night he'd pull out the headphones on his Walkman and crank the volume so we could listen to whole albums, like *Purple Rain* and *1999*, and we'd talk. He loved Kate Bush, too.

"But Nena's hotter," he said.

"Who?"

"'99 Luftballons.'"

"Oh yeah," I said. "I could see that. Tie."

"But you know who I have the biggest crush on? You know the video for 'Venus' by Bananarama?"

"Yeah."

"Watch the brunette on the left, like, how she dances. If you watch closely at the beginning, she trips and swears and they all start laughing."

"Are you serious?"

"Totally. But you know who's absolutely gorgeous?"

I was thrilled we were talking about this. I actually started to get the tinglies.

"The lead singer of the Bangles."

"I know, hey?" I said. "'Manic Monday.'"

"Yup, 'Manic Monday' forever. That thing Susanna Hoffs does with her eyes just knocks me out."

"How do you know her name?"

"Don't you read magazines?" he asked. "And I can tell you're shocked that I think women are hot. They are. It's just that men are hotter for me."

I nodded. "I'll be honest," I said. "I am surprised."

"You know who my favourite teacher was and will always be?"

"Mr. Harold!" I said.

"He was the best," Cody smiled.

Every night we'd talk about music, videos, movies. He told me *Porky's* was his all-time fave movie. That shower scene had changed my world forever, with all that glorious nakedness. He told me that he loved seeing all the men's bodies. He also confided in me that he didn't own a thing of his own. Not even his clothes. They were all borrowed or hand-me-downs. All the TV he watched was at his auntie's at the old folks' home. When things got rough at home, he'd sleep over there. He told me he was on his own for food and safety.

"Why does Silver hate the world so much?" I finally asked.

"He feels that he's cursed."

I shook my head. "With his leg?"

He nodded. "Yeah, and his asthma. Mary is going to show me how to make a traditional medicine for his lungs. Maybe that will help. But our dad is still hosting his hate feasts, when he just turns our people against certain families. And Silver listens, and he can be so cruel and ruthless, you know? He does exactly what our dad tells him to, and it's just so sad."

Lester Cranes was always in the paper talking about the Chipewyan, how they weren't getting their fair share of things in town. I was too young to understand the treaties and the land claims and the politics, but he always seemed bitter. The Cranes residence used to be a gathering place for the Chipewyan families in town. They had a microphone and speaker system, and when Mr. Cranes got going on how the Chipewyan were the true leaders of the North, the other Chipewyan families would listen. People said that he would call down the Slavey, the Gwich'in, the Inuit, the Métis, the Bush Cree and, of course, the Dogrib. Then there were those mysterious house fires that started after these meetings targeted certain families, and it was rumoured that Silver and his father started the fires together.

"Silver's asthma," said Cody. "When he gets his asthma attacks, he can't breathe. But when it passes, he goes deep into himself and comes back meaner. Don't ever tell anyone I told you this, okay?"

"You got it," I said. "So how will you . . . escape?"

"Escape?" He sat up. "What do you mean?"

I sat up too, and was careful with my words. "How will you escape to be the real you?"

"The real me?" He put his war face on. "How do you mean? Being gay?"

"Not that," I said. "I see you so happy here, collecting medicine, learning, helping out. You don't have to be who your family says you need to be."

"And you can stop being your mom's son."

"What?"

"I see how close you are. You think I don't know no one else wanted to bunk with me?"

"Cody," I tried, "I think this is also about honouring the treaty."

"The treaty . . ." Cody said. This was the first time he'd ever really said anything about it. "You know, I heard this Elder say a long time ago that life was hard. It was tough. You trapped and hunted and fished all year, and when the fur buyers came, you'd see your friends who'd been gone for months in the bush. They'd place their hands on each other's shoulders and say, 'So you're still alive.' That's how we used to greet each other. Can you imagine being gone for months, surviving with your family on the land? Imagine war on top of that, where your family is being attacked—and the raids and the killing."

"We can't break the treaty," I said. "We're supposed to be walking together side by side."

"Silver's convinced we have to beat the Dogrib, the Slavey, the Inuit, that we have to be the best, the strongest, the most brutal."

"But what if we just all help each other?" I asked.

"I like that, but that's not his way."

"My folks call me a Yabati, which means 'protector' in Dogrib. How do you say 'protector' in Chipewyan?"

"Dene Sorulthen," Cody said. "My mom taught me that."

"Dene Sorulthen," I repeated. "That sounds so ancient."

"So does Yabati," he said.

We were quiet for a while.

"I want my brother's love," he said quietly.

It was the first time I had ever heard somebody's soul wish.

I nodded. "Then I hope you get it." *But is Silver capable of love?* I wondered.

He shook his head. "He calls me his AIDS brother. He soaks all of my dishes with bleach. And in our town, you're remembered in one of three ways: you're either a good man, full of BS or a gaylord. I think we both know how I'll be remembered."

"So change."

"From being gay?" he asked with an edge.

"No," I said. "Why did you have to break into the elementary school?"

"Yeah," he said. "That was dumb. I got drunk and the next thing I knew, we'd destroyed the school."

I was quiet and hoped he'd say more. I was so surprised that he'd had a hand in the vandalism.

"Even the way people say my name in town," he continued. "I can feel their pity and their hate. I just feel that by being gay . . . I've shamed our family even more."

"Take it easy," I said. "You are who you are."

"I got expelled, Lawson," he said. "When you're born a Cranes, it's like you're born . . . with less. You'd think with all the family pride Stanley commands with his sports, Lester would be happy, but oh no, Silver's long silver hair was our hope. Lester said that when a child is born with silver hair, they've been here before, that they're reincarnated, and they, in this lifetime, are supposed to be a shaman or a prophet. But Silver's not. He's just angry and bitter like our dad."

*I wonder why he calls his dad Lester.*

"I'm on your side," I said. "Cody, I'll never fight you, I promise. Side by side, remember? I'm here to help. We all are. Be the medicine your family needs."

Despite himself, he started smiling. "I like that."

I was surprised by what I'd said. Where do my words come from? How come my spirit suddenly speaks? Mom was famous for that. She'd blurt the truth, and it was always surprising how it would come out. I didn't know what to say next.

"What's the sexiest man video?" I asked.

"That's easy," he said. "'Rain,' by the Cult."

"Really?"

"Ian Astbury is a god. That hair. Those lips. Have you seen how many times he licks that microphone?"

This conversation felt luxurious and dangerous. I felt so giddy from this kind of connection.

"You know, Cody," I said, "I think you are at your freest when you're dancing. I love watching you dance. We all do. I honestly think you're going to have the most amazing life of us all."

He smiled. "Thank you. I'd hug you but I have a half chub."

I laughed, shocked. He put his arms up and mimicked a hug.

I put my arms up in the air, as well. "Spiritual hug."

A bird-like whistle sounded through the trees.

"Gotta go," he said.

I watched him as he stood up and started getting dressed. He was slender with broad shoulders. He'd been wearing track pants and a muscle shirt. He pulled on a long-sleeved shirt that he'd hung on a nail. He checked his face and hair in a small mirror we had set up for brushing our teeth.

"What was that sound?"

"My Scout." He winked.

There was a camp for Beavers, Scouts and Venturers on the other side of the island.

"Tell no one about this," Cody said. "Keep it on the keemooch—that's Cree for 'on the sneak.'"

"Deal," I nodded.

"Lawson," he said, looking serious. "I haven't told you my biggest secret yet, but I will before we head back to town, okay? Just in case anything happens?"

"Okay," I said, concerned. I wasn't sure what he meant.

He pulled on his runners and left quietly.

# Mother Stands for Comfort

TO MY HORROR, THE NEXT MORNING WHILE WE WERE SWIMMING, someone wrote FAG AIDS TENT with charcoal on the side of our tent. My mom wanted it washed off, but Cody said no—this was a reminder of how ignorant the entire camp and town were.

"Leave it up," he said. "Welcome to my life."

My mom was furious. So was I.

Some of the students looked down at their shoes while others looked around.

"I'm so sorry, Cody," I said.

"Well," he said with a sigh, "now you know what boys like me are up against."

Every day my respect for Cody deepened as he and Mary vanished into the bush to gather more medicines for town. Every night we talked and played our newly invented game, "oh my god I totally know what turns you on." At Tsu Lake, nighttime couldn't come fast enough.

On the last night, around our sacred fire exercise, Mom shared a story I still think about all the time.

"Life," Mom said, "is about respect, saying yes to good things, and gratitude." She looked at all of us. Cody leaned against me. He was tired. He had snuck back from his visit with his Scout at around five that morning. "We need to talk about įk'ǫǫ̀, or 'medicine power' as we call it," she continued. "All of you walk in two worlds now." She looked at me and smiled. "Lawson does. Cody does."

I sounded out the word in my head. *Inkwo.*

She came to us and placed her hands on our shoulders. "I am happy and proud that my son sits with Cody Cranes. Cody is a descendant of Akaitcho, the great Chipewyan war chief, through his mother, Therese. My son is a descendant of the great Dogrib war chief Edzo, through me. A friendship treaty was born despite war, despite hunting one another, despite rage and hate. It makes me happy to hear my son laughing at night in the tent he shares with Cody. We are living side by side, as our ancestors wanted. Our peace treaty is nezį. Good. And it is a treaty of forgiveness and helping one another. Our treaty with each other is a treaty of hope that others can learn from, and we need to protect and honour that. Mahsi."

*Nezi.*

She motioned for Cody to stand, and he did. Handsome Cody. She hugged him close. "To see Cody and Lawson together as friends is all the proof I need to trust in our ancestors' plan and know that they only wanted the best for us together in peace. May we all learn to live together in peace. Sigha naxixè welè."

I'd never heard her say this before and wanted to ask what it meant, but Cody raised his hand. Mom was surprised, as Cody rarely spoke during the camp gatherings.

"Auntie," he said, "can you tell us the story of how the Dogrib came to be?"

Mom smiled and nodded. "I will. A long time ago, when the world was new, the people travelled together. They had to follow the animals. Medicine power—įk'ǫǫ̀—helped the people. They say one of the women gave birth to six puppies and was banished because the leaders—the men—feared her power. She was fine, she was happy and she did her best to raise her puppies as her babies. One day she caught them playing as human children. Three of the five babies never turned back into puppies. Those three were the first Dogrib Dene. We are their descendants."

The students all got quiet and looked into the fire.

"Thank you. Mahsi," said Cody thoughtfully. "Does every family have medicine power?"

"In their own way. Yes." she nodded.

"Can you lose it?" he asked.

"Those who drink alcohol lose it." She thought about it some more. "Or when you talk or brag about it. If you have įk'ǫǫ̀ or are being offered įk'ǫǫ̀, don't ever tell anyone, okay? It is a precious gift that is not to be spoken or bragged about."

Dave and Mary Prince approached the fire with their three helpers, who brought fresh bannock, jam and butter. They also had Labrador tea.

Mom pulled Cody and me close and gave us a squeeze.

"My boys, promise me that no matter what, you two will always protect each other."

"Deal," Cody said and held his hand out. "Side by side. In peace."

"Promise," I said, shaking his hand.

"Bless the Dene Sorulthen," I said and nodded.

He nodded back. "Bless the Yabati."

She patted our shoulders twice. "Nezį. Good. Let's eat."

---

IT WAS OUR LAST NIGHT AT TSU LAKE. CODY AND I LAY IN OUR beds.

"Lawson," he said, "I have something to tell you. And this is between you and me, okay?"

"Okay," I said.

"I'm afraid of Silver. Like, really afraid. When we were kids, he was always sneaky and really into dark stuff, like the Ouija board and making offerings to beings no one worshipped anymore."

I nodded. Mom said to never have anything to do with the Ouija board. There was a reason we closed the curtains as soon as it got dark out. We never wanted spirits looking into our homes.

"I remember hearing my folks talk one night," Cody said. "As proud as they are of Stanley as an athlete, they were convinced Silver was reincarnated or a shaman because of that streak of silver hair he has. For us, it's a sign of reincarnation. Lester thought if one of his sons was a shaman it would make us royalty, that people would have more respect for us. I remember Mom warning him that not all of the spirits out on the land are kind. But Lester was convinced that Silver would lead our family in a new way.

"Lester kept taking Silver out to the bush and leaving him there. Silver never had to do chores like the rest of us. He was revered. They wouldn't let anyone touch his hair or his head. Lester kept taking him to the bush and leaving him overnight, kept taking him, kept taking him. Stanley and I were worried. Mom was so worried too. She thought Silver was too young to be left alone, but Lester insisted. Silver started to fast. He started to bury himself out there. He said something was waiting. Lester was pleased.

"Then one day, Silver came back and said nothing had happened, no one had spoken to him, but, you know, I didn't trust him. I remember that day. It was the most beautiful day, and the second he came out of the truck, I had a thought: He's changed. There was something wrong with his eyes. They were so cold. So mean.

"As time went on, Silver started to hurt us. There were always accidents. My parents put locks on his door so he couldn't sneak out at night, but then we'd hear him talking to someone. I remember one day he told us to put locks on the inside, too, so that the Dead One who came to him out on the land couldn't come inside our home."

I felt cold. Instantly cold. "Holy, Cody," I said. I was freezing. "The Dead One?"

He nodded. "I think Silver made a deal with it for power, and now it's commanding him, demanding that he do things. Horrible things. I can only do so much to protect Stanley, but I think I'm next on Silver's hurt list."

"Jesus," I said. "So what's your plan?"

"Your mom and I made a promise, and we need you to honour it, too. If I run away, you have to do your best to save Stanley, okay?"

"Okay." I nodded, confused.

Cody looked worried. "Can you please try to get Stanley away from Silver? I've tried to protect him, but Silver's mean to him." He shook his head. "I really do feel that my life's in danger sometimes. Silver sets up these things for me to do, and there are always these near misses."

I winced at hearing this. I had no idea things were so sad and dangerous at the Craneses' house.

"So if you ran away, where would you go?"

"Edmonton," he said.

"Why Edmonton?" I asked. "You need money for the city. Who'd take care of you?"

"I have a different dad than Silver and Stanley," he said.

"Seriously?" I had no idea.

"You can never tell anyone about this, okay? I'm telling you because you're a Yabati."

"I swear on my mother, Cody. I won't tell anyone."

He nodded. "Our mom left Lester a long time ago, after she met someone else. She spent a summer with that guy in Edmonton, and that's when I was conceived. Lester came down and brought her back, knowing I was not his son. That's why he's always hated me. And I think he told Silver even though he swore to Mom he'd never tell anyone and that he'd raise me as his own. But everyone could tell I was not his son by the time I was eight. That's why I don't call him Dad."

I let my breath all the way out. "Holy, Cody."

"Yeah," he said. "So my real dad has told me that I'm always welcome in Edmonton with my other family. I have three sisters. Sisters. Can you imagine?" He smiled with tears in his eyes. "My real dad runs sweat lodges and the sun dance. That's where I belong—in ceremony, where people like me are honoured."

"Cody," I said, filled with hope for him and his future, "you have to go. You've got to get away from here."

"Find a way to stop Silver if you can." He shook his head. "If I ever vanish from town, I'll call you when I'm settled."

He looked at me again, this time with worried eyes. "I'm scared of Silver. I feel cold in our house sometimes even with the wood stove cranked. I think he's called something back into the world that shouldn't be here. He's got this jar filled with dying things: mice, bugs, minnows. He huffs it. I can hear him breathing into it, inhaling it. And then he trances out. If I start to feel like Silver is going to hurt or kill me, I'm gone."

*Gross*, I thought. "Okay. Call me."

"I don't know if I can call. What if he hears me?"

"Hears you?"

"There's so much you don't know."

"So tell me," I said.

"Look," he said, "whatever you do—no matter what happens—don't break that treaty. Silver's counting on you to break it. If you do, you'll give him permission to start the war that he and Lester have always wanted. I know it's what this thing—this Dead One—wants, too."

"I promise. On my mother. On our ancestors. I promise. Why would I break it?"

"There's one more thing I have to tell you, Lawson, but I'm worried you won't believe me."

*Oh frick*. "What?"

"I get the sense sometimes that Silver can tell what I'm thinking. I think Silver can read minds now because of the Dead One."

I shook my head. "That's impossible."

"I hope I'm wrong," he said, "but a few times I've caught him watching me, and it's like he's always two steps ahead of me."

Cody said something next that I would never forget: "Medicine power was here long before Jesus. It'll be here after the world is gone. Nothing is impossible."

—

MOM WAS HELPING ME PACK TO LEAVE TSU LAKE THE NEXT day when a chickadee called out behind our tent: *chickadee-dee-dee*. Mom started to chuckle.

"What?" I asked.

"You're growing so fast, my boy," she said.

I nodded. I'd been hearing that a lot lately: from Dad, from Mom, from Sonny.

"Have you had any medicine dreams yet?" she asked me.

I looked at her. "Nope. I don't think so. How would I know if I had one?"

"Oh, you'd know," she said. "Remember what I told you. Now that your voice is changing, things will come to you."

I frowned. "Things? What things?"

"Medicine dreams. Remember, medicine can come to you—"

"—In a dream, from a person, an animal," I said. I slowed my voice down to sound like an old Dene Elder. "You always have to be ready, my boy. You always have to be ready. Medicine can come to you at any time."

She looked at me, surprised that I'd been paying attention.

"I listen, Mom. I do." I stood up and pretended to be her. "And always call everyone honoured guests, and always bring food and gifts."

She started laughing. "There's no way I sound like that."

I sat down and decided to cool it with being cheeky.

"So why are you heading to Rae tomorrow?" I asked.

"The Friendship Centre in Rae has funding they need to spend," she said. "We get to teach there what we've just taught here, and I arranged to bring Stanley Cranes with me."

"Stanley?" I asked. "Why?"

"We need to keep him away from Silver as much as possible," she said. "Something's not right in that house and we need to protect him."

She took out her caribou medicine bag. It was full of fresh fireweed.

"Look at this," Mom said proudly. "Cody and I went for a medicine walk today and he showed me how to harvest fireweed. Did you know that a long time ago we used to use fireweed as tobacco? We could also mix it with grease and make a salve."

She let me smell the bag. Oh, it smelled so good.

"It's yours," she said.

"What?" I said, surprised and pleased. The caribou hide was so soft.

"My boy," she said, "I want you to know that Cody and I have worked on something for you. I pray you'll never need it."

I blew my breath to lift the bird feathers that decorated the top of the bag. "What is it?"

"Cody and I gathered fireweed and made a promise to protect you."

I smiled. "Really? Mahsi cho." Then I paused. "Wait. Protect me from what?"

"I hope you never know," she said.

"Okay." I shrugged, confused.

"I love you," she said, and hugged me. "I am so proud to be your mom."

I hugged her back. "I love you too. And I am so proud to be your son."

Looking back, I am so grateful I got to tell her that, because a week to the day after we shared that hug, she was gone.

---

BY THE END OF THOSE THREE WEEKS OUT ON THE LAND together, I felt like Cody and I were true friends. We came back tanned and freckled, our shoulders peeling from sunburn, all of our clothes smoky and drenched with the smells of various bug sprays. The Twin Otter arrived to take us back to town as Dave Prince and I were taking the canvas off the kitchen tent. He handed me a homemade slingshot similar to the one he had given Cody and patted my shoulder.

"Thanks for being there for Cody. He has his own medicine, that one," he said and pointed with his lips to where Cody was helping to roll up the canvas tents.

The slingshot was awesome. It was wrapped in so much tape that it felt spongy but firm. It had a grip, and it was so centred that you would hardly ever miss if you even half tried to aim.

"Mahsi cho, Uncle." I smiled and shook his hand. "Wait. Cody has his own medicine?"

Dave touched his thumbs together and used his fingers to flap like wings. "He's a healer."

I watched Cody with awe.

"That Silver is trouble," Dave said. "He's always wanted to be the boss of those brothers, but you know who would make a great war chief out of all those brothers?"

"Stanley?" I asked.

He nodded. "You bet. I would never want to see that boy angry. It's a good thing he's found his way through sports. Imagine him on the battlefield."

Stanley was fierce when he competed. That was the reason half the town showed up to watch him: no hesitation, just pure determination—though he had a temper just like his dad, just like Silver. Heaven help you if you ever hurt any of his teammates. Play fair and everyone would do just fine. Break the rules and "the Arm" would get you.

"You know," Dave said, "my grandparents told me about how bad things used to be with the Dogrib and the Chipewyan." He clicked his tongue and shook his head. "When they were children, they came across a camp that the Dogrib or the Chipewyan had discovered. Their parents told them to look away, but of course they peeked. There was blood everywhere. Was it Dogrib or Chipewyan bodies face down? You could see some had tried to run. Even the dogs had been killed." He squeezed my shoulder. "Keep protecting each other. Remember the treaty, because it wasn't just the Dogrib and Chipewyan who made peace. Your treaty set an example for other tribes and many families about what's most important: sharing what you have and living in peace."

While Mom and the other kids and instructors loaded up the plane, Mary stood with Cody down at the beach. Mary held a large red pillowcase stuffed with something. Pamper moss? Hornets' nests? Fungus? Rat root? I wish I had taken a picture. Cody had jars of goose grease mixed with something—maybe ground hornets' nests or fireweed or yarrow. Mary spoke with Cody, who nodded and smiled. When she was done speaking with him, it looked like he was making a promise. She hugged him and held him tight.

"Mary said that Cody has a gift she's only ever seen once before," Dave said, nodding. "Everyone says that Stanley is the hope of that family. It's actually that one." He pointed with his lips to Cody again before lighting a hand-rolled smoke.

I smiled. "Did Mary tell him that?"

"I believe so," Dave said, and then he looked at me. "It's nice to see the descendants of Akaitcho and Edzo as friends."

When we arrived back at the dock at Four Mile Lake in the Twin Otter, Silver was waiting. I held the caribou medicine bag Mom had given me and watched Cody as he ran to Silver with the jars of goose grease and the medicine in that red pillowcase. He started speaking, offering Silver the jars and the medicine, but Silver slapped him hard and yelled at him. "Get your faggot AIDS hands away from me!" Silver threw all the jars in the water. My jaw dropped. So did everyone else's. I could see Stanley the giant pacing on the shore.

Cody never looked back at us. But I looked at Silver with such hatred, my face burning, my hands not knowing what to do. None of us, out of fear of Silver, knew what to do.

It wasn't just me. Our whole town was afraid of him.

# Sledgehammer

DAD HAD A BRUCE LEE BUILD, AND HE WAS HIS OWN KIND OF handsome. He had wide cheekbones and a long nose. He had nice teeth and a kind smile, but his eyes seemed to keep you at a distance. He was smart, always reading the room. You could feel him scanning—he was always processing something. He met my mom through basketball. He can't really see without his glasses, but during basketball tournaments he'd sometimes just whip them off, give 'er down the court and shoot like crazy. It was that blind courage that caught Mom's sweet eye.

"Hey, Mr. Serious," she called out to him after a game. "How can you see the net when you're squinting so hard?"

He just shrugged as he put his glasses back on, looked at her and beamed. "I squint, pray and do my best. But I sure am glad I can see you. Hello!"

And that was how their romance started.

Because of all the teasing he'd suffered due to his squinting, he took boxing when he was a teenager and he never backed down from a fight. He drove a few people into tomorrow with what he called "the Kiss of the Dene Hawk."

My pops worked at the federal building as a bookkeeper during the day and helped people in town with their taxes, but after Mom passed he also signed up to be a server at the Legion and at Moccasin Square Gardens to get out of the house. He was also the best bingo caller in town, so he was requested for fundraisers and full-on bonanzas. Basically, if you wanted to know where my dad was, all you had to do was watch the community channel and track the bingos and dances on TV. The only thing about this was that I always worried my dad would end up in a brawl. Before the accident, my dad had knocked out Sonny Nets with one punch from the Dene Hawk for saying something to Mom at the Legion.

"What happened?" I remember asking him when he came home with a towel wrapped around his fist.

"Some people shouldn't drink," Mom said as she plucked some dried yarrow that had been hanging on strings from the ceiling. "Sonny Nets is one of them."

Dad put on water to boil and reached for a jar of bear grease in the fridge before Mom shooed him away. Dad sat down.

"That mouth of his is just gonna keep getting him stretched out until he sobers up," he said.

Sonny and my dad had to apologize at the Legion and shake hands in front of all the veterans and management or be barred for life—and nobody wanted that.

After Sonny's second wife left him, he showed up at our house with a big pot of moose nose soup that he'd made all by himself. You could smell the spuds, onions and carrots. He even brought his lucky salt shaker. Well, how could Mom and Dad turn him away? It was a Fort Simmer delicacy that had ended many grudges. It was crunchy and good. The cartilage popped in my mouth. It was kind of like caribou tongue. He also made blueberry bannock, pan-fried in a cast iron skillet.

"In bear grease?" Mom asked him, smiling despite herself.

"I know that's how you like it," he said. "I am sorry for what I said, Roberta. I am so, so sorry."

Mom nodded, got up and hugged him. "Thank you, Sonny."

Dad stood up and shook Sonny's hand, and they hugged too.

Sonny then looked at me, and I looked to Mom and Dad, and they nodded.

I stood up and shook his hand. He hugged me. That was also the night he called me nephew.

"Nephew, we are Dogribs. You know what that means? We have six times the national average of digestive enzymes in our stomachs. We can eat what most can't and thrive. We also have six times the natural reflexes of any race. That is the power of our ancestors."

"Wow," I said.

Dad rolled his eyes, but Mom shushed him.

Sonny continued: "You know we come from a woman who gave birth to six pups, hey? You know we are half spirit and more than human when we need to be, and that we can call on her when the chips are down. Don't worry about Jesus, Mary and Joseph. They're more than busy. But our mother"—he waved his hand parallel to the ground—"our mother is always ready to help her children. Heh eh." He nodded. "Nezį."

"Nezį," Mom said. "Good."

After that forgiveness feast, we started having supper with him now and then, but he'd always show up with Tupperware and leave with all our leftovers. When Sonny drank, my dad would have nothing to do with him. When he was sober, they were like brothers. They'd go skidooing together in the winter, and they'd go moose hunting in the fall. If we missed Sonny when he stopped by, he'd set up the firepit in the backyard with twigs, old man's beard and sticks so Dad would only have to drop a match in, and it would light every time.

When my dad's heart was hurting, he'd go to Sonny's garage (a.k.a. the Wallow Pit) and play Elvis hymns on a record player or with Sonny's guitar, and they'd sing for hours, leaning on an old piano that Sonny had won in a card game. They called it a singing. It was kind of like an unofficial Alcoholics Anonymous meeting. Other men driving by would see their trucks and mosey on in, joining them in chorus before starting a backyard cookout. Dad always had a gruff voice the next morning, but there was an ease about him. Sometimes he smelled like cigarettes and woodsmoke. That fellowship was why our freezer was always full. We had caribou, buffalo, bison, pickerel, moose, duck, whitefish—even muskox. People who attended Sonny's singings showed their gratitude all the time, and when they had extra food, they'd share it. When we had too much, we dropped some off at the old folks' home. Dad let me drive the Green Death when we did that, and I loved it. I had my learner's.

As far as I know, Sonny and my dad never talked about the punch again—not even to joke about it.

---

DAD LOOKED AT THE COMMUNITY ANNOUNCEMENTS IN THE paper and shook his head. He had a fresh haircut and was looking pretty sharp.

"Still no word on when the school will open."

"Nothing?" I asked.

Paul William Secondary had big tarps around the entrance. A team of asbestos removal workers from the south were up with huge white vans, and we were all waiting to hear when school would reopen.

For my final year, grade twelve, I would have physics, art, social studies, gym, math and bio. Every day on my timetable would be a variation of the same routine, but I had double art on Friday afternoons. It was rad that I finally had spares, too.

"Okay," he said, "if you're ever bored out of your tree, you can join us for a singing. And you know you can always talk to me, hey?"

I motioned to Dad's new haircut. "Did you burn your hair yet?" Whenever we used to go for haircuts, we had this tradition of burning our old hair in the firepit in our backyard. That's what I did with a bit of Mom's hair after the funeral. We did this so our enemies couldn't take a single strand to use for bad medicine. We did the same thing with our nail clippings, but we usually just threw those in the fireplace.

He looked at me, surprised. "I took care of it."

I would have seen him in action if he had done it in our backyard firepit.

"You took care of it?" I frowned. "Where?"

"Don't worry about it, Junior. Poppa Bear took care of it."

I shrugged and took him at his word. Maybe he'd done it at Sonny's.

It was then suddenly and strangely quiet. We'd actually run out of things to talk about. He drummed his fingers on the table and cleared his throat. He leaned back to check the time on the clock, and I remembered something I'd been meaning to ask him.

"Hey, did you get the truck's tape player fixed?"

"You bet." He grinned. "Benji really souped it up. You should hear how loud she gets now."

The Green Death, Dad's green truck—which should have died years ago—had the second-loudest sound system in town, after Sonny's truck. At his singings, Dad would sometimes crank open both doors and turn up his cassette player. You could just sing along to whatever song he wanted you to learn.

I was allowed to take the truck when Dad wanted me to get the pot-bellied wood stove in Sonny's garage going before the singings. I'd crank "Taking My Chances" by the Outfield and "Shout" by Devo. I often listened to Kate Bush's "Hello Earth" when I was alone, because I always felt like it was Mom and her guardian angels singing down to me. I loved "Cars" by Gary Numan, Bronski Beat's "Smalltown Boy," Duran Duran's "Save a Prayer," and Billy Idol's "Rebel Yell." I loved just about anything that could pull me out of my head and out of Fort Simmer.

---

THE LAST TWO YEARS HAD BEEN HARD. TRULY HARD. ALONE hard. Brutal hard. Loner hard. I hadn't gone swimming since the accident, and Dad and I no longer visited the graveyard together. In fact, I didn't go at all anymore. To go would have been to accept, and I still wasn't ready.

People wonder what this kind of grief is. She was gone. My mother was gone. The church couldn't help me. God couldn't help me. Friends, family, cards, flowers, food left on our porch—it was all in the way of my bed and headphones. I was numb and I was alone.

After we lost Mom, I slept for a year and mumbled in my sleep. So did my dad. He forgot things. I'd come home and find the house keys still in the lock. Sometimes the Green Death would still be running. He lost four pairs of gloves that first winter. I lost two. I had to keep telling him to change his clothes. He kept showing up for breakfast wearing the same shirt, the same pants. With this kind of grief, you're just tired all the time. It's like trying to walk with an elephant standing on your shoulders. You have to learn to think through a soup. My grief came in waves and landslides. I'd be fine in class, only to sag in the hallway en route to my locker. I used that small shelf in my locker to hold myself up, pull myself up, many times.

My bed became my island. I still slept in Mom's sleeping bag that she took to the bush for all those winter and summer culture camps at Tsu Lake. It was returned to us after they found her body. Her sleeping bag smells like her—or maybe that's just grief memory—and I use her scratchy Hudson's Bay blanket because it has three long strands of her hair in the fabric. I touch them every night before I go to sleep. They look like spiderwebs now. I felt guilty about keeping them for myself instead of burning them, but I wasn't ready to let them go.

Then there's Mom's spice rack. We don't use it. To take anything left of the spices, to me, feels like I'm spilling out her ashes. Her cookbooks with her notes and her lovely handwriting in the margins. My heart aches every time I look at them.

Thank God I had drafting last year. I focused on lines, lines, lines. Those I could control. Thank God for music. Thank God for Corey Hart's "Sunglasses at Night." Thank God for Whitesnake and Iron Maiden and Metallica. Kate Bush's "Running up That Hill" was my get-up-and-go anthem in the morning whenever I had to hurry to get to school on time.

Because Mom passed away on the job, it was ruled a workplace accident. There was a settlement, and Dad gave me half. It's thousands. We had to set up a bank account. I have enough to go to college or university. I don't spend much.

I think my grief is also what made me such a good cook. Dad just didn't have it in him. All the food we received—it would just keep coming from family and friends: duck, fish, caribou, moose.

It was up to me to take care of Dad, and I learned that no matter what was happening, if you could focus on cooking, an hour would pass by and then you could just dive into a great meal. You had to eat. And we often ate without a word, just country playing on the radio.

I remember one time Sonny came over with an uncooked moose roast. Dad and I were in a daze. It was early, before lunch. Sonny took one look at us and went to work. He seared the roast in butter after he patted it down all over with a dry rub of onion soup mix. He then sliced and diced carrots, onions and celery, and added a major sprinkling of pepper and salt. He fished around, found some chicken stock and added that to the Crock-Pot, which we hadn't used since Mom passed. He turned it on low for the day.

"Take it easy, boys," he said and closed the door behind him.

It was Mom's recipe and the house smelled like her cooking. Dad and I watched TV. I couldn't even tell you what was on. Then, at four that afternoon, Sonny returned with spuds and a two-litre of ginger ale, some grenadine, orange juice, and a big bag of ice. He mixed us some Shirley Temples as he sliced the spuds, which he added to the Crock-Pot that smelled so good.

He sat with us in the basement and watched TV for a bit before going upstairs to do our old dishes and tidy up. Then he set the table and called us for supper.

It was the best meal we'd had in such a long while. He insisted on doing those dishes, too, and he even vacuumed as Dad and I went back downstairs.

When he was done, he came over and hugged my dad, then hugged me.

"Have a good sleep," he told us both and vanished into the night.

"Mahsi cho," my dad said. I could hear it in his voice: his love, his whole light had been stolen. Mom was gone and this was the day we couldn't pretend or wish it away anymore. She was gone, and Sonny was there when we didn't realize how much we needed him.

# Silent Running

A WARM LATE-SUMMER DAY FOR THE ANNUAL NWT TERRY FOX Run. The first time I really left my cocoon since Mom's accident. She admired Terry Fox, and I wanted to honour them both that day. Fort Simmer was raising money for folks fighting cancer, and we were doing our best to raise more money than the folks in Hay River, Fort Smith and Yellowknife because that's what we do: we compete.

To my surprise, Uncle Sonny strutted onto the small stage outside the Northern Store as the day's emcee with a huge honkin' purple hickey on his neck. He was wearing a moosehide vest with a nice white long-sleeved shirt and nice pants—probably from the Northern Store—and moccasins with moccasin rubbers. He was tall, like me, five foot nine, and he still used Brylcreem in his hair. His nose, however, told the story of the few fights he'd lost, and he had a deep scar under his left eye that I had always meant to ask about. Actually, as Sonny turned to speak to us, I saw a cluster of hickeys on the other side, under his jaw. *Holy geez, Uncle, all those passion bruises.* That's what the townies called them.

Uncle Sonny took the microphone. There were about two hundred of us, and it was going to be a deadly awesome day.

"Ladies and gentlemen, my friends, cousins, and everyone I owe money to, welcome to the 1986 Terry Fox Run. Today we honour the life and legacy of a Canadian hero, Mr. Terry Fox, who united this country through his courage and through a strength that most of us hope to have when we need it most. I still can't believe this brave young man began his journey of courage at the age of eighteen—" Sonny stopped and covered his eyes for a second. The crowd hushed. Was he going to cry? "Sorry," he said. "As a father, I can imagine his family's worry for him." He stopped again and looked up to the sky as if to gather strength. The crowd grew silent. I didn't know the whole story, but Sonny had lost his sons in a house fire when I was a kid, and it was just so brutally tragic.

"Now," he continued, "if you look up and to the left, to where I'm pointing, you'll see Halley's Comet, which will be soaring above us tonight."

We all looked and, sure enough, there was the ghostly outline of something far away in the sky. Maybe I was imagining it, but I could see something.

"Can I ask everyone to wave at our runaway cousin?"

We all waved at Halley's Comet.

"CBC was saying that our cousin in the sky will return every seventy-five years. That means that the next time our friend returns will be the year 2061. Now, as you know, we are a quadrilingual town, but we have, what, eleven official languages in the North? I think it's more than that, so who here knows how to say 'Venus' in Bush Cree?"

"Ogeenanz!" an Elder to my right yelled out.

"Ogeenanz," we all repeated.

Sonny nodded and smiled. "Thank you, Auntie."

Sonny then looked at me and to where Cody should have been standing. He stopped smiling. "Nephew," he asked me, "how do you say 'northern lights' in Dogrib?"

"Naka," I said, blushing.

"Naka," everyone echoed.

He nodded and gave me a quick, puzzled look. He was probably wondering where Cody was. The two of us had to honour the treaty right after the run. The Elders would be waiting for the food we were to bring together to the old folks' home. This was the Yabati and Dene Sorulthen tradition.

I shrugged. *I don't know.*

He again pointed at the comet. "Okay, so in seventy-five years, when our cousin in the sky returns, will we as Dene still continue our traditions?"

"Yes!" we cheered.

"Will we still be speaking our languages?

"Yes!" we cheered.

"Will we still be honouring Terry Fox?"

"Yes!" we cheered.

"And will the most beautiful women and the handsomest men still come from Fort Simmer, Northwest Territories?"

"Yes!" we all cheered and started laughing.

"Okay." He clapped his hands. "Follow me in my muffaloose-powered hot rod. Volunteers in blue shirts have water and snack stations set up along the route. Hydrate, pray for strength, and mahsi cho for honouring Terry Fox and his family and for anyone fighting cancer today. Let's raise funds together for those in need. Mahsi!"

As Sonny smiled, bowed to our applause and waved before leaving the stage, I heard a man say to his friend next to me, "That guy should be our mayor."

"Too bad he's such a sad drunk," the other replied.

And that was it: that was the classic Fort Simmer sting.

We could be so brutal to each other and so sweet at the same time.

We all went to the starting line and, as the mayor raised his starter's pistol, I saw Sonny give a tourist a wink—a brunette—and she blushed. She was pretty, wearing a shawl, jeans and sandals. Lots of freckles and, sure enough, she was sporting a hickey, too. A few of them. They must have had a wild night together. Sonny was always on the keemooch. His prowess came and went in the crests and troughs of his drinking.

This year's Terry Fox Run started downtown by the drugstore and the Legion. We hoofed it down McDonnell, our main drag, took a right at the big brown house onto Fox Drive at the welfare centre, then all the way down Robin Avenue. Our high school was surrounded by big trucks and workers in space suits. They were removing asbestos from the walls and ceilings. I think only Jesus, Mary and Joseph knew when school would start.

We made our way by Panty Point to the banks, then began our return. I was relieved that our route was one street away from the graveyard. *Not today, Mom,* I thought. *Sorry, but I just can't visit you right now. It still hurts too much. I hope you can forgive me.*

To run with two hundred townies that day actually felt good. And I needed Sonny's motivational speech. I needed to be reminded what a jewel our town was. As I looked at the water tower with the huge FORT SIMMER painted on it, and the huge Roman Catholic church downtown, I could smell the river and I knew I was home. I was Dogrib. Our relatives lived thirteen hours up the road in Fort Rae and Edzo, but I didn't know them at all. Simmer was where I was born and raised. I loved it here because when you grieved Fort Simmer grieved with you. We were the hickey capital of Canada. We were the nickname capital of Canada. We were a truck town, a tough town, a rugged beauty of a town. We were the beginning of Highway 5, where everyone listens to the *Saturday Night Request Show* on CBC North and watches *Night Tracks, Fraggle Rock* and *Good Rockin' Tonight* with Stu Jeffries.

Our official town mascot was the muffaloose. Fort Smith will tell you that they thought of it first, but the truth is we did. Every few years, someone claims they have seen one. A muffaloose is half buffalo and half moose. On every muffaloose T-shirt, the animal has a goofy big-toothed grin. The muffaloose that Benji and the mechanics had mounted front and centre on the hood of Sonny's black '49 Ford F1 had a focused snarl. I loved Sonny's hot-rodded F1, a.k.a. his war pony, Ragged Glory. Every time I saw it, I whispered one of my favourite lines from *The Road Warrior*: "The last of the V8 Interceptors." The truck looked like it could race through the fires of Hades and come out unscathed. It looked like it had been forged by trolls. It was dark and dangerous looking. I loved that truck. I loved its running boards. I loved its rims. I loved how it was small as a two-seater but big enough that you could drive around with a buffalo standing in the back. Every time Sonny fired it up in our driveway, my blood rippled with pleasure. I never got tired of looking at it. It was so urban and completely USA, so not from anywhere near here. It looked a lot like the truck on the cover of ZZ Top's *Afterburner* album, except Ragged Glory was a dusty black. It was something out of *CARtoons* magazine. When Sonny cruised, ZZ Top's "Rough Boy" was his tape-deck anthem, his get-up-and-go. It is such a sad song, but a classic. He was a rough boy, all right, and I hated it when he drank. He was funny, but sad funny, if that makes sense. And he'd always end up crying into his hands.

---

SO THERE I WAS: LOOKING FOR CODY CRANES AT THE TERRY Fox Run while my uncle Sonny Nets cranked AC/DC's "Who Made Who" and led two hundred of us down the streets of Fort Simmer from behind the wheel of his "muffaloose-powered" hot rod. This run was important, as cancer was on the rise in our town and all over the North, but my mind was elsewhere. The entire time I was running, I was just about kinking my neck looking for Cody.

Thank God Silver was in jail.

The nunchucks I had? I'd stolen them from his yard one day when I found them behind an old log pile. Want to know what he'd written on each handle? WAR and CHIEF. That should tell you plenty about how he saw himself.

The Dogrib and the Chipewyan were never supposed to raise our hands against each other, but Silver never cared about that. When my dad made me sign up for boxing, Silver got one of the Ratskin boys to punch me so hard that I ended up peeking through two puffy blue shiners for a week. "Didn't break the treaty!" Silver called as I was being tended by the coach.

Then there was the time I decided I wanted to join hockey so I could go to tournaments in Hay River and Yellowknife and maybe even Grande Prairie. Silver sent a townie to cross-check me into the boards. "Didn't break the treaty!" Silver yelled as they brought the stretcher out for me. As I looked to the stands for my dad, I spotted Mr. Cranes smiling and having a good chuckle at the spectacle of me stretched right out while a coach from Hay River held the back of my neck straight. Silver had never touched me, but he'd had me hurt many times over the years.

Those Elders would now be waiting for the food we were supposed to deliver—caribou stew, bannock and salad. So where was Cody, for frick sakes? If he didn't show soon, I'd have to bring the food to our Elders alone. Had Cody made his escape to the city? If so, why now? Had something happened at home?

The Elders didn't deserve to wait, so I would have to lone-wolf it. While I loaded the food on the wheeled cart loaned to us by the curling club, I could hear scratchings and scritches from the ravens steadying themselves against the wind on the roof of the Catholic Church, where Cody and I were baptized and confirmed, and spent our winters as altar boys. I wondered if my mom was watching me from Heaven. Not long ago she had been one of the organizers of the Terry Fox Run.

As I pushed the full cart with my seventeen-year-old math arms, I looked around with pride at our little town. Up above soared a few pelicans, a few ravens. Cody had told me that if he ever left town it would be because he knew he was in danger. Maybe he was helping his brother Stanley. Stanley had been with my mom when the canoe tipped. My mom didn't make it because she gave him her life jacket. After the accident, Stanley only came back to himself halfway. He was never the same.

Because of the way that cart worked, I had to back out carefully to turn it. I held the door open and turned and got it safely out, but when I looked up, there was Silver Cranes. He had his back to me and was working on something. He was tanned from nothing but being full-blooded Chipewyan. I suddenly realized that he was in the process of breaking into the Legion. He was prying back the grate covering the side window with a screwdriver and leaning on it with his full weight.

Stanley was standing watch. He was wearing his PWS jersey from the Territorial Track Meet, where he'd won gold for shot put, javelin and baseball years ago. He spotted me with those dim eyes of his and grunted, motioning to Silver that they'd been spotted. How was Silver out of jail already, and why was he with Stanley? I had heard there was a no-contact order between Silver and his giant of a brother, Stanley.

*This is why Cody didn't show today. He must have fled town.*

Maybe Silver wouldn't see me. Maybe I could run. There was no way he could catch me if I hopped that fence. Silver had gotten TB when he was younger, and it had warped his left leg. He walked with a limp. His leg was so curved that townies called him Banana Leg, but never to his face. The door closed and locked behind me. Loudly.

*Oh god . . .*

Silver spun around and looked at me, surprised. There were those cold, deep-set black eyes and the immediate reminder that the threat of violence was always around him. Silver was three years older than me, twenty, and his eyes always freaked me out when he looked at me directly. They flickered with something cruel. The look he gave me was one I knew instantly: Silver was going to hurt me for catching him.

"Lawson!" He gripped his screwdriver and approached me, blocking my exit through the gate. "Where's Cody?"

Stanley stood still, blinking slowly like some mindless ape. He was nineteen, but his body had gotten soft. He was still a giant but no longer the all-star sports champion we all used to cheer for. He was a mountain of soft muscle and flab.

"Where's Cody?" Silver repeated. He held the screwdriver like a gutting knife. "I need him. Now."

*What is that stench?* I looked around for random rotten fish that may have been tossed in the grass. I swallowed dryly and started breathing through my mouth. I'd keep my promise to never tell Silver where Cody was. This was the day Cody had warned me about. He must have fled town because his big brother was hunting him down to hurt him.

"I don't know," I said and stopped pushing the cart. I'd need both hands if he decided to break the treaty and fight me. Maybe the stew could save me. This was food for his Chipewyan aunties at the old folks' home. Before I knew it I heard myself say, "You're not really gonna break into the Legion and take the money we raised to fight cancer, are you?"

Silver twirled the screwdriver in his hand, showing off. He'd gotten big in jail: more muscles. A tight white T-shirt showed off his dark skin and—what was this? The long strand of bright silver hair that he was named for was gone. I could see a bald spot where it had been cut or yanked out. Silver looked me right in the eyes and said, "Don't waste my time, Lawson. Tell me where Cody is and I won't hurt you."

*Too late,* I thought. *He's going to hurt me no matter what.*

"So that's a yes," I said, deciding to just face him and use the treaty as a shield. "You just got back to town and you're already up to no good?" I gestured toward Stanley. "You should be helping Stanley, not getting him into more trouble."

I decided to be like my dad in a fight and keep Silver on the defence.

*Never back down,* Dad's voice told me. *Stay focused, and remember: God hates a coward.*

If I stalled for time, someone walking or driving by would see us and stop this. I said in my loudest voice, "You know what I think? I think you've both forgotten where you came from and just how incredible you are. Your grandfather killed a grizzly with a long pole. Sonny Nets told me the deadliest story about your grandpa. I love this story."

Stanley looked at me with surprise, and I decided to go for it. I had to dazzle them with the truth. It would buy me time to be rescued.

"What he did was—Stanley, raise your arms and pretend to be a grizzly."

Stanley did exactly what I said. He raised his arms.

"Stanley, don't listen to him," Silver scolded.

"So," I said and pretended I carried a large spear, "what your grandpa did was, the grizzly charged him out on the Barrenlands when he and a bunch of teachers were taking kids out for science camp, and your grandpa had a long, sharp pole. Your grandpa knew that when a grizzly stands, he can't back up, so your grandpa stood and raised his arms to challenge the bear. The grizzly stopped and stood. Your grandpa flexed and made a motion to stab the bear." I pointed to where my ribs meet. "He aimed that sharpened pole right here. Then your grandpa ran away. But this was a trick. The grizzly dropped down to chase him only to realize he'd been impaled through the heart. The grizzly died right there. That's how amazing your family is—*not* by doing this dumb breaking and entering. We have a treaty to protect and Elders to feed."

Stanley blinked slowly and looked at Silver.

"Lawson," Silver spat. "He can't hear you."

There I was, standing in my track pants, my Platinum Blonde *Standing in the Dark* T-shirt, my Asics. I had to keep stalling so someone could help me—Sonny, the cops. Sooner or later the cops, bylaw officers or town workers would come by to pick up the pylons off the street. And there was the library. Someone had to see us from the library or the drugstore. My dad was a two-minute walk away, in the federal building. Maybe the mayor would come back and check up on me.

"I need Cody, and I know you know where he is." Silver flipped that screwdriver up like it was a knife and started walking toward me. *Wait.* He wasn't limping. His leg wasn't bent anymore. He was taller, bigger. Did he get an operation to fix his leg?

I had to think fast. "Why didn't you let Cody cure you?"

"What?" He stopped walking.

I wanted to be like those moths that can throw sonar but dip and fall while the bat lunges for where they used to be.

I pointed at Silver. "Cody gave you the cure for your asthma from Mary and Dave at Tsu Lake and you threw it in the water."

"Dave and Mary are Cree," he said. "We don't use Cree medicine." He then pointed at Stanley. "Stanley, get behind him. Last chance, Lawson. I need my brother—now."

Stanley's head jerked around at the sound of Silver's command, and he did as he was told. He walked toward me with those dazed eyes of his and loomed behind me.

"Hi, Stanley," I said, looking up to meet his eyes, but he wouldn't look at me. "Uh, remember what I said about your grandpa. That's the power you have. You don't have to do what your brother tells you. Silver, I have food for your aunties and the other Elders at the old folks' home. Let's just go and bring it to them." Then I raised my voice so Silver and anyone in the vicinity would really hear me: "AND HONOUR OUR PEACE TREATY TOGETHER LIKE OUR ANCESTORS HAVE ASKED US TO, okay? Please."

"It's too late." Silver shook his head. "Listen to me, Lawson. Listen. We're wasting time."

"Silver," I said gently, "I won't narc. That money's for folks with cancer. Come on. Don't be like this." I pointed to the giant standing behind me. "Your brother needs you to look out for him."

Silver shook his head. "But that's the thing," he said, with his war face back on. "If I just do what I'm told, I can save my brother." He looked at me. "Unless..."

"Unless what?" I asked. "Silver, let me help you. Just stop whatever you're doing."

"But I can't," he said, and it was the way he said it that worried me. He was scared of something, desperate almost. "And that's why I need Cody. I—"

Then everything changed.

Silver's eyes glazed over and his mouth hung open the same way Stanley's was. The rotten fish stench surrounded me again and filled my pores. Silver staggered backwards and began to speak—but not to me. Whoever it was that he was talking to, I couldn't see them.

"Yes, I know, Father. I promised. I know. I know. I just need more time."

Stanley started to whimper.

Silver turned and looked at both of us with flickering eyes, and then he focused on me.

"I need you to tell me where Cody is. Lawson, you have no idea what's going on, so help me get Cody and stay out of my way."

"Silver," I said. "Are you okay? What's going on?"

Silver approached me. "You know where Cody is. I have to find him. Please."

*Please?* This wasn't like Silver at all. He was desperate. I raised both my hands and backed away from him.

"Why? Why do you want Cody?" I asked. "You were so

mean to him when he was here."

"*When* he was here." Silver thought about it. "So he's not here in town. We need him. This is the only way I get Stanley back. Where is he? I have to hurry."

I had to keep stalling. Surely soon someone would see us and intervene. "Come on. The Elders are waiting. Those are your aunties in there. Help me deliver the food. We can do this together."

He focused on me, and I felt something around him grow.

"You're not listening. I made a mistake and now Stanley's life is on the line."

I knew Cody was in Edmonton, but I didn't know exactly where.

"Edmonton?" Silver asked.

"What?" *Oh god. He heard my thoughts.*

"You just thought 'Edmonton.'" he grinned.

"How the—?" *Oh no! Cody had warned me that Silver could read minds.* "How did—?"

"With his Cree family."

"Silver, can you . . . read minds?"

"Father," he said, his eyes glazed over. "Yes, I'm working as fast as I can in your name. Cody is in Edmonton. I swear it. Please."

Then I felt hands inside my head as Silver tried to steal into my brain and read more of my mind. It was like ice water pouring into my body. Then the hands inside my head became fingers, and they started to rifle through my thoughts and memories. I glimpsed Tsu Lake. I saw Cody in our tent laughing it up. I saw Cody confessing, telling me—*Oh god!*

"Get out of my head!" I heard myself yell. Out of complete panic I lunged and tackled Silver, but he was ready for me. He wheeled around and put me in the guillotine. His arms were steel. I couldn't breathe. My face grew hot and I started to see sparks. The screwdriver he'd been using for his B and E spun on the ground before coming to rest under my leg.

Stanley paced back and forth making strange throat sounds, as if he were choking and not sure what to do. I clawed at Silver's arms trying to pry myself from his python grip. He was squeezing me so hard he started grinding his molars. It sounded like rocks trying to crush rocks. I could smell his rotten-fish breath and something else—smoke from a campfire.

*Wait.* I had made first contact! I had broken the treaty! My eyes bulged in their sockets. I. Could. Not. Breathe. Who was he talking about? Who was this "father"? Their dad had died over a year ago. My eyes begged Stanley to help me. I even reached out to him with my free hand. Stanley made fists, and he started to moan as if he were crying. I brought my chin down to suck air.

"Stanley, frickin' help me," I gasped. "My mom died saving you."

Silver tightened his grip and whispered, "I made a mistake. Stanley's going to die if I don't bring Cody back. What do I do, Lawson?"

I was choking. My face was burning. I had broken the treaty by tackling Silver. I was starting to pass out, but then I felt something as I scrambled for balance. *The screwdriver.*

I had to do something. With my free hand, I found and gripped the screwdriver. I aimed it, ready, with the sharp tip pointing up. *What do I do? If I don't defend myself, he'll choke me to death.*

"Do it," Silver said. "This is the only way to save us."

I had to do something. Everything was starting to dim.

"Do it," Silver pleaded. "I can't do this alone."

*Is this what dying feels like?*

"This is the only way. Trust me."

I was drowning.

"Lawson," Silver whispered, "stab me so I can take you there. You have to break the treaty."

I was drowning and I had no choice.

*I'm sorry, Mom,* I thought as I slammed the screwdriver up, knowing I was breaking our ancestors' peace treaty forever. My arm felt the full impact of the jab as he let out a roar of pain and fell backwards, covering his face. I spun around, scrambling to my feet to get away, but instead of running and hopping the fence, I had to say sorry. I'd definitely broken the peace treaty now, and he needed to know I was sorry. Silver was stunned. His eyes watered and his left nostril started to bleed. Silver was furious and started yelling, "That's it? You were supposed to stab me in the eye or something. We have to break the treaty all the way. Now he's not going to believe us."

*What? Who is he talking about?*

I held my hands out as a sign of surrender. "I'm so sorry, but you were trying to kill me." I wanted to run, but decided to try to help him. "Frick, man. I am so—"

"Lawson." Silver wiped his nose and saw blood on his index finger. "You ruined this—*everything*! You're wasting time!" Silver pointed at me. "You're coming to the forest. Stanley, knock him out."

Stanley's eyes flickered like a Cylon's when he heard Silver's order. He swung his huge arms out and locked eyes on me. He twisted his neck sideways and started marching toward me.

I stood slowly and raised my hands to protect myself as I started to walk backwards. I wanted to run, but the gate was locked and the fence, I realized, was too high.

"No, no, no, no, no. Stanley, we're friends, remember? My mom saved your life!"

"Break him, Stanley!" Silver ordered.

Stanley lowered his head as he looked at me, and he changed. Everything changed as Stanley put on his war face. I raised my arms to say I surrender, but Stanley grabbed me, swiftly picked me up and flipped me, smashing my head into the—

*Bang!*

That was my skull that made that sound. A high-pitched whistle screamed in my head as I fell away.

# Eyes Without a Face

I WAKE IN A CLEARING IN A FOREST OF TWISTED SPRUCE AND pine trees leaning and bent in all directions. It's winter. Definitely not Fort Simmer. I can't feel my legs. I can't feel anything.

*Am I dreaming? Can you dream with your eyes open?*

The sky is grey. Something is rotting.

*Are all these trees dead? There's something wrong with them.*

A long, sharp pole lies by a small fire in front of me. In the middle of the fire is wood and red-hot coals. I can't move, and snowflakes brush soundlessly against me as they fall.

My hands and feet are tied to poles with ropes of black hair.

I'm crucified.

I hear a rattle in the brittle leaves as the wind kicks up.

In the trees are crude suspended bundles—altars—displaying chunks of meat, fat and teeth tied and hung with what looks like more human hair. An eye looks back at me through a splintered rib cage in one of them. In another altar, an animal has been ripped and folded inside out with its snout pushed through its own jaws in a frozen scream.

The altar closest to me is glazed with ice that looks as if it has been gnawed by mouse teeth, and hung with a tangle of hair and torn hide. What it holds looks like grey freezer-burnt meat. I count seven altars to my right, but I can hear more clinking in the trees behind me. The altar hanging highest to my left is definitely fashioned from an animal. From its cage of bones hangs the wing of a bluebird. From another, the ears of what I think was a bear or a large bat. Yet another displays a small skinned hand. Human? The one to my right looks human. *Oh god, I hope it's not human.* What animal is closest to human? Dave Prince out at Tsu Lake told us it was bear. It must be bear. I see a pyramid of at least eight animal jawbones with missing teeth swaying from a branch and clicking like wind chimes. This is a place of ritual or ceremony, and these are death bundles. I'm in hell. This has to be hell. I didn't know that it could be winter in hell. But it has to be.

*Wait. Is this a medicine dream?*

Silver Cranes stands in front of me, facing Stanley, who stands still, gazing up with dim eyes. Silver is using what looks like a rolled-up moose caller of yellow birch to scoop burning coals from the fire and funnel them down Stanley's throat.

"That's it," Silver says to his brother. "Just like medicine. I'm so sorry. I didn't know. He never told me."

I can hear Stanley suffering. I can hear him wanting to run or defend himself. Smoke puffs out of his nostrils. The coals are burning him inside.

Stanley keeps trying to raise his hands to stop what's happening, but Silver pushes them back down. "Stop it," he says. "Stop fighting. If we don't do this, you die. Lawson's here now, and he's going to help us."

Stanley gags and I can hear his insides crackling as the coals make their way down. He groans. I hear a giant animal walking in the snow behind me, but then it stops. I see something glowing blue on a piece of black cloth. It's like a fire burning a fuel of some kind. It flickers and pops brighter each time Stanley swallows those coals.

Silver looks around frantically.

"Keep looking up," Silver orders his brother. "That's it. I took this too far and I'm sorry. We'll find a way, brother. I promise. I swear." He looks around at all the chalices made of rib cages, pieces of rotting meat and jawbones before cursing under his breath.

I look up and see something black swirling around a faint light, high in the sky. It's Halley's Comet. *Why is it like that?*

Silver works quickly to take one of the sharpened poles and hook something high up in the tree beside Stanley. He then kneels and unwraps a flickering blue fire in a black cloth. "Okay," he says. "Good. We're good for now, bro. Hang on. You're still here." He wraps the flame back up in the black cloth, then uses the sharpened pole to lift it high and place it on a spruce bough nearest to Stanley. Stanley faces this tree with his head up. I can see his throat move as he struggles to breathe. Silver points to where he placed the blue light in the black cloth, then raises his finger to his lips, gesturing to me to keep this a secret.

Silver walks across the crunchy snow toward me. He's wearing a Slayer T-shirt, jeans and Nike high-tops. There's a splash of frozen blood across his lip and chin from where I struck him. And there's that pink bald spot where his long silver hair used to be. I can see a wound where it was removed. It looks like it was ripped out of him. He takes a big breath, and before exhaling whispers, "Lawson." He looks around. "This is his den and that's my brother's soul. Find a way back here. Get Stanley's spirit and put it back inside of him. He's coming. When he arrives, do not listen to him—no matter what he promises you." He glances around quickly. "Watch everything and get us out of here. Please."

Silver leans toward me and that foul smell makes me gag and cough. "I had to bring you here." He points to my right. "Look."

I try to turn with all my strength to see what he's pointing to. To my surprise, the most radiant speckled chickadee looks at me with glittering eyes, then turns its attention to something approaching us in the snow. A bird in hell?

The chickadee flies to a higher branch as something walks beside me.

The biggest black wolf—must be from the Barrenlands—stalks slowly toward us. Its back is curved, and its muscles ripple as it makes its way. Its paws are huge. The wolf curls its body and its hackles rise so that its back becomes even fuller and more spiked.

"Who is that?" it asks Silver. I am stunned. A wolf who can speak? This is definitely a dream—a medicine dream. This is exactly what my mom told me about. What did she say, that this is where I would be offered medicine power? Holy.

"You tell me," Silver asks, pretending not to know. "Were you followed?"

"This is no good," the wolf growls, turning its focus toward me. "Why did you bring him here?"

"Because he has medicine." Silver grins.

*What?* No, I don't. I don't have medicine. If I do have it, you can take it. Just take what you need and get me out of here. *I have to get out of here.*

The flesh altars in the trees start to sway like chandeliers. The teeth in the jawbones start to rattle from a wind that blows rotten. Something evil starts spilling over the land around us. The hair on my arms stands straight up, and I am suddenly filled with terror.

The ground beneath my feet starts to shift, pop and split. Something is moving, diving underneath the earth. It's huge. I'm tilted sideways along with the tree I'm tied to as something tunnels underground like a giant snake. I watch as a whole section of trees sways far to the right. Bark, roots and branches pop. I hear entire root systems tear and snap as whatever this is hunches the land from under itself, ripping the flesh of the earth around us. I see an opening appear. From this raised opening I see steam or breath or both. This is a push-up, like muskrat make on the ice so they can come up for air before diving back under. I see the land lift as something huge takes a big inhale before it turns and dives slowly under the land again, creating a new push-up hill in the distance. The land tears and splits as steam rises. Whatever this is, it is massive, and it sounds and feels like a rumbling underground thunder as it circles all the way around, pushing up directly behind me. My heart pounds so hard I think blood is going to shoot out of my ears. I am now liquefied fear.

The wolf and Silver both kneel with their heads bowed as something crawls out of the earth behind me.

"Father," they both say, looking down. Silver is shivering.

It rises from under the earth on what sounds like four stumps: *chuck, chuck, chuck, chuck*. I feel the cold seep into my very bones. My heart seems to switch from pumping blood to pumping a terror juice that fills me and squeezes me at the same time. I hear whatever is behind me chewing with blasts of breath that blow against me as it works its jaws back and forth and side to side. I hear *crunch, pop, crunch* as it devours whatever is in its mouth. Then I hear dripping. Whatever it is that's dripping causes a hissing sound as it hits the snow. I dry-swallow, listening and closing my eyes. Whatever stands behind me spits something out. It's a bloody tooth. Whether it's from an animal or a person, I don't know.

I gag again and peek to see what Silver's doing. He and the wolf bow even lower in fear of whatever's behind me. They are terrified.

I then hear it make a new sound: *chick chick chick.*

Each time it clicks its teeth together, the teeth in the jawbones in the altars around us rattle. It lets its breath out for a long time before speaking.

"Oh, look, in the tree, in the tree, in the tree," it whispers slowly and deeply. Every leaf in every tree and branch trembles as it speaks. "We have guests. A bird and a boy. A boy and a bird. I wonder who they are and who brought them here, and will they warm me?"

"Father." Silver stands and points at me. "This is Lawson Sauren, a direct descendant of Edzo. A Yabati. Sworn to protect the treaty. He just broke it, and he has medicine power. My work is done."

The thing looms closer and sniffs my neck. I feel cold teeth press against each side of my neck, firm as a vice. The coldest breath finds my soul, and I nearly freeze before it backs off.

"Useless," the voice says. "I can't eat him. You say he broke the treaty?"

*That's me: useless and gross tasting. Can I leave? I won't tell anyone. Just untie me and let me get out of here!*

"Yes, Father," Silver says. "I promise you. Our treaty is broken. He hit me with a screwdriver."

"This one has no medicine. Where's Cody?" the voice asks. Fear squeezes my spine, and my back arches involuntarily. *What is this thing behind me? Wait. Is this him? Is this the spirit that Cody called the Dead One?* The rotting smell grows even thicker until I'm dizzy. I switch to breathing only through my mouth. *It must be the Dead One standing behind me.*

"And where are my warriors?" the Dead One asks Silver.

"Father," Silver says and points to me. "Lawson Sauren is a direct descendant of Edzo. That has to count for something. Take him instead of Stanley. I'll bring you Cody."

*What? What! Trade me?*

"You can't trade deaths," says the Dead One.

I feel both dread and relief flood my body. *You can't trade deaths?*

Silver pleads, "I am your most loyal servant. I was working on getting money to fly your warriors up, but Lawson interrupted me." Silver looks in fear to the Dead One behind me. "I'm sorry, Father. I got Lawson to break the treaty as you requested, and I found out that Cody is in the city. We know Cody's in Edmonton. I just need more time."

"And I helped you enter Lawson's mind," says the Dead One. "This was our trade: a slave, a new leg and fresh lungs for you, and I get Cody. I need new skin."

"I just got out of jail," Silver pleads again, this time more panicked. "I need money to fly your warriors up, and they want to be paid to help us. But I have a plan."

"Promises!"

"I will get Cody, and I'll bring back warriors for you. I've done everything you've asked."

"Silver, you called me, and what I have given you? I can take it all back at any time."

"But I shot my teacher in the eye. I united gang members while I was in jail. I gave you my braid."

"Yes. Yes, you did," the Dead One says calmly. "But I still don't have Cody's medicine, and I need new skin."

Silver's energy changes. He puffs up his chest, stands firm and faces the Dead One. I can see him summon his courage.

"Screw this," Silver curses. There was his temper. "You're just using me for Cody's medicine."

"Maybe," says the Dead One playfully. "Why do I think you're deliberately trying to delay delivering my request?"

"Because you lie to me," Silver says with an edge. "You keep making these damned promises. You keep changing the rules. And now I have to keep feeding Stanley like a damned guppy or he dies? You told me that you'd give me what I wanted."

"And, so far, I have. You're wasting time."

Silver points at Stanley. "So how long do I have to feed Stanley like this?"

"For as long as you want your puppet."

"I never wanted a puppet," Silver says angrily. "I just wanted him to not be so good at sports. You never told me any of this at the beginning."

"You were jealous of Stanley," says the Dead One. "Now you're not."

"I'm a hostage to him now, and he's fading!" Silver yells. "I have to keep finding my way back here and hoping he's still alive. He's getting weaker. What happens when his spirit goes out?"

"Oh, I don't think you'd want that," says the Dead One. "Let us hope it never comes to that. How could you live with yourself?"

Silver looks to Stanley, whose eyes stare blankly, his mouth wide open. "Damn you," Silver says. "Damn you, and to hell with you for lying to me."

"Power demands sacrifice. You knew this was coming," says the Dead One. "Bring me Cody or you can go back to being the crippled little boy who begged for me in the forest. And you better hurry, or Stanley will die here without his soul. You can be a beggar again in your own land or you can be the war chief you've always wanted to be—or was that a bluff?"

Silver points to his leg. "So turn me back into a cripple if that's what it takes. Take my leg back. Take my lungs back. Do whatever you want with me, just let Stanley go."

"Oh, it's too late for that," the Dead One says calmly. "We are bound. Bring me Cody and you will have more power than you ever dreamed of, war chief. And I'll return Stanley to the world."

Silver looks past me with the saddest eyes. "You'll bring him back all the way? Like how he used to be?"

"Oh yes," the Dead One says slowly. "I'll show you how. Bring me Cody and enough warriors, and you can have Stanley. But you better hurry. Stanley will get weaker every day that you're not here."

"Okay, I'll go. But what will you do with Cody once you have him?"

"You despise him," says the Dead One, "so I'll let you watch."

"Watch what?" Silver asks, with genuine worry in his voice.

"Enough talk," says the Dead One. "Go to Edmonton. Bring me your half-brother so I can feed."

Silver says, almost begging, "Wait. Let me talk to Lawson. I need to find out where in Edmonton Cody's hiding."

"Return here with Cody—and don't you fail me," says the Dead One.

"Can't you just take Cody's family medicine without hurting him?"

"Cody," the Dead One says in a long breath, clicking his teeth a few times. Something wet falls and I hear hissing as it spatters in the snow behind me. "I'm going to feast on his medicine after Slitter kicks him to death from the inside, then my pack can fight over Cody's stomach lining."

*Gross! Who or what is Slitter?*

"No." I hear a sob come from Silver's throat. He's scared. To my surprise, Silver covers his eyes and starts to cry. "I never should have listened to you."

"You wanted power," the Dead One reminds him. "This is the price, and you better hurry back, or Stanley dies. Slitter, come. You are needed."

The wolf starts to whine and whimper. Its entire body starts to shake and shudder, and I see its hide loosen from its joints and bones. It throws its head back and starts to yelp and scream in pain. Its belly hangs lower and lower, then splits open. I hear a wet *schlop* as something falls to the ground, and the smell of rot fills my nose completely.

Then I hear something crawling around on the snow. I am shocked to see a small creature—it looks like a skinned bear cub—using its knuckles and thumbs to manoeuvre while dragging its short body away from the staggering wolf who shakes in agony, yet somehow has survived the tearing of its underbelly.

The skinned creature looks like something that didn't develop right. Every cell of me turns inside out with revulsion. This little devil turns and focuses on me, its face now like a giant frog's but with a hooked beak smeared with blood. It has the most hateful eyes, which peer at me through red slits. It looks like someone has smeared dead bugs under its mushy, mottled skin. It hisses at me with pure hatred.

One of the creature's arms is longer than the other. On one hand its fingers are tar-brown knuckled stumps, while the other has long claws like a wolverine. It sniffs the air before shifting around to study me and Silver. Oh, it wants to lunge and tear me apart so badly, and I cannot back up or defend myself. Its tongue darts in and out of its mouth, and I realize that it has two tongues folded on top of each other. One could scoop up as the other pulled down. The creature licks its lips and twists its neck to look up at the Dead One behind me. It wants to kill something. Anything. Then it looks directly at me again and starts to back up, preparing to charge.

"Slitter," the Dead One commands, "go with Silver. You two go to Edmonton and find Cody. Bring him back to me alive. Remember, Silver, if you don't feed Stanley, he'll die without his soul, so you'd better hurry. Remember our plan."

"I don't need that thing to lead me to Cody," Silver says with worry as he assesses the creature called Slitter. "Someone has to feed Stanley. He's getting weaker."

"Well, you better hurry then," says the Dead One. "Time to declare war on other tribes and destroy their peace treaties. Run along now. Your brother should last, oh, a few days without his feeding tube."

"Damn you," curses Silver.

Suddenly, with a roar, a black fist dives down from the sky. Thousands of birds swirl and twirl their small-boned bodies together to pound the wolf and Slitter over and over again, attacking and clawing as their deafening cries daze them. It is like a winged hurricane of greys, blacks, claws and beaks. Swallows.

Silver and I watch in surprise as a lone chickadee and hundreds of swallows work together to create a giant wheel, their heads and wings tucked in, swiftly gaining momentum. They slam and dig into the wolf and Slitter again and again like a buzz saw, a blinding blizzard of winged assault. The birds peck, punch and pierce the Dead One's servants relentlessly. Both the wounded wolf and Slitter snap their jaws, trying try to pull the birds from the air, but the swallows dodge, using their claws to swipe and stab before swooping back up into the wheel for the next round of attack. Again and again, the birds gather group strength and plunge to strike the wolf's and Slitter's faces. Their wings are loud—like ptarmigans when you surprise them—and both Silver and I are buffered by the air as their wings whoosh like a blurred blanket of force to push the wolf and Slitter away from us. Fur, skin and feathers fly. The wolf starts to yelp and bark. Slitter, face down in the snow, starts to howl in pain from the hundreds of peck wounds on its hairy, lumpy back.

Silver suddenly races toward me and speaks quickly. "Lawson, don't look in his eyes. That's how he gets you. Save my brothers. I'm sorry. For everything. Put Stanley's soul back. I showed you where it is. This thing feeds on war, and it wants Cody's medicine power. Don't let it get Cody. And, if you can, save me—please!"

The birds spin and soar back into the air before flying away. The wolf has collapsed, bleeding heavily from its left eye and legs. With huge scratches and hundreds of peck gashes, Slitter lets out a cry of rage from its frog-like face. Its long tongue laps at the wounds on its ripped and glistening flesh.

"See?" declares Silver, pointing at me. "I told you Lawson was protected."

"Where did they come from?" the wolf pants as it looks in the direction of the Dead One. Patches of fur hang off its body in chunks. I can see its yellow bones peeking through its torn hide.

The Dead One rises once more from the earth behind me. The smell of its rotten body fills my nose and I gag. I hear skin and bone, gristle and muscle popping as he expands. Silver and the wolf back up and look skyward as this thing towers over all of us.

"Well now," says the Dead One, "it appears that our Lawson does not have medicine power, but he *is* protected by spirit helpers. You knew this and brought him here on purpose!"

"No," insists Silver. "I had no idea."

"Lies! You showed him too much."

"No, Father. I would never betray you."

"More lies. Slitter, inhabit Silver so he does as he is told. Be my eyes and ears. See to it that you don't return without Cody."

From the snow, Slitter spins on its knuckles, gathers momentum and becomes as small as a squirrel before launching at full speed into Silver's mouth. Silver gags and tries pulling out Slitter's body as it weasels its way down his throat. Silver's body arches back and forth as he tries to breathe. Once the little devil has burrowed its way inside of him, Silver stands straight and quiet. His eyes roll all the way back, then I watch the same fog that I saw in Stanley's eyes take over.

"Bring me Cody, Silver. Bring me the warriors you assembled while you were in jail. And come back soon. We're starving, and we need new skin."

*We?*

Silver begins walking into the forest. I want to call out to him to stop, to fight whatever is inside him, but I pause when I see the injured wolf trying to pull its hide back together using its teeth. The hide keeps slipping off its yellow bones. It limps weakly and whimpers as it tries its hardest to pull itself back together.

"My Lord," it asks, "can I go now? I'm so weak. Release me. I want to go home to my family. You promised me."

"Oh dear," the Dead One says soothingly to the wolf. "You're hurt."

"I gave my body for you," says the wolf. "I've served you for years."

"Oh, I know," says the Dead One. "I know."

I see large, clawed hands reach out and stroke the wolf's fur. On one of the Dead One's fingers, I see a ring: a ring of silver hair.

That's where Silver's silver strand of hair went. That's how this thing—this beast—is controlling him. I always thought it was only a myth that if your enemies got their hands on a strand of your hair they could control you.

I hear crashing through the snow to my left. Two large tundra wolves approach the Dead One and stop. The larger of the two, a male, is black. The other is a red female. She is simply the most stunning being I have ever seen or imagined. Her coat is gorgeous, her eyes are a fiery yellow, and her paws are the colour of honey. I am hypnotized by her grace and power. *You are so beautiful.* She pauses to look directly at me. I can tell from that look that she needs help. As I think this, her eyes widen. *Can she hear my thoughts?*

"My Lord," says the black wolf, "the leaders you asked us to check up on are drinking and weak. They've forgotten their treaties and are ripe for reaping. Is the Dogrib and Chipewyan treaty broken?"

"Oh yes," says the Dead One. "Lawson Sauren here did my work for me. War has awoken in the North, and I'm starving."

"Who is this one?" the black wolf asks as he approaches the wounded wolf that birthed Slitter. The wounded wolf limps and shivers, still half bone and half shredded fur.

"This old thing?" the Dead One asks. "Spirit helpers sent from the living world broke him. He's no good to me anymore. Kill him."

"Master!" the old wolf pleads. "Please. You promised me—"

The red wolf addresses the black wolf: "Don't, brother, this is our chance to fight this thing."

Without any hesitation the black wolf tears into the injured older one. The red wolf turns and closes her eyes. The old wolf lets out cries of fear and agony. The black one tosses the old wolf's upper body into the air before descending on him and tearing into him even more aggressively. Fur flies. Bones snap. I hear the chewing of gristle. When it is done, the black wolf approaches the Dead One with its ears back and its neck low, its snout dripping with blood.

"Forgive my sister," the black wolf says to the Dead One. "Please. Our family is promised to you."

The red wolf shakes her head sadly. "No. You made this promise. Not me."

The black wolf snarls at her. "This is the only way for our clan to be the most feared, sister."

"Keep saying that," the red wolf counters, "and sooner or later, you'll hear your own words and know that we have been lied to. This is not the only way to save our family."

"You and I will talk later," the black wolf says sternly to his sister. "For now, we have work to do." The massive black wolf assesses me and licks his lips.

*Please let this be a dream. I don't want to be here anymore.*

The red wolf pushes past her brother, approaches me and sniffs the air.

"No," she says. "Whatever this thing is about to ask you to do, don't do it, brother. Even our enemies call this one 'the poison root.' We can still leave."

"You can't leave," the Dead One says to the red wolf. "Kill the Yabati. Show me you stand with your brother and what's been promised for your family."

*Kill the Yabati? Me? He is talking about me.*

"No," says the red wolf, "I won't." She then turns to her brother. "And you won't either. This is what it does. It keeps asking us to kill. For what? For the hope that we will be the most feared family in our territory?"

The black wolf's hackles stand up in thick, sharp spikes as he growls and prepares to attack his sister. "We have to do this. We've been promised. Kill the boy."

"Uh, hi, everyone," I say. "I can just leave. Nobody needs to kill anybody."

"No." The red wolf lowers her body and prepares to launch herself at her brother. "I won't. And you won't either. I'll fight you for him."

The two wolves tear into each other, and the Dead One starts to laugh. This is entertainment: It doesn't matter who lives or dies, as long as there is war.

"Stanley," the Dead One commands, "make me an altar out of the old wolf. I've always loved his tail. Make sure you pull it all the way out and display it so can I remember him. Good boy."

The black wolf uses his paws to grab the red wolf's neck and bites down on her nose with a snarl that scares me. The yelps and cries from the red wolf make my soul hurt. She curls into a ball, then, before her brother can bite or grab her again, she zigzags away and dives into a huge crevice in the disturbed earth. The black wolf looks around for her, sniffing, but he is simply too large to go where his sister has gone. I see patches of her red fur blow over the ice where he's yanked her coat out in tufts.

The black wolf gathers his strength and approaches the Dead One slowly. I can tell the wolf is questioning everything that is happening but he says, "I'll find her, my Lord. I serve you. For my family."

"I see that," the Dead One says, "and I am pleased. Watch what happens to those who fail me. Watch and learn."

Stanley walks backwards through the snow, letting out a small moan as his eyes roll back. I hear him twist and snap the dead wolf's ribs with his bare hands. It looks like he is wrapping a present, the way he moves. His strong hands wrench the wolf's joints apart before reaching for the head. Then he yanks off the tail and weaves it through the guts. I close my eyes in disgust.

And then a sound from behind me jolts me fully alert. Something like a whip—or a long tongue—shoots straight out to my right, grabbing one of the older bundles. I hear the crunch of bone, cartilage, gristle and antler.

"I'm growing and I need new skin," the Dead One purrs. "Bring me twenty of the fattest caribou."

"I will, my Lord." The black wolf bows.

Stanley grabs what is left of the dead old wolf. He produces a rock and begins pounding something soft and bloody, splattering the rocks and snow around him.

"That's it," the Dead One says approvingly. "Brains. His memories. His past hunts. Just the way I like it. You grind them up so perfect." I hear its lips smack together.

I look around and, to my surprise, I see the red wolf's eyes as she watches from her crevice in the earth. Her eyes catch mine, and I nod to let her know that I can see her. I can tell that she is considering running back through the forest in the direction they came from. I shake my head. She is wounded, and I think the Dead One's lightning-fast tongue might grab her.

I hear more chewing of bone and gristle, then the Dead One says to me, "Lawson Sauren, you broke the treaty. You have betrayed your ancestors. You are a disgrace. Before Stanley pulls you apart, what do you have to say for yourself?"

*Pulls me apart?* I have to say something. I can't move, but I decide to challenge the Dead One with the only thought that comes to mind.

"Stop!" I yell. "My mother died saving Stanley. She did this to defend the treaty."

"And now look at him." I feel the Dead One's cold breath on the back of my neck. "My perfect slave. Just like Silver. Soon we will find Cody in the city, and once I have his medicine power, we will only become stronger. This Dogrib–Chipewyan peace treaty is broken, thanks to you."

The ancient Dogrib and Mountain Dene blood in my veins starts to roar. I want to fight. All these years of being told not to fight. I burn with a rage I haven't felt since I lost my mom. I want to be untied so I can face the Dead One. What it said isn't true. The Dead One broke the treaty by letting Silver read my mind.

"As if I would break our treaty!" I yell. "As frickin' if!" *God hates a coward.* "This cheap liar behind me broke our treaty," I continue, addressing the black wolf. "We didn't. Your sister's right. He's lying to you."

The black wolf listens. I know the red wolf is listening too.

"How?" the Dead One and the black wolf ask together.

I feel my old cheeky self start to return.

"You let Silver read my mind," I explain. "I defended myself after Silver started choking me. I was defending our treaty, and none of this would have happened if you hadn't intervened. We didn't break anything, because you meddled. Where's your honour? And why would anyone follow you? It's all trickery."

"Is this true?" the black wolf asks.

"No," the Dead One insists.

"You're a liar and you know it." I look to the black wolf. "Your sister's right. You're going to end up in one of these altars after he kills you."

The black wolf bares his teeth and draws closer. "If this is true, I attacked my own sister for nothing. You cannot take full command of us. We are promised to you, but we are not bound—yet."

Oh, this is good. The alpha stands, challenging the Dead One now.

I glance back to the red wolf and see that she is watching me. I feel a connection building between us.

The black wolf studies the Dead One with bared teeth. "Does the Dogrib tell the truth?"

"Frickin' right he meddled," I said. "When I hit Silver, this cheap wannabe boss was inside us both at the same time, reading our thoughts."

The wolves look at me, then both stare intently at the creature standing behind me.

"You did lie," says the black wolf. "You told us the treaty was broken. But if they did not break it themselves, it has not been broken."

"Back on planet Earth," I say, "they call this outside interference. The treaty still stands."

The red wolf limps toward her brother. "He's right, brother. The poison root lies. That's all it does. We cannot proceed. It tricked our father into handing us over. No more. Let's go."

The Dead One finishes chewing and swallows. "Silver was taking too long to bring me Cody and those warriors."

*Yes!* "See? He meddled, and he's a liar. The only reason we fought was because he broke into my mind and I was forced to defend myself."

The two wolves look at each other. I can sense some form of telepathy between them. The black wolf knows now that the Dead One is not the leader he makes himself out to be and that his sister has been right all along. The Dead One must sense this too.

"You two will never leave here," he says to the wolves. "In fact, you two can starve to death."

"Oh no," the black wolf challenges, "we have a say in what happens next." He goes to comfort his sister.

"You like games, Lawson Sauren?" the Dead One asks with menace. "Let's play. Let's see who can return here first: Silver with Cody, so that I get Cody's medicine and break your treaty forever; or you, Lawson, who must find his own way back here and face me with a Chipewyan to demonstrate that the treaty still stands."

Stanley approaches, his eyes dead and his mouth completely open. His hands are covered with blood and guts.

The two wolves come toward me. "We too accept this challenge," says the black wolf, "but for a new leader. What's done is done. Silver is on his way to the city to find Cody Cranes and bring him back. Slitter cannot be stopped. You, Lawson Sauren, must find a way back here, and find a way to free Stanley Cranes with a Dene Sorulthen. If you do this, you will be our leader."

"What?" spits the Dead One.

"I accept," I say, before the wolves have a chance to change their minds. "I will find a way back here, I will free Stanley and Silver, and I will face whatever gross, lying thing is standing behind me."

The wolves consider my words. My dad always says that when the leader doubts, the group suffers. But what if you make the group doubt the leader?

"When I return," I continue, "I'll face this liar, and I'll not only free Stanley, I'll free you, too."

The wolves are shocked.

"Shut your mouth," says the Dead One. "I haven't accepted these terms."

The wolves look to him and growl. "So what are they?" the red wolf asks. "What are your terms?"

The Dead One pauses, and the forest grows quiet.

The black wolf lowers his snout to the snow and again bares his teeth. "You heard my sister. What are your terms?"

"Lawson cannot tell any adults about this," decrees the Dead One. "He must find his own way back here and face me. If he fails, I get Cody's power, we proceed and I get Lawson's life."

The wolves look to me. "Do you accept? No adults?"

I close my eyes. *My life? No one knows I am here. He already has me. If I can get away, maybe I can figure out what I need to do to get back here and save Stanley. But how will I keep all of this from my dad and Sonny? I'll just have to. I have to do this. Silver showed me where Stanley's soul is hidden. I have to free Stanley.*

"Deal," I say.

"Lawson, I want you to know that when you fail, I will steal your life. I will suck your eyes out while you scream."

The red wolf looks at me, and I send a thought: *I will free you. Hold on.*

She nods, and I feel the weight of her life on my shoulders. I can't fail.

"Stanley, let him down," commands the Dead One. "In the meantime," he says to the wolves, "bring me twenty caribou for a feast of feasts."

"No," the red wolf replies. "I say we wait. Everything under this forest is hollow, like your words."

The Dead One speaks directly to the black wolf: "Come. Look into my eyes and let me tell you what I can give you while we wait for either Lawson Sauren or Silver Cranes to return."

Stanley works at cutting my ties loose with the sharp edge of his brain-battering rock.

"Stanley," I say, "it's me, your buddy Lawson. My mom saved you, buddy. I'm coming back to get you out of here."

I see pain in his eyes. As he cuts the hair that ties my right hand to the pole, I look down at where Stanley's footprints have revealed ash and bones under the snow. We are standing on a carpet of frozen hair, animal fur, bones and ash, all matted together. This is a field of slaughter built on lies. This forest is a killing place.

*What did Silver say? Don't look in its eyes? How can I do that? How can I see what the Dead One looks like?*

*Stanley. Stanley's eyes. A reflection.*

"Stanley," I say, "look at me."

Stanley does, and I see my reflection in his hollow eyes. I focus and squint to see the Dead One, our captor, standing behind me.

What I see reflected in Stanley's eyes—just as he cuts the hair binding my left wrist and I start to topple face first toward the snow—is something larger and thicker than a silvertip grizzly, wearing a fur cape crawling with maggots. It's wearing a rotting bear skull as a mask, and it sees me studying it. I am frozen by the gaze from behind its mask. I look into its pulsing diseased eyes. In that instant, I can tell that it's sick and needs strength. Yet it's like it could seize my soul and squeeze it. Its eyes freeze me with so much hatred. It's here to kill, and it will kill everything and everyone who no longer serve it.

Thank God I was falling when it looked into me, because the freezing grip it had on me had to let go.

# She Sells Sanctuary

WHEN I CAME TO, MY EARS WERE RINGING AND THERE WAS grit in my mouth. The smell of rotting meat was gone, and it was summer, and I was no longer in the forest of the Dead One.

I sat up slowly. I spat the dirt out and looked up as I took another deep inhale. I had seen the medicine world, where animals could talk! I'd never believed any of our stories before, but I did now.

I wiped my mouth with my sleeve and looked around. I was back at the Legion in Fort Simmer. *It better still be frickin' 1986.* There was the church. There was the drugstore. There was the library. *Thank God!* All the muscles in my neck felt wrecked. My skull felt cracked—actually cracked. It was like I'd been struck by lightning, like all the plates in my skull had mashed and melted together. I ran my hands over my chest to make sure there was nothing and no one inside of me but myself.

I could see the metal screen that covered the Legion window was open. Silver and Stanley were gone. Silver had done it. He had robbed the Legion and had taken all the money we'd raised—thousands in cash. Thousands for his warriors' return.

He had tried to trade my soul for Stanley's.

I rolled over and tried to stand. I had to kneel. The world blurred sideways. The screwdriver we'd both used was gone. Blood pounded in my ears.

Silver Cranes and whatever he served could read minds. I had just travelled to the forest of the Dead One. And Stanley was there. Standing and being force-fed. It was Silver who was responsible for the way Stanley was now—not Stanley almost drowning with my mother. Silver served the Dead One. There was a little devil inside him, and talking wolves existed, and a tornado of birds had protected me.

*I don't have medicine power, but I was protected. Was this what Mom was talking about at Tsu Lake when she said she hoped I'd never know? When those birds attacked Slitter, the old wolf and the Dead One, was that Mom and Cody working together to protect me? I think it was. Holy! Thank you, Mom. Thank you, Cody. You may have saved my soul.*

I looked up at the sky but it was too light out to see Halley's Comet. It had been black and cold and swirling slowly where I was in that forest. My god, I had to warn Cody. But how? I didn't have his number. He had mine. Silver was coming for him with gross and lumpy Slitter.

The cart carrying the caribou stew was still there beside me. I had to act like nothing had happened. On the sidewalk, I saw a tiny trail of blood from where I'd jabbed Silver's nose.

I gathered my thoughts. The Elders at the old folks' home would be waiting for their stew. The cart's four wheels helped me find my balance as I pushed. I was in a daze, but I made it there. I remember blubbering excuses when Stan the Man, the guy who manages the place, answered the door and gave me a dirty look.

"Took you long enough," he barked as he wheeled the stew into the building. "I'll take it from here. Where's Cody?"

"I'm sorry," I heard myself say. "I don't know. Sorry I'm late."

He looked at me and shook his head before he shut the door. I caught a glimpse of three Elders in wheelchairs at the window, with blankets over their legs, watching me. Two of those Elders were Mary and Freda. They had loved my mom so much. They all waved. I raised my hand and waved back. I half staggered toward the potato field but had to stop. The world started to tilt. *Silver read my mind. He made a deal with darkness and evil. Something that killed peace treaties. Something that wanted to break the world.*

I heard a truck pull up beside me. Oh, I felt weak. I had nothing left. I heard Joan Jett's "Bad Reputation" blaring and a voice call out: "Lawson?"

I put my hands on my knees and started mouth-breathing. The world started to spin again.

"Lawson?"

I looked warily to my left. It was Shari Burns, in her dad's truck, wearing dark sunglasses. *I thought she was still in Calgary.* I hadn't seen Shari Burns in almost two years, but holy cannoli—freckles galore, green eyes and light brown, almost reddish hair—even in my current state, she had my attention.

I remember in grades eight and nine, Shari, in her black leather jacket and tight blue jeans, would want to dance with me. She was always so not awkward, maybe even forward with me. Looks from her made my forehead sweat. She was like the Métis Joan Jett or Pat Benatar: skinny, big attitude, big eyes, slender lips.

"Lawson, what happened to you?" she asked as she pulled her sunglasses up to focus on me. "Get in."

I felt nausea roll inside of me as I pulled myself into the truck and buckled up. My mouth tasted like I'd been licking batteries in a wet basement.

"Lawson," she repeated. "Are you okay? What happened to your face?"

"Silver Cranes," I said. "He stole all the money we raised for the Terry Fox Run." I barely had the strength to pull the door closed.

"Are you serious?" she asked, pulling her sunglasses back down. "Why would he do that? And why is he out of jail so early?"

"I, uh, I just need to rest," I said. "I need to think about everything I just saw."

My nostrils filled with the smell from the air freshener hanging from the rear-view mirror. What a relief it was after smelling the Dead One's rot. The air freshener was in the shape of a pine tree and had the words "Midnight Toker" stencilled on it.

"Okay," she said. "You have one minute and then you better tell me everything. Do not cheap out, because I have something to tell you in return that you probably won't believe."

I was so sleepy. *Why am I so sleepy? Is this shock? Do I have a concussion?*

Before she had left for Calgary, Shari had earned the nickname "Body Finder" after she went to the cop shop and told the constables exactly where a world-famous kayaker had recently perished. The story goes that he came to her in a dream and gave her the location of his body. He had not drowned while kayaking. He'd passed in his tent after having a heart attack. He had heard the search planes overhead and the search parties calling to him but had been unable to call out, and in such dense wilderness he had remained undiscovered. Until Shari. The kayaker told Shari that he wanted his ashes returned to his family overseas. With the support of the Rangers, the RCMP found this gentleman's body exactly where Shari said it would be, and Shari was catapulted to celebrity status—with a price. Everyone wanted something from her.

Soon after, she terrified and mystified everyone in grade eight biology. Mr. Bicksley was going through a slide show when Shari stood up, clutched her chest and yelled, "Mr. Bicksley, your wife is having a heart attack. Go home. Now!"

Mr. Bicksley told her to sit down and calm down.

"She's dying. Sharon's dying. If you go now—we can call the ambulance—you can save her. She needs CPR. It's a heart attack."

It was the way Shari spoke: direct, firm, confident. I had no idea that Mr. Bicksley's wife's first name was Sharon. None of us did, I don't think.

Mr. Bicksley turned and ran out of the school, hopped in his truck and raced across town. Shari ran to the office and called the ambulance. Nobody—not even the secretary—argued with her. Shari knew exactly what to do. When the ambulance arrived at the Bicksley residence, Mr. Bicksley was giving his wife CPR. He was credited with saving her life, but the school knew that it was Shari. That's when people started to become afraid of her. And it was shortly after that that she and her family moved to Calgary.

I leaned my head against the glass. It was cold. I felt like I was starting to doze off.

"How did you know about Mr. Bicksley's wife?" I asked groggily.

"Hey," she ordered, "don't fall asleep. Just talk to me. Here. Drink this."

I opened my eyes, and she handed me an ice-cold Pepsi.

"Frickin' Silver," she said. "Thank God Stanley has foster parents now."

I opened the can and got sprayed. I didn't care. I drank it and washed down the grit and grossness.

"Frick sakes," she said. "I'm telling my dad. We should go to the cops."

"No adults," I said. I had to keep my promise to the Dead One and to the wolves.

"Lawson," she said, "I'm so sorry. Your eye looks frickin' brutal."

Again, I just wanted to sleep. I needed to forget the horrible ugly evil face of that imp that was inside Silver. "I know how Silver is keeping Stanley weak."

"What?" she asked. "Wait. Let me pull over."

Shari pulled over at Kelly's Canal and went down the back road, a service road. This was where a lot of bush parties took place.

"Lawson," she said, "you can't fall asleep. You hear me? If you do, you might never wake up."

I nodded. I felt my body rolling.

"Here," she said and stopped the truck's engine.

She unbuckled and gestured that she was going to lay her hands on me.

"Your spirit," I heard her say, "is way, way out of your body. Let me help."

I nodded and she placed her hands over my eyes. "I borrow from grace," she said. "I pass you light here," she said, and I felt a blue humming light fill my skull. The shiner I had from Stanley started to pulse. "I call light, I call light, I call light."

She lowered her hands and placed them on my chest, over my heart. I could not open my eyes. I was stunned with calm, and warmth spread through me.

"There. I pass light from the grace. I give you light from the grace. I pass light. From my heart to yours, from my universe to your universe, I call you back, Lawson. I call you back. I call you back. Take what you need. Take all the light that you need. I call you back. I call you back. I call you back. Take what you need. Take what you need."

I felt a healing light calm my soul, calm my spirit, calm my heart.

"There," she said.

I do not know how long I sat there. I felt gently lifted in the most soothing way.

"There," she whispered.

When I came to, she was watching me to make sure I was okay.

I looked at her, at all her freckles, in complete peace. The terror had left me. My heart was back to pumping blood. I blinked a few times and looked around. I felt brand new!

"What did you do to me?"

"Oh now," she said, "let's just say I gave you a little bit of universal love."

I blinked hard to clear my head. "How did you do that?"

"I'll tell you about it another time. What did you say about Silver keeping Stanley weak?"

"I think I had a vision," I said. "Like a medicine dream."

"Did you see your hands?" she asked.

"What?"

"It's not a dream if you can see your hands."

I thought back. "Yes, I could see my hands."

Because she'd just brought me back to myself somehow, I decided to tell her everything. We hadn't spoken for two years, but I'd known Shari since kindergarten. She'd seen a dead kayaker, she'd saved the life of Mr. Bicksley's wife, and she'd just somehow healed me. I told her how Cody had told me about the Dead One visiting Silver, and about how the Dead One had given Silver new lungs and a new leg, but in exchange Silver now had to bring Cody back so the Dead One could steal his medicine. I also told her about Slitter diving into Silver's mouth. I did not tell her about the wolves and about my immediate connection with the red wolf. If this had been my medicine dream, I did not want to lose anything from it. I knew I sounded crazy, and I thought she'd kick me out.

Instead, she went quiet and whispered with closed eyes, "Shh." She nodded. "I'm trancing." I could feel a shimmer around her and didn't know where to look. *Trancing?*

"The words I'm picking up," she whispered, "are *vessel* and *servants* and *soul stealer*."

"Who did Silver make a deal with?" I asked. "Who or what exactly is the Dead One?"

"Oh, Silver, what have you called into the world?" She shuddered, then said, "He's bound to . . . some sort of resurrected demon—a soul parasite is feeding off him. It never stops. It just keeps feeding."

"Silver said not to let it grow."

Shari nodded. "That's what it does. It steals power through false promises. All the while it grows."

*Cody,* I thought. *Silver's been ordered to bring Cody back, and Slitter will make sure this happens.*

"It feeds on war," I added. "Here in the North, it will test every single peace treaty, starting with the Dogrib and the

Chipewyan. All my life I was told I was a Yabati, a defender of our peace treaty, but I never believed it."

"Well, I hope you believe it now. We're going to need help."

"I made a deal that no adults can be involved in what happens next. You can't tell your dad," I said. "If the cops catch Silver, and Silver can't get back to feed Stanley, Stanley dies."

"Okay. But your dad's going to flip when he sees that shiner."

I looked in the rear-view mirror. My eye was so puffy. I thought of Silver and his pleading eyes.

"Silver begged me, Shari. He knows he's been used all this time. This thing doesn't want him. The Dead One wants Cody's medicine power."

"The Dead One wants to twist it and use it to cause sickness," Shari said. "That's what it wants."

"Oh no," I heard myself say. "Listen, there were birds—a chickadee and hundreds of swallows who worked together to form a wall between Silver and the Dead One so Silver could talk to me. Who sent them?"

*Maybe she can confirm it was Mom and Cody. I want her to confirm it was Mom and Cody.*

Shari closed her eyes and shook her head. "Spirit helpers. Your family? Your ancestors? I'm not sure." Shari looked at me. "You said you saw Silver place something in a black cloth, right? That's Stanley's spirit. So if you go back there, you can get Stanley's spirit back to him."

"Yes," I said. "I think so." I could not believe I'd seen where it was, or that I'd seen the ring made of Silver's hair around the Dead One's finger.

"How do I go back to that place and, like, how do you know about this soul parasite stuff?"

She nodded and closed her eyes. "I could feel it here this morning. Cold. I felt soul cold. Silver called it forward and made a deal with it."

I shivered. "Silver heard my thoughts. He heard me when I thought about Edmonton after he asked about Cody. Now that Slitter is inside Silver, he can't stop even if he wants to."

# Broken Wings

DAD WASN'T HOME. I NEEDED A TYLENOL FOR MY HEAD. I HAD the worst headache. I went to the bathroom and pulled open the right drawer beside the sink. No Tylenol. The drawer was still filled with Mom's makeup, her combs, scissors, nail polish, her lipstick. Her beaded moosehide hair clip still smelled like her. I sniffed it.

My headache was getting worse. I decided to look in Dad's room.

Their wedding photos were still up. Mom had been buried with her wedding ring on, but there was the little spruce box it used to shine in.

Dad's bed wasn't made. Beside it were more pictures of Mom: a few camping ones, her graduation photo, them together holding hands. There was his shortwave radio and his tape player with a stack of cassettes: all Elvis or George Jones. A few shirts were laid out on the bed. He had arranged three pillows on the side where Mom used to sleep and dream. She used to say, "We heal fastest under blankets." Whenever she was sick or worried about someone, she'd pull as many blankets as she could over herself and pray. Whenever Dad or I was sick, we'd wake from naps with blankets she'd somehow placed over us and—*poof*—our fevers would have vanished, or we'd be healed from the colds that had been trying to take hold.

There it was: a bottle of Tylenol on Dad's nightstand. I took one and dry-swallowed. On the top shelf of Dad's closet, which was filled with work shirts, was the flare gun kit that Mom had ordered for the last trip she'd ever make. The kit came with five flares. It had arrived the day after we returned home without her—as if it would have even helped her in the daytime when the canoe flipped. The photograph of Mom and Dad together on Dad's nightstand just devastated me.

The advice that I most held on to as I clawed, sank and cooked my way through grief surprisingly came from Shari's dad, Mr. Burns, Fort Simmer's Métis president. He came up to me in the graveyard on the day of the funeral. I was holding Mom's cross. He'd lost his mom, too, just a month before. The whole town went to both funerals. But this time I wasn't just watching alongside my father and the other attendees. I was standing with Dad while Mr. Burns and Shari watched. Mr. Burns approached me, squeezed my shoulder and said, "I am so sorry this happened. Take it one hour at a time, Lawson." Then he added, "There is no wrong way to grieve. Stay busy, and don't hold back when the tears find you."

These were the words that saved me. As fierce as he was, all I saw was tenderness in his eyes, and I felt it in his voice.

But it all felt so weird. It felt like my life became a movie that I was watching. I'd be like, *That's me eating, pretending I can taste my food . . . That's me pretending to smile at all the funny scenes in* Fast Times at Ridgemont High *and* Pee-wee's

Big Adventure . . . *That's me crying into my pillow in the closet with the doors closed, because . . . What are we supposed to do now?*

Our family constellation was supposed to be Orion's Belt. Dad was the bottom star on the left, lifting us all with his quiet strength. I was the middle star: my job was to rock out and trust that I had only inherited the best from Mom and Dad. Mom was the top star—the leader star, guiding us all. She was our lighthouse.

After Mom passed and Stanley was released from the hospital, he started his strange ritual of shuffling to the banks every morning to watch the sunrise. For the first month, Cody joined him. Then Cody left him to watch it by himself. According to Cody, Stanley would watch and smile and mumble to himself in whispers no one could understand. It was like he was talking backwards. Then, once the town realized he was all alone, folks would come out and sit in their trucks with him. Some kids would come and play around him. Some of the Elders would braid his long hair and talk to him, soothing him. But we were all invisible to him. Once the sun reached a certain peak, he'd turn and shuffle back to Indian Village, where I assume he'd wait for Silver to order him to do whatever it was that Silver wanted his mountain of a brother to do.

---

I REMEMBER ONE NIGHT IN THE RAIN AND SLEET, WE COULD hear honking, over and over.

"Sounds like a parade," said Dad. "Want to go see?"

"Sure." I shrugged.

We hopped in his truck and followed the sound.

The whole town eventually showed up at the school track, where Stanley was running laps by himself in the cold. Some of the kids ran after him in their coats and gumboots, chanting, "The Arm! The Arm! The Arm!"

There was nothing Stanley couldn't do when it came to sports. He was our town champion at the Arctic Winter Games and at our community track meets—javelin, shot put, baseball, basketball. He was an all-star athlete. Even when playing darts at the Friendship Centre.

People cheered. "Yes, we can! Yes, we can! Fort Simmer pride! Fort Simmer pride!"

Stanley half raised his arms and looked off toward the water tower.

Some of the teens started running with him.

Then some of the adults.

"Look at that," Dad said, turning off his truck. "It's like his body remembers."

For a moment we all held our breath. We were all thinking, *This is it. This is the night Stanley Cranes wakes up and remembers who he is. This is the night he tells us everything that happened out on Slave Lake. Why did the canoe flip? How did Mom die? Why did he only come halfway back to who he used to be?*

But then Stanley dropped his arms and looked off into the distance, and we watched that blank face wash over his features. We saw the strength leave his body. He was back to zombie mode. Stanley turned and walked home.

"What the hell was that?" asked Dad.

"Maybe he'll come back," I said. "Maybe he'll tell us what happened to make that boat flip."

But as soon as I said it, I felt horrible. I felt like I'd slapped my dad with the last moments of Mom's life. "Sorry," I said.

"S'okay," he said, putting his hand on my shoulder. "It's all right."

Whenever I saw Stanley, the same six words came to me in a rush: *My mother died to save you.*

That night I felt like asking Dad if he wanted to go to the graveyard together, but something stopped me.

"Let's go home," he said.

I nodded and we, like everyone else, turned on the truck and went home. Stanley "the Arm" Cranes was a ghost in his own skin.

---

I WOKE TO THE SOUND OF POTS AND PANS CLICKETY-CLANGing together and the smell of frying bacon and eggs. I heard the toaster pop, and I could hear CBC North playing. Dad was whistling along to "Papa Don't Preach." I hadn't heard him whistle in years. I listened to Madonna sing and decided to change the lyrics: *Papa don't preach, I've been losing sleep, but I made up my mind, I'm keeping my treaty. I'm gonna keep my treaty. Ooh. Mmm.*

I must have dozed off, and I needed a glass of water big time. My mouth tasted like Tylenol dust. As soon as I came around the corner, I spotted Mom's medicine bag. This wasn't a nightmare. I'd survived something that would haunt me for frickin' ever, with Slitter leaping into Silver's mouth and burrowing down his throat. I had to face Dad.

"Here we go," I heard myself say. He had his back to me and was cooking away—eggs, toast, hash browns, bacon. I braced for what Dad would say when he saw my shiner. "Morning," I said.

"Holy," he said as he turned. He froze, holding a spatula, when he saw my swollen eye. "What the hell happened to you?"

Sporting his fresh haircut, he looked younger somehow.

"Just wait until I have a glass of water."

He eyed me while I made my way toward him. He was wearing jeans and a nice shirt that looked freshly ironed. He was even wearing his moccasins. There were two plates set up for the afternoon feast he was preparing, and I could see a battalion of bacon on two paper towels to catch the grease. *Wow. What are we celebrating?*

Most important was a fresh pot of coffee. I pretended to look out the window as I guzzled the water. Mom's moccasins were by the balcony door below her caribou medicine bag that was filled with the fireweed she and Cody had picked together one day on a medicine walk at Tsu Lake. Mom and Dad's wedding photos were on the wall.

"Okay, so you gonna tell me what happened?" he asked while switching his wedding ring from one finger to the next. He did this when he got nervous or was dwelling on something.

"Coffee first," I said. "Hey, that's a nice haircut. Who cut your hair?"

"I need to hear right now what happened to your eye."

I took my time pouring the sugar and stirring in the Carnation.

Dad sighed, eager for an answer. He was like a heat-seeking missile. I could feel him thinking.

"That shiner wouldn't be related to Silver Cranes being on the run with all the money he stole from the Terry Fox Run, would it?" He asked. He was finding his coordinates.

*Why are there no secrets in this town?*

Dad flipped the eggs on the cast iron pan and watched me.

"The RCMP are looking for him," said Dad. "Frickin' guy never learns. They had security cameras in the kitchen, and they got it all on tape. Any news you'd like to share? There's probably a reward, if you need to make quick money."

"I guess he likes jail," I said, and shrugged. I didn't know what to do with this information. I wanted no part in playing a hand in his arrest—which would likely lead to Stanley dying.

Dad looked at me. "Weren't you there with Cody delivering food to the Elders?"

He was on to me. "I delivered the food. Cody never showed."

"No? Where was he?"

I shrugged. "On the keemooch, maybe." That coffee couldn't pour fast enough.

Dad sighed. "Just tell me what happened. I can't protect you if I don't know. That blood on your shoes"—he pointed with his lips to the porch, where I'd left my shoes—"is that yours or Silver's?"

*Blood on my shoes?* I looked and frowned. He should have been a detective.

"Dad," I said firmly, "let me deal with this."

*No, no, no,* I thought. *I cannot involve adults.*

"We're locking the house from now on," he said, placing the eggs on the plates. "Use your house key. I have a feeling we'll all pay for whatever happened."

"Deal," I said.

"They'll catch him and put him back in the pokey," said Dad. "I guess he loves the crowbar hotel with three hots and a cot, hey?" He chuckled to himself and I grinned.

"Thanks for cooking," I said. I was still confused about Silver. *How did he know that by knocking me out he'd bring me to the Dead One's forest?* I had so many questions, but I was also aware that the clock was ticking on Stanley's life. I couldn't return alone.

The wolves I'd spoken to were promised but not bound. I had no idea what that meant. Could I get them to help me?

We ate quietly for a while before Dad spoke.

"Big shindig coming up for Simmer," he said, "and this affects you." He handed me the newspaper. The headline read DENE PEACEMAKER VISITS FORT RAE AND EDZO WITH HIS FAMILY.

I saw pictures of an old man standing with his two adult daughters. His name was spelled *K'aílaza* but the story said it was pronounced like *Kalazaa*. K'aílaza had long hair and wore a gorgeous moosehide jacket with beaded gauntlets. Both the jacket and the gauntlets had fringes. K'aílaza was dark and his face was long. He had a sharp nose, but what I noticed most were his eyes. They were kind. Even though in the pictures, he and his daughters were smiling, I could see that he was on guard and watching, reading, sensing.

I read: *Inspired by spiritual visions, K'aílaza of Mesa Lake , a direct descendant of Chipewyan and Dogrib leaders Akaitcho and Edzo, is set to visit key communities throughout the North with his daughters, to share in celebrations of Dene honouring their peace treaties and thriving together.*

"Looks like he's coming here next," said Dad. "He's also asking that each community prepare something special so people can feast together and celebrate. It says that in Fort Rae it's dry meat and caribou stew. For Fort Simmer, he's hoping to have the finest moose nose soup."

"Moose nose soup?" I frowned. "Do you know how to make it?"

He shook his head. "Sonny does. His grandma was crazy for it."

"So this Elder is a revered peacemaker?" I asked. This was interesting timing. There was no way this was a coincidence.

It was a bannock slap from my ancestors, letting me know that my rematch with the Dead One wasn't a stand-alone event. A great peacemaker was on his way here while Halley's Comet could be seen above Fort Simmer and I had just toppled out of the Dead One's den. Plus, I had just had my very own medicine dream, and I swear I could feel my red wolf thinking about me. I got the shivers.

Dad made a point of looking at my bruise. "Your mother would have done everything to prepare a feast of feasts for K'aílaza and his family at the centre."

I looked at him and thought of Mom. I looked at her medicine bag and her moccasins. "Do we know when he's going to arrive?" I asked.

"He says he's being guided in dreams," said Dad. "I bet the mayor's reading this and scrambling to figure out where they can put him up and host him."

Maybe K'aílaza and his family could help me—but how could they, if I wasn't allowed to tell them about what was happening or what I'd seen or been told?

I had to chew my toast with strawberry jam slowly, as my right eye hurt badly.

"Cool," I mumbled.

"Cool?" Dad asked. "He'll want to meet you and Silver and the Cranes brothers."

"Us? Why?"

"Because you are the descendants of Edzo and Akaitcho. He'll ask you if the treaty has been honoured." He paused. "So, just rehearse a little. I see you sporting a shiner, and there's dried blood on your shoes, while Silver's on the run with all that Terry Fox money. How's that peace treaty coming along?"

"Dad," I said firmly. "Trust me, okay? I'm handling it."

"Handling it?" he scoffed. "You're sitting across from me with a black eye, and you're asking me to let you handle it?"

*No adults, no adults, no adults.*

"Yup." I nodded.

Despite his frustration, Dad started to smile. He tapped his knuckle on the table.

"You're one tough cookie sitting there, you know that? You realize that, as a Yabati and as a direct descendant of Edzo, it will be you who has to make him moose nose soup, right?"

"I don't know how."

"Sonny will. Ask him."

Dad started to focus on my eye. I had to throw him off my trail.

"I'll handle this, okay? *And* I'll learn how to cook moose nose soup, if that's what K'aílaza is asking for. *And* I'll deliver it myself as a Yabati."

*What did I just agree to? Why was I such a blurter?*

"Okay, you said it. I'll hold you to your promise. The other thing K'aílaza wants to see is the North the way he remembers it, so there'll be competitions."

"Like what?" I asked.

"Jigging, fiddling, drum dances, hand games, all the fun stuff. I bet the mayor will stop by the federal building tomorrow to ask for soonyows." There are a lot of Cree here in Simmer, so we sometimes use their words. *Soonyows* is Cree for money. *Moonyows* means white people.

This was my chance to ask more questions about the peace treaty. I had to keep Dad talking.

"Sonny knows way more than I do. You should talk to him. You know his great-grandmother lived to be a hundred and five, right? She spoke no English, only Dogrib. Sonny told me she was awake at four every morning, ready to go, because that's when the Chipewyan would attack."

I looked at Mom's picture on the wall. There she was: head tilted, smiling, snow falling around her, her long hair sweeping over the back of her hood.

"It's hard to stomach even just thinking about traditional warfare. The treaty was made in the 1820s, I think. Your mom was working on a big grant to bring everyone up to Mesa Lake so we could all be reminded why it is important to honour the treaty."

"How many treaties are there here in the North?" I asked.

"Dozens," he said.

I remembered what the black wolf told the Dead One: that the North's leaders were drinking and weak. I had to stop the Dead One. Maybe I could learn something from K'aílaza that might help.

I thought of Silver, him begging me for help. He had made my life so frickin' miserable. What if I could find out more about Mr. Cranes?

"Dad," I asked, "do you think it was Silver's dad who turned him wicked?"

"Maybe," said Dad. "Let me tell you a story. Lester Cranes, that old battle-axe, wanted to be the first Dene mayor here in Simmer. You know who won against him every time?"

"Who?"

"This handsome Cree who wasn't born here. Charlie Snow."

"Okay," I said.

"And guess what else Mayor Snow won? Therese. Lester Cranes' wife."

My jaw dropped.

"Oh yeah." Dad smiled. "They had a little somethin'-somethin' on the side, but then she got pregnant. And guess which son of hers definitely looked like a small version of the mayor?"

I had to act shocked at this, but I already knew what Cody had told me out at Tsu Lake.

"Lester was humiliated," he continued. "Therese took off to Edmonton to be with Charlie Snow and his people. She soon found out Charlie had a few other women on the go, so she came back here with Cody."

"Holy," I said.

So the Dead One knew Cody's secret—that he had a different father than Silver and Stanley, and that he had his own medicine power and family. I prayed that Cody was safe from what was coming for him.

When Cody got in trouble with the law, it was all because of Silver.

"Dad, do you think Silver knew those cameras were recording when they broke into the elementary school?"

"Damn straight. Silver knew that if Cody got caught with him, he'd get expelled, get a criminal record and never graduate. Silver never wanted his little brother to succeed."

I put down my fork. "Because if Cody graduates, Cody leaves town."

"With Stanley the way he is, who would take care of him? Not Silver," said Dad.

"The whole Cranes family lives a lie of sorts."

"How?"

"Mr. Cranes told everyone that he was a direct descendant of Akaitcho—yeah right, he wished he was a direct descendant of Akaitcho. It was Cody's mom who was the direct descendant."

"Mom mentioned that at Tsu Lake."

He shook his head. "According to Mr. Cranes, the Craneses were supposed to be Chipewyan kings. He was owed. He tried being chief and mayor, but he never won. He got bitter as he got older, and he was cruel to those boys. He'd go into these rages. Social Services was over there quite a bit. The boys were covered in welts from getting whipped by that big willow he always carried with him."

"Geez," I said, remembering that big willow stick Mr. Cranes had at his side every time I saw him.

Silver had been a hellraiser growing up, back when everyone called him Banana Leg. He had twenty-three charges against him by the time he was seventeen, but he knew he was largely untouchable because of the Young Offenders Act. He'd sneak into your house during the day to rob you and take your car keys. He'd come back at night and steal your car and destroy it on a joyride. He shot a teacher, Mrs. Thornton, in the eye with a BB gun the day before her wedding. She lost it, too. She was in her backyard working on the final touches for the reception. Silver said he was target-practising and that he must have shot through his backstop, but everyone knew that was untrue. That's why he went to jail.

"Frickin' Silver." Dad pointed at my shiner and held up his fist. "Remember, if Silver ever comes back for another fight, your first move is the stunner. Smile, be loud and make fun of him. If that doesn't work"—he held up his other fist—"go berserk and give him the Kiss of the Dene Hawk." He flexed his right arm and kissed his muscle.

I wanted to laugh but my face hurt from my black eye.

"Everyone I ever fought," said Dad, "I just used what they already showed me against them. Fighting's a thinking man's game. Understand that and you'll never lose. And I am proud of you. You stood up to a bully, and now he'll think twice about tangling with you."

I was grateful for how cocky my dad was. His cockiness gave me courage.

Dad looked at the big plate of bacon, eggs and toast left on the table.

"Look at me. Two years later and I'm still cooking for three."

"Fine with me," I said and held out my plate. As much as my face hurt, I was starving.

# Talk It Out

THAT AFTERNOON SHARI SHOWED UP IN HER DAD'S TRUCK and told me to get in. We drove to the landslide and parked. The Slave River was calm today, and I could see the trees starting to turn. A few pelicans were off in the distance. It was so peaceful here, and I took a big breath. I'd had my medicine dream. I had seen so much—too much—or maybe not enough. I didn't know. I needed Shari's help.

"Okay. Let me think about this." She grew so quiet I thought she had fallen asleep. I marvelled at her features. Her face looked perfectly sculpted. "Have you met the Cree family who just moved here?" she asked.

"No, what Cree family?"

Shari raised her sunglasses and looked at me. Those green eyes of hers were like lasers.

"You haven't seen the most gorgeous Cree woman who has ever walked the earth?"

"What?"

"Oh my god. You're going to fall in love."

Suddenly, I was interested. "Sorry. What's her name?"

She pushed me and teased, "You're already breathing heavy. Get ready, Lawson. You won't even be able to handle it. She's a devastator."

I was intrigued by Shari's description. *Who is this supposed new goddess in town, and why haven't I seen her yet? Oh, I know: it's because I haven't left my house in almost a year, and when I did I got knocked out and went to a twisted forest where souls were traded like hockey cards, and I met an evil spirit called the Dead One who told me that I don't have medicine power but am protected by spirit helpers.*

Shari turned on the truck's tape player. A bizarre little song came on, with pianos and fingers being pulled across strings, then a little chorus of jazzy voices.

"Being serious, this thing of yours—this . . . beast—doesn't just feed on war. It feeds on medicine power. But we can face it. I'd been wondering why the Valentines moved here, but now it's clear to me that we need them." Shari rolled down her window. "Roxanne's in grade twelve. So's her brother—who is also stunning, I must say. Whatever family medicine they have, we need it to beat this soul parasite."

I motioned with my lips to the tape player.

"The song's called 'The Caterpillar,'" she said.

"Cool," I said. "I like it."

I realized that I was finally myself again. Whatever Shari had done by passing me her light the day before had saved me.

"I'm so sorry about what happened with your mom, Lawson," she said as she turned the music down.

"Thanks."

She sighed. "Even in Calgary, I wondered about you. I just . . . it's just so sad. I . . ." She looked at me and touched my arm. “I didn’t know what to say. I’m sorry. Oh, look at you. You’re so beat up.”

I felt the lump on the side of my face. “It’s okay. It’s been two years, and I still don’t know what to say about it.”

“I can see your mom’s features in you. You’ve gotten handsome, Lawson Sauren.”

I blushed. I wanted to look into her eyes again but she’d pulled her sunglasses back down.

“Are you sure we need the new Cree family?” I asked.

“I know we do. The Valentines have something we need to face the Dead One and his wolves. Something the North needs. New medicines. I can feel it. Go meet them, and the signs will reveal just how we’re to take on this beast. What do you say?”

“Okay,” I said. She was the Body Finder, so who was I to argue with her visions and whatever other powers she had?

“We’ll call this Operation Cree Love.”

“Operation Cree Love?” I asked, confused.

“Find out what family medicines they have. The Dead One won’t see this kind of Cree medicine coming when we face him.”

I had a flashback of the forest: the ribs hanging from ropes of human hair and the rattle of jawbones clicking together as the Dead One approached.

“*We* face him?” I repeated, suddenly hopeful at the thought of not having to do this all alone. “Thanks, Shari. You just gave me hope.”

“Well, what do we know for sure? We know that it feeds on souls and medicine power in order to grow,” she said. “But what does it want to grow into?”

*It kept saying that it needed new skin. Gross. For what, though? It was huge, whatever it was. Does it moult like a bird?*

*Does it shed its skin like a snake? What does it need new skin for, and how can we kill it? And why was it wearing a cape of crawling maggots? How can something be rotting and alive at the same time?*

"You said Silver's hair—his spirit—is on the ring finger of the Dead One, and Stanley's spirit is in a tree?"

"Yes," I said. "That's exactly what I saw. Silver showed me where Stanley's spirit was hidden so I could go back and save him."

"Okay. You have to get that ring. Then that creature won't be able to control Silver," said Shari. "And you have to get Stanley's spirit back inside him."

"Silver begged me to help him," I added. "Silver is scared and, if he can, he will help us—if we can get Slitter out of him."

"And we *will* help them," said Shari. "If he's scared, that tells me everything. You know it was his frickin' dad who made him like this, right?"

*That's right: Shari and Silver used to hang out.*

"What do you remember from when you two were friends?"

She shook her head. "It's so sad. Remember how his dad never got to be chief or mayor? He took it out on his sons."

"Dad told me," I said.

"I snuck a look at Silver's journal once, and he had a list of poisons he wanted to try on people. When I told my dad that, I was forbidden to hang out with Silver and told to quit wasting my time trying to reason with him. My dad said he'd down Silver or his dad if they ever came near me."

Shari's dad is huge. He is a hunter, trapper and proud Métis, always wearing his Métis sash and a jacket that he calls a capote. I would not want to ever mess with him.

"I have prayed so hard for Silver," she said. "And Stanley."

"Stanley is Silver's zombie," I said. "The Dead One has made it so that Stanley may die if Silver doesn't come back with Cody and feed him soon."

Shari thought for a long time before she said, "I don't know how yet, but you have to return to the Beneath."

"The Beneath?"

She nodded. "That's the word that keeps coming to me. Beneath. Your mom knew how to go there. Did she ever tell you about it?"

*The Beneath.*

"No," I said. *How on earth does Shari Burns know all about this stuff? I have so much to learn from her, and I'm really starting to have a crush on her.*

"Stanley and I were friends once too," she said, "and I think he still remembers me."

The image of Silver funnelling burning coals down Stanley's throat came back to me.

"If we can free Stanley in the forest, he can help us," I said.

She nodded. "The Beneath is how you return."

"Okay, how do I even do that?" I asked. *Do I even want to do that?*

"We can stop this, but we need the Valentines to help us."

I looked at Shari. "How do you know all of this?"

She smiled and patted my leg. "Stick around, Lawson. I have guides and so do you. But I don't know how your people pass their medicine power on to each other. Isn't it through animals? Or is it the land? Is it in dreams, or through touch? Maybe your dad knows."

I would have to ask him. Through animals? I thought of the red wolf and our connection. Maybe she would offer her medicine power to me. What could I do with her įk'ǫǫ̀?

"Oh shoot. I have to work," Shari said, pointing at the truck's clock. "I'm taking you home."

"Where are you working? The drugstore?"

"Yeah right," said Shari, "and have everyone ask me if their dearly departed is standing next to them?"

I looked at her and realized that, yes, everything must have changed once the town nicknamed her the Body Finder.

"Sorry," I said. "I just remember you used to work at the drugstore."

"We have a home office, and I'm registering the Métis here for their health benefits."

She must get so lonely working from home, unable to work jobs around town and visit with people without them expecting something from her. Howard Jones's "Like to Get to Know You Well" came on and she turned it up.

I was so happy to be able to share with Shari what had happened to me. Who else would believe me? Shari was Métis and proud of it. Growing up, she and her dad had won every talent contest with their jigging, but that all stopped once everyone knew she was psychic.

"You've been through hell, Lawson. But it's nice to see you again—even if we're taking on a soul parasite."

Shari took me to my house and pulled up to the driveway. She walked around the front of her dad's truck. Now that she was standing, I could see she was wearing a black Metallica *Ride the Lightning* T-shirt. She handed me a tape labelled LET'S ROCK MIX, a Memorex dBS with ninety minutes on each side.

"Okay, Lawson. Give me your fave songs *not* on the tape, the best Canadian song, best American song, and best international song."

"Okay," I said. "Why?"

"Because," she said softly, "if you wow me, you get to ask me to the graduation dance."

This was random. She was just back from Calgary and already on the keemooch. It was August. The grad dance wasn't until June, ten months away.

I didn't know what to say and I could tell she knew it, too.

"Sorry," she said. "Is it too soon for a little romance in your life?"

"No," I said, "you just surprised me."

I was blushing and she smiled when she realized that she was the reason I was blushing.

She then looked at me seriously. "Tell no adults, Lawson. Go meet Isaiah Valentine. He'll be at the grad fundraiser dance. Find out what family medicine they have, because we need it—and try not to fall in love with Roxanne, okay? She already has a boyfriend. Gotta go."

She took her time climbing back into her dad's truck. Her licence plate read METIS. As she sped away, she cranked "Battery" by Metallica.

I was exhausted. Beat. And I was surprised that Shari Burns had directly flirted with me. I needed to rest and regroup, and, apparently, I needed to meet the Valentines. How on earth did Shari know that Isaiah would be at the upcoming grad fundraiser dance? I shook my head. She was psychic, that's how—and I had a sense that she was right: we needed his Cree power from down south. This was the key to getting Silver his soul back. From there we could save Stanley, too.

I needed to sleep again. Could I sleep? I lay down, started to doze, and suddenly remembered that I'd won a tennis racquet at a track and field meet a few years ago. I got up slowly and pulled it out of my gym bag, where I had also stashed Silver's nunchucks.

“Silver, Silver, Silver,” I whispered, “you sure did it this time. Why did you have to call this hell beast back into the world?”

I’d never used the racquet before. I held it like a war club. If Slitter came scuttling toward me to jump into my mouth, I’d frickin’ whack it into next week.

# Dancing with Myself

I PRACTISED BEFORE ANY DANCE BY REWATCHING *Breakin'*, *Footloose* and *Flashdance* on VHS. In our basement bathroom, I'd put on Dad's wool socks and practise the moonwalk. I just needed the right tunes. Would DJ Muffaloose finally play "Reckless" by Ice-T? Man, I had a whole dance routine planned out in my head. I had a whole love affair planned with the night. In my fantasy, I'd start with "Ain't Nobody" by Rufus and Chaka Khan, then launch into "Rockit" by Herbie Hancock, then end with "Reckless." After that, I'd dance with whoever wanted me the most.

That was the fantasy. The reality was, well, I'd sit and watch and, if I was lucky, someone who'd been turned down by the person they actually wanted to dance with would see me sitting there, and we'd dance. I was okay with that. I was. Actually, I kind of sucked at dancing.

Because Paul William Secondary was out of commission due to the asbestos removal, the grad fundraiser dance was held at Joseph Birch Elementary. The teachers and grade elevens had done a great job for us: there were streamers and fog lights and a light system that blinked pinks and purples. GRAD 87 was all done up in hundreds of balloons.

That's right: we would graduate the next year, in June 1987.

The gym was filled with Dene students from all over the Northwest Territories. There were white, Gwich'in, Slavey, Bush Cree, Inuit, Métis, Chipewyan, a few Dogrib who never spoke to me, and northerners. The room was pretty rank with Calvin Klein's Obsession, assorted toothpastes, and Aqua Net hairspray. I hoped that no one would light a match. With all the fumes emanating from people's poofy hairstyles, the whole place would blow up. Geez, this town. Everyone here wanted to smell like the kids at West Edmonton Mall.

I was an outsider, and I felt it in every one of my molecules as soon as I walked into the gym. It was decorated in a Halley's Comet theme. The rest of the students at Paul William Secondary had gelled over the past two years while Dad and I were grieving Mom. I'd missed the bush parties, the house parties, the make-out sessions at Panty Point. The teenagers who sat in various separate groups looked like those from my favourite movies. There were stoners, preppies, athletes, nerds and—ever since "Into the Groove" came out—there was a squadron of Madonna wannabes. And then there was me: Lawson the loner.

The dance started awkwardly with "Papa Don't Preach" and "Girls Just Want to Have Fun." Nobody danced. Even with the greatest tunes—even with everyone all gussied up—we still needed the Cody Cranes tradition, him getting out there and dancing first, giving the rest of us permission to let loose. His courage in being gay and not hiding it somehow abolished the shyness in all of us. When Cody would slide out onto the PWS dance floor, it was literally Fort Simmer's version of *Footloose*, that scene where Ren McCormack slides onto the dance floor and yells, "Let's daaance!" and everyone just gives 'er. We all copied Cody's moves. Even the teachers. Most everyone loved Cody—until he broke into JBE with his brothers. *Cody,* I prayed, *I hope you're safe wherever you are.* I prayed his family on his birth father's side was protecting him and keeping him safe.

Starting with Bon Jovi's "You Give Love a Bad Name," we watched as the handsome new Cree student, Isaiah Valentine, asked girl after girl after girl out to the dance floor. They all said no shyly because they didn't know who he was. Then Shari Burns walked right up to him and asked him to the floor. Man, could he dance. Shari could, too.

Isaiah had this strut. Was it his hips? Was it the way he moved his shoulders? What the heck was it? All I knew for sure was that Cody had quickly been forgotten, and Isaiah Valentine now reigned supreme. Those previously shy young ladies I had grown up with since kindergarten now lined up to dance with him. Isaiah smiled and looked into his dance partners' eyes as they gave 'er to "Relax" by Frankie Goes to Hollywood and "Venus" by Bananarama. Unlike me, he actually talked with each of his dance partners. He'd touch their arms and lean toward them to speak into their ears. He had them laughing as he did the pharaoh to the Bangles' "Walk Like an Egyptian" and shimmied to Springsteen's "Dancing in the Dark." He was all about his hips for "Why Can't This Be Love?" by Van Halen, "What You Need" by INXS, and "If You Leave" by OMD. He actually danced like Michael Hutchence in "What You Need." With his gorgeous brown skin and black Cree hair, I knew that he'd be the new talk of PWS. Girls in acid-washed jeans and leg warmers lined up waiting for the chance to dance with him.

I could tell nobody wanted to dance with me. Maybe because no one knew what to say about my mom drowning. Maybe I was just one big pity party and it was easier to ignore me. I was swallowed by loneliness. I went outside to look at the stars. I could hear the last dance of the night being announced: "Take My Breath Away" by Berlin. I hated that song. Like, *as if* you could even dance to it. Porridge rolling down a hill moves faster than that frickin' sad and slow song.

Halley's Comet was faint in the night sky. There were no northern lights yet, but I could see Orion's Belt—Mom's star, Dad's star, my star. I suddenly felt so left behind by life.

I returned back inside just in time to see Shari rest her head on Isaiah's chest. She closed her eyes as they slow danced. They were practically grinding.

After what she had predicted in her dad's truck, this left me keemoochly confused. I was the one who was supposed to fall head over heels for Isaiah's sister. It wasn't supposed to be Shari falling for Isaiah. I kept trying to make eye contact with Shari. *Hey! Remember me? You passed the power of the universe to my soul, remember?* I felt something: a mean trickle. Was it jealousy?

And where was Isaiah's sister? I wanted to see the so-called devastator.

"Lawson," Shari said as we all returned to our chairs to grab our jackets when the dance ended, "make sure you get Isaiah to invite you over for a sleepover. Whoa! What is up with your face right now?"

"Uh, having fun?" I surprised myself with my bitterness.

"Hey," she said, "I'm a free agent until you invite me to the grad dance. Lawson, look at me. I never leave my house.

Do you have any idea what it's like for me to just have fun? Isaiah Valentine can sure dance, and what girl wouldn't want to dance with him?"

"You could have asked me to dance, you know," she said.

"Okay, okay," I said. She was right. I could have and I should have. So, Shari rarely left her house. I knew all about that. And it was all suddenly so sad to me.

I touched her arm and said, "I'm sorry you hardly leave the house."

"Thanks. It's just . . . easier."

"I, uh, that just makes me sad."

She looked at me and nodded. "Okay, just go and make friends with Isaiah and we can talk about this another time."

My left eye was still swollen, and I'm sure it would go over like gangbusters when I asked to get invited to a sleepover by someone who I hadn't even met yet.

---

"HEY," I SAID, CATCHING UP TO ISAIAH AS WE WALKED HOME from school. "I'm Lawson."

"Lawson? Hi." he smiled. He was wearing a Def Leppard "Rock of Ages" T-shirt. "What happened to your eye?"

"Welcome to Fort Simmer," I said, ignoring his question.

We shook hands. He squinted to get a closer look. "Did you at least get one good shot in?"

I looked down. I decided to push ahead despite my blushing face and ask, "Want to camp over next weekend at my house?"

He looked up at the comet. "Camp over?"

"Yeah, it's a tradition here to welcome new students by hosting a supper, watching movies and sleeping over—just to make you feel more at home and welcomed as an honoured guest," I fibbed. "Where do you live?"

"Willow Street," he said.

"We live one street over." I pointed with my lips over to our street.

"You wouldn't happen to have an Allen wrench set, would you?" Isaiah asked me. "And a hammer?"

"Yeah," I nodded. "Our junk drawer is a toolbox."

"How 'bout you bring those and camp over tomorrow night?" he said. "You can meet my family."

*Oh wow! This is going to be easy.* "Okay." I was beaming inside.

He looked at me sideways. "We're still unpacking, so you gotta help set up beds and a table, okay?"

"Sure," I said. "So, are you going into grade twelve or what?"

"Yup," he said.

"Me too." I smiled.

"Cool," he said.

The stars were out and we were both glancing upward.

"Do you believe in aliens?" I asked.

He nodded. "Yup."

There was Orion.

"Sasquatch?"

He shrugged. "Sure."

"People being able to read minds?"

He looked at me and frowned. "I wish I could do that."

"Cool."

"Did you hear when they're going to reopen the school?"

I shook my head. "Nope."

"Okay, come over tomorrow night for supper. You can meet my mom, my brothers and my sister, okay?"

"Okay."

"Don't forget those tools," he said. "You can sleep over but remember you gotta set up your bed and stuff."

I nodded. "Deal."

"You like moose meat?"

"Love it," I said.

He held out his hand. "Good."

We shook. He pointed to his house. "Number seventeen. Come by at five."

"Okay," I said. "Mahsi cho. See you then."

"Yup," he said. "See you then."

I was now invited to the Valentines' for a sleepover and, from there, I would enlist their help in facing whatever darkness Silver had made a deal with. Operation Cree Love would soon be in full effect!

# Our House

SATURDAY NIGHT DAD WAS HAPPY BECAUSE I WAS HAPPY. DAD had an early supper—caribou stir-fry—before he went to work a dance at the hall, a.k.a. Moccasin Square Gardens. With this new haircut of his, Dad no longer looked like he was wearing a puffy helmet of fur. I was looking at a very handsome man. His hair was less black, but there was still way more pepper than salt, as Sonny would say. Dad was playing "On the Other Hand" by Randy Travis. For my dad, country and Elvis were church. I'd hear him play Elvis's "How Great Thou Art" every morning in my parents' room as he got dressed for the day. At night, he'd play Elvis's "Crying in the Chapel." Then I'd hear him fiddle with his shortwave radio and find a channel far away. He needed it to sleep. I almost needed it to sleep.

But tonight was sleepover night at the Valentines'. I was so excited. I'd set the Allen wrench set and our hammer by the door so I wouldn't forget them. I could help set up beds as we watched *Night Tracks*. This was my chance to claim Isaiah as my new best friend and see what kind of medicine power he had—but I'd have to find out if he even believed in medicine power first.

One street over, a few knocks, and I was at the Valentines'. Their porch was stuffed with workboots, gumboots, winter boots, Reeboks, Nike high-tops, high heels, sandals and jackets—so many jackets. I could smell a moose roast cooking as soon as I walked in.

"Thanks for bringing the tools," said Isaiah.

"No problem," I said as I untied my shoes.

"Lucky for you, Linus found our Allen wrenches last night, so we spent all day putting everything together."

"Really?" I acted disappointed. "Oh, man. And I was so looking forward to helping."

He motioned for me to enter the living room. "Come meet my family."

Yes, there were two of Isaiah's younger brothers in the room. Yes, there was their mother. But most importantly, there was Roxanne Valentine. Miss Cree Saskatchewan in four years? Shari was right: Roxanne Valentine was a Cree goddess.

After I shook everyone's hands, we sat and played Crazy Eights Countdown while listening to ABBA's *Voulez-Vous*. I had to keep my eyes from continually wandering back to Roxanne. She was beautiful, heavenly beautiful.

The Valentines wore stunning moccasins. The colours were brighter than what we wore up here, and the living room smelled like smoked moosehide. The entire Valentine family had sharp features. I had a soft face, my mother's face. I was grateful nobody asked about my shiner, but I saw them exchange a look that said they'd talk about it later, and that it was up to Isaiah to find out if this was from my folks or what.

Isaiah's brothers were Linus and Patrick. Linus, in grade five, had a pigshave haircut with big ears poking out. He wore a blue shirt that said TUBULAR! Linus was small, but he was built like a wolverine: solid. Patrick was in grade seven and had long hair swept over his face. He wore a Teenage Mutant Ninja Turtles shirt and had a Transformers Time Warrior watch. The brothers were sharing a huge bag of salt and vinegar chips. Roxanne was curled up on the couch resoling a pair of men's moccasins. On the left one, the beadwork said COME, and on the right one it said HOME. At her feet were several small bowls—each containing a different colour of beads—and a pile of college and university applications. She kept glancing at the rotary phone.

There were stacks of Choose Your Own Adventure books on the shelf beside me. The one nearest me was *Sugarcane Island*. It looked like Mrs. Valentine was a reader, too. She had *The Thorn Birds* and *The Prince of Tides* on either side of where she sat, each with a beaded flower moosehide bookmark indicating where she'd left off.

Of all the artwork in the living room, the piece that kept stealing my gaze was a blown-up framed photograph right above the TV. It was a full-colour image of a Cree man with his braids flying. He was wearing grass-dancing regalia, including a headpiece made from what looked like wolverine fur and two eagle feathers. The photo was a blur of fringes, tassels, bells and a proud, handsome man wearing white moccasins or mukluks. It was a portrait of grace and power.

The bookshelf displayed the same headpiece seen in the photo, along with sage, sweetgrass, buffalo horns and beaded moccasins.

"That's Isaiah's grandpa," Mrs. Valentine said when she saw me looking. "My dad."

"My mushom." Isaiah nodded. "Harold Valentine."

"Best grass dancer there ever was," Roxanne said.

The Valentines grew silent. I was sure he had passed. The headpiece was magical to me. It was unlike anything I'd ever seen before. I stood and approached it.

"Can I ask what it's made of?"

"My boy," Mrs. Valentine said to Isaiah, "show your friend."

Isaiah stood and lifted the headpiece. He held it up gently and showed it to me. He then put it on. "The headpiece is deer hair that goes around, then porcupine hair that comes down, and then from the inside there's a roach spreader." He wiggled his fingers back and forth and the plumes on the end started to move. "These are grasshopper antennae. That's how they would respect the insects."

He took it off and handed it to me. "Here. Hold it. You have my permission."

I held it and was in immediate awe. The work that had gone into the headpiece was incredible. I could smell smoke and old sweat. The fur tickled my wrists as I turned it around.

I handed it back to him and bowed. "Wow."

He nodded. "Beautiful, hey? Mushom gave it to me before he passed. See this?" Isaiah held a pouch filled with something. "This is a tobacco offering from my mushom's worst enemy."

Isaiah handed it to me. It was either moose or deer hide filled with tobacco so old it crunched when I held it. I sniffed the hide and could tell it had been brain tanned—it probably smelled so sweet with smoke years ago.

"My mushom got into politics back home and had a lot of enemies," Isaiah said. "His worst was Frank Summer. Folks used to show up at band meetings just to watch those two fight. Tables and chairs flew, and they came to blows many times." Isaiah's voice lowered. "When Frank got cancer, he asked my mushom to dance for him at his memorial. As much as they hated each other, Grandpa could not refuse this offering."

"Because of the tobacco?" I asked. "Even though they hated each other?"

"Once you choose the way of the grass dancer," Isaiah said, "your life is no longer your own. You can be called upon anytime anywhere to dance, but the offering has to be for a good cause, to help others."

"Oh wow. That's so beautiful," I said as I handed the pouch of tobacco back. "Mahsi cho for sharing that with me. What a great man."

"He was the best," Mrs. Valentine said tenderly, and motioned to Isaiah. "Isaiah's a grass dancer."

"Semi-retired," Isaiah said shyly as he placed the tobacco back beside his grandfather's photo and sat down.

"Semi-retired?" I asked. "Why?"

Isaiah gestured toward the town. "Do you see any other grass dancers up here?"

"No," I said, "but I'm looking at one right now, and we may need you to dance here."

"Yeah right," he said, gesturing for me to stop joking. I wasn't. This was not the time to ask him to help us just yet, but now I had the key. I needed tobacco to do this properly, and I needed a pouch to offer it to him in. This was good. This was fantastic.

"Isaiah," Mrs. Valentine said, "I'd love to see you dance here. Maybe at the reopening of the centre?"

"We'll see, Mom," Isaiah said. "Okay?"

She nodded but looked to me and gave me a thumbs-up.

Patrick snuck up behind Linus and yanked his pants down. Linus fell on his side and scrambled to assemble himself under his shirt. He was embarrassed but started laughing, too. Everyone howled but looked away out of respect. You could tell the Valentine family was used to this.

"What's Dad's ETA?" Linus asked as he pulled up his pants.

"Yeah," Patrick said. "When's he coming home?"

"He's doing his best. He just picked up another load."

"Cheap," Patrick said. "He better not miss my birthday."

Roxanne sighed. "Can Dad just get here already?"

The room grew quiet for a bit. Was this grief or sorrow or both for not having their dad around?

Roxanne kept looking at the phone. She was wearing a long-sleeved Beaver Canoe pullover. I couldn't tell how long her hair was because her braid was tucked behind her. I wondered if it went down past her waist.

"Are you gonna play that card or what?" Isaiah asked me, pointing to my hand. "And quit checking out my sister."

Roxanne raised her eyebrows and smiled.

"What!" I blushed. "Not even." My face immediately felt like it was melting. The lump under my eye started to throb.

Roxanne cast me a side glance and went back to sewing. I went back to watching her over my cards. In the kitchen, Mrs. Valentine was slicing moose meat off the bone. It felt like home. It was my kind of bonkers, and I was already in love with the Valentines. Operation Cree Love was a pretty easy assignment.

"How do you like Fort Simmer so far?" I asked as we played on.

"I'm excited for Isaiah and Roxanne to finish high school here," Mrs. Valentine said. "Have you heard anything about when they plan to reopen?"

I shook my head. "No. Dad says they have a crew up working around the clock, but it's slow, you know?" The community channel had said they were hoping for the end of September, but it seemed uncertain.

"Well, we love it so far," said Mrs. Valentine, "and we're grateful for our home."

"And our extended summer break," added Linus. Patrick cheered.

The Valentine house was nice, even though it was low-income row housing. My buddy Kenny had stayed in one of these houses with his mom before she got a new boyfriend and he frickin' betrayed me by moving with them to Hay River. There'd be three rooms upstairs and a bathroom. The tub would be orangey yellow with red flecks in it. Like rust. Like someone had used their thumbnail on it. I bet the bar that was supposed to hold up the towels would be rickety, as if it had been pulled off its holder time and time again. The basement would be cold and musty, but at the same time it would smell like dryer heat. The whole place had been repainted with that same yellow-white paint they always used for these houses. The Valentines had already decorated the main living room and kitchen walls with ceramic plates showing wolves and bears, and paintings of long-haul trucks on black velvet. There were doilies and huge dream catchers all over the place. There were licence plates from Nevada, Idaho and Saskatchewan. One licence plate read WELCOME TO MUFFALOOSE COUNTRY: FORT SIMMER, NWT, and featured a silhouette of a smiling muffaloose with buck teeth.

There was also a beaded moosehide bag filled with eagle feathers. There must have been fifty feathers—spotted eagle and golden. I kept looking at it. This was definitely proof of their medicine power.

Isaiah noticed me checking out the feathers. "My mom," Isaiah started. "Ever since she was a girl, eagles have dropped their feathers for her. One time we were canoeing and a spotted eagle dropped a feather. Mom caught it in the air."

"I saw that with my own eyes," said Patrick.

"Me too," Linus added. "These have never touched the ground."

"You caught all of these in the air?" I asked.

Mrs. Valentine smiled. "Most of them. And usually there's an eagle feather outside our door when there's a major life decision to make." She pointed her lips to a single feather on one of the shelves. "That one told me it was time to move here and take this job."

Shari saw eagle feathers in her vision of the Valentines. We were on the right path. I was exactly where I needed to be.

"What do you do?" I asked Mrs. Valentine.

"Mom's the new executive director of the Friendship Centre," said Patrick.

My stomach dropped. That was my mom's old job.

"Mom's gonna set up back-to-the-land programs and language immersion," Linus added.

"She's going to reopen the Drop-In Centre," said Patrick.

"Cool." I nodded. "We need that."

The Drop-In Centre was padlocked now. There were rumours that Gordy—the last youth worker and stand-in for my mom as the town tried to get things back to normal after her death—had stolen a pile of money that was supposed to be used for upkeep and to bring the centre back up to code. *How could anyone do that to my mom's memory and all her hard work?*

"When is the centre going to reopen?" I asked.

She sighed. "We'd love to host a community feast for the Elder and his family coming to town. Do you know anything about K'aílaza and his family, Lawson?"

Everyone looked at me.

"He's coming here to celebrate peace in the North," I said. "And probably to share stories."

"Stories? What kind of stories?" Linus asked. "Myths and legends, or what?"

"For the Dene. I think he knows about all the peace treaties, I guess," I said. Roxanne watched me while I spoke, so I puffed up my chest a little and used my hands to talk, like Sonny when he really got going with his storytelling. "The Chipewyan have a peace treaty with the Dogrib because of our ancestors, and K'aílaza is related to both sides."

"Are you Dogrib?" Roxanne asked.

I nodded. "And Mountain Dene, through my dad. My mom was Dogrib."

I could tell everyone sensed what had just happened. I had spoken about my mom in the past tense.

"Mom," Roxanne asked, "do you think I could make this Elder some moccasins?"

Mrs. Valentine nodded and smiled. "I think that would be so sweet, my girl."

"It said in the newspaper that K'aílaza means 'moon' in Chipewyan," Mrs. Valentine said. "He wants there to be friendly competitions and community feasts in every community he visits. In Fort Simmer, he wants to see who can make the best moose nose soup."

"Ew," said Linus. "Really?"

"I'd try it," said Roxanne.

"Me too." Patrick shrugged and pushed Linus. "You don't say no to food."

Linus pushed Patrick back and folded his arms tight around himself. "It sounds gross."

Isaiah frowned. "If that's their way, that's their way." He thought about it. "I'd try it."

"I'll need to trace his feet," Roxanne said.

"I can help," I offered. As soon as I said it, I was like, *What?*

*How are you going to do that?*

"What's the holdup with the centre anyway, Mom?" Linus asked.

Mrs. Valentine sighed. "We keep having problems with contractors. They're all working on the Northern Store, and there have been so many house fires here. But it's beautiful what's been done so far. I want to bring in a counsellor on-site and in the school. You kids deserve a safe place and better gym, board game night, cards. I'd like to have sharing circles and community feasts. Maybe we could bring in motivational speakers. I also want to offer short classes like breakdancing and beadwork and photography."

"Breakdancing?" I smiled. "Cool."

"What do your parents do?" she asked.

"My dad works for the government," I said. "He's a bookkeeper. My mom passed away a while ago."

"Oh no," she said, bringing her hand to her face. Everyone looked at me, and the house fell silent. I felt the energy leave the room.

"My dad also calls bingo," I offered.

"Lawson," Isaiah said, "I'm so sorry. I didn't know."

"Was your mom Roberta?" Mrs. Valentine asked.

Was. *There's that word again. It's like she was just here a moment ago.*

"Yes."

"Oh god," she said.

"What, Mom?" Roxanne asked immediately. "What's wrong?"

"Lawson, did your mom . . . pass on the land?" Isaiah asked quietly.

I nodded.

Mrs. Valentine continued. "Lawson, I was told about all the good she did for Simmer. All the programs out on the land. She's a hero."

"Summer camp," I remembered. "Winter camp, Tsu Lake, Slave Lake."

"She is a legend. She did so much fundraising, not only for this Friendship Centre but for others across Canada. I have pretty big footsteps to follow. Every morning when I walk in, I see her words, 'Make Yourself Proud,' on the wall in big letters. In my office—sorry, her office—it says—"

"'Lead with love,'" I said gently. I remembered now. I remembered that. I remembered the day she painted that on her wall.

"Lawson, we have boxes of gifts at the centre that other Friendship Centres sent once the news of her passing spread. There are seven star blankets that were sent from across Canada to honour her and her family."

"Wow," said Roxanne.

"Holy," said Isaiah.

I looked at Mrs. Valentine. "Star blankets? I'm sorry, I don't know what those are."

"When you're ready, I'll tell you all about them. They're safe in my office, and there are other boxes of her stuff, as well. We can deliver them to you when you're ready, or you and your dad can come pick them up. No pressure."

I winced. I'd never be ready.

"Okay," I said. "Thank you."

After Mom passed, they got an artist to stencil her words on the walls in the gym. I started to feel grief close in. "Um. Can we play please?"

"Of course," she said and nodded to Roxanne, who spoke

Cree to her brothers. They resumed playing, but they were quiet. "Her words are still up," said Mrs. Valentine. "We've kept them even through the renovations."

I could feel her watching me, analyzing me. I didn't like it.

"Can I ask," I said, "did you ever see what happened to those Elder photos she had taken a long time ago?"

Mrs. Valentine thought about it. "Were they framed?"

"Yes. They're black and white, and the photographer was really good. They had them blown up huge and framed so nicely. They used to hang in the gym, like in that one foyer. People would come in from Fitz and Fort Smith just to look at them. Everyone wanted copies."

"I've seen them," she said. "They're stacked and covered in clear tarps in the library."

What a relief. "So many of those Elders have passed now. It would be cool once the gym is done to hang them up again."

"I like that," she said. "Lawson, may I make a suggestion?"

I looked at her. "Sure. What is it?"

"When we reopen the Friendship Centre, what if we renamed it in memory of your mom?"

I felt my soul blush. Everyone looked at me.

"Think about it. She's a hero. She gave her life to save another. The Roberta Sauren Friendship Centre. What do you think?"

I found myself smiling and wanting to burst into tears at the same time.

"Wow. She'd love that," I said.

"I can start the paperwork, but maybe you'd like to talk to your family first."

I needed some time to process this. "I, uh . . . I need to talk to my dad about this."

She placed her hand on my arm and gave it a squeeze.

"Of course. And, like I said, wait until you see what we're doing with our renovations. You will be amazed."

"You know we're only here for a year, right?" Isaiah asked me.

"What?" I asked, confused.

"Mom's job is to get the Friendship Centre back on track financially and then get someone local to run it."

Mrs. Valentine smiled and shrugged. "That's what I do."

"Where will you go next year?" I asked.

"Wherever they want me."

"Unless," Patrick said, "we love it here. Then we can stay, right?"

She nodded. "If we love it here, I can ask for an extension."

*Frick sakes! These guys are all going to leave me in a year?*

I noticed there was a lit candle under a photograph of Isaiah's dad. He was standing in front of a huge truck with his thumbs up. He wasn't smiling. His black hair was slicked back with Brylcreem. He wore an open-chested long-sleeved shirt with a pack of smokes in the breast pocket. He was stacked with muscles and jewellery. One of his hands was a fist, the other held a lighter. He looked tough. I sensed no joy in him at all.

"Is your husband sick?" I asked without thinking.

Everyone turned to me with worry in their eyes.

Mrs. Valentine looked at the picture and then back at me. "Oh no. He's a long-haul trucker, so we light the candle to send our love and protection."

"Dad's moccasins will be ready tonight," Roxanne said. "He needs to just come home now."

"Tapwe, my girl," Mrs. Valentine said. "I'll tell him that."

"*I'll* tell him that," Roxanne said firmly. "And he better bring me more moosehide."

I'd walked into a complicated family, and I loved it. I felt warm with them. Safe. But it was obvious something was up with Mr. Valentine.

The moose roast smelled so great. It was the aroma of high berry and deep earth. "Joey." Roxanne put the moccasins down and pleaded with the phone. "Frickin' call me."

"Told you," said Patrick. "You shoulda broke up."

"I hope you don't go back to Saskatchewan for university, sis," Isaiah said. "Stay away from that loser."

"Yeah," Linus said. "Dad calls him a bonehead."

Roxanne pulled the moccasins close to her chest and moved a table lamp closer so she could see better. "You never gave him a chance."

"Let's eat," Mrs. Valentine said.

"Go ahead," Roxanne said. "I'm not hungry."

We feasted, and we devoured everything. Mrs. Valentine had made mashed potatoes and had boiled up frozen vegetables. She apologized for not having any dessert, but nobody complained. Gosh, it felt so great to be hosted and cooked for. Linus and Patrick behaved at the supper table and cleared their plates as soon as they were done. Each of them hugged their mom after and thanked her. Then Isaiah pointed with his lips for us to get to work on setting up his bedroom.

Mrs. Valentine took a sip of her tea and said, "Set up that fold-out bed before you guys wind down. Don't stay up too late, and keep it quiet, okay? No wrestling in the house. Got it?"

"Got it," Isaiah and I agreed as we cleared our plates.

"Boys," Isaiah said, "it's your turn to do the dishes."

They let out a collective groan but got to work.

"Good night, everyone," I said. "Thanks for having me. That was delicious, Mrs. Valentine. Mahsi cho."

She smiled and nodded. "Mahsi cho," she called back.

I snuck a peek at Roxanne. Goodness, she was so beautiful. That bonehead Joey was sure a lucky guy.

Isaiah and I headed upstairs.

# Tormentor

SILVER LET OUT A GROAN AS SLITTER TIGHTENED ITSELF inside of him. He looked around. Where was he? What was he doing here? They were on the bus. It must have been heading to High Level—he recognized the road, the signs. They'd have to switch buses in High Level to get to Edmonton, where he'd done his time in jail, and gather the warriors he had promised to the Dead One.

He had to find Cody. Once he found him, Slitter would know what to do. When they brought Cody back, the Dead One would let Stanley go.

This was a good trade. Now Lawson believed what he'd been told. Everything had been set in motion, and Silver carried his father's medicine inside of him.

Cody was an imposter: not full-blooded. Not a true Cranes. Not worthy of being included in his father's resurrection.

Slitter surfaced inside of Silver and looked around before settling, waiting, plotting.

You could not trade deaths. That was Silver's father's law.

What was done was done, and Silver's new body was a marvel. He finally felt as strong and as huge as Stanley. No more bent leg. No more searing lungs. He could do anything with his body now. All of his dreams of becoming a war chief were coming true. As his father had promised, the North would kneel when his name was spoken.

He just had to find Cody. And he would find Cody through Cody's father, Charlie Snow.

Charlie would be easy to find. He worked at the Friendship Centre on Ninety-Fifth Street. They would go there. Slitter would leap from Silver's mouth into Charlie's, and Charlie would lead them to Cody. After that, the Dead One had a plan for bringing Cody back to the den quicker than the others. All Silver had to do was trust and do his part. His father would take care of the rest. Once he and his warriors returned, they would turn their focus to the man they called K'aílaza.

Cody's and K'aílaza's medicines would give the Dead One the power he needed to make the North theirs—through war, through fear, through suffering, through pain.

Slitter's tail snaked slowly inside of Silver, searching for new ways to twist around his guts and bones to squeeze and torture him whenever he doubted their master's plan.

"Stop it," hissed Silver. "I know the plan. I know where Cody's dad works. You can have Cody when we find him, so stop frickin' hurting me. Sleep, Slitter. Rest. We'll need you ready to attack when we meet Cody's dad. He's protected, so you'll have to work fast. Take him over and get him to lead us to Cody."

Slitter loosened its grip. Silver attempted to clear his mind. He dimmed his thoughts and slowed his breathing, just like he had done to tune in to his father's words when he was in jail.

Slitter finally dozed inside of him.

Had it sensed doubt?

Silver knew he was being driven by something cruel, something that fed off war and terror, but he welcomed it. This time next year, the Dogrib, the Bush Cree, the Inuit, the Mountain, the Slavey—all of the Dene—would fear him and pay him the respect and tributes he deserved. He would make the laws in Denendeh. Silver Cranes would be as respected and feared as Akaitcho. His very name would strike fear into the hearts of those who might plot against him.

The bus hummed along toward its destination. Silver had been so tired for so long. All his life he'd been waiting for power, and now he had a new body, new strength. It would be so good to see his Chipewyan warriors, his gladiators, the ruthless lot of them. It would be so good to command them and bring fear and terror to the North like his dad had always wanted.

He must trust his master's plan and lead his master's return to the world through Cody's medicine. There would be no stopping this magnificent god who had chosen him, Silver Cranes, to rule the North.

Silver spoke the prayer he'd worked so hard on, learning in Chipewyan to call the Dead One forth: "ʔetao t'ası neba serástthën sį́. Neba hế̃snąu sénaolnı. Sedarıyéne beghą k'ohıldḍhër. Neghą́nıtą́h." It was a simple prayer and a calling prayer. Slitter loved it whenever Silver recited it. Simply, in English, it translated to "Father, I serve you. Use me and remember me. You are my god now. I love you."

Silver Cranes smiled as he looked out the bus window. He could feel Slitter purring inside of him.

# Send Me an Angel

MY MISSION WAS TO CONVINCE ISAIAH TO UNITE WITH US FOR Operation Cree Love, so why, ten minutes later was I going berserk and twisting Isaiah's neck in a WWF headlock before hammering his arms with Sally Cows and legs with charley horses as he tried to donkey-kick me from behind?

"My neck!" he said, wincing. One of his moccasins flew across the room. I straddled him from behind and put him in the sleeper. "Submit," I said. "Frickin' say it."

"No—wrestl—ing . . ." he gurgled.

The walls of his room were covered in heavy metal posters: Iron Maiden's *Somewhere in Time,* Metallica's *Master of Puppets,* Black Sabbath's *Seventh Star,* and Megadeth's *Peace Sells . . . But Who's Buying?* There were also Iron Maiden flags: *Killers,* "Run to the Hills," "Aces High." It was rad. Derek Riggs' paintings of Iron Maiden's mascot, Eddie, were incredible.

"You're frickin' moving in a year?" I asked him.

"If we want to stay—we have—to—fill—out—an—appli—ca—tion." He grimaced.

He tried a few nerve holds, but I oozed sweat to make

myself slimy, and wiggled around so he couldn't get my wrists or tendons.

"Frickin' secreter!" he said. "You kinked my neck!"

I pushed him away and rose quickly so he couldn't fishtail me. He gripped his neck and rocked back and forth.

"Smooth move, Ex-Lax," he said. "You kinked my neck."

"Oh, man," I said, and sat on his bed. "I am so sorry."

Out the window, I could see Joseph Birch Elementary with the lights still on. I could also see Halley's Comet in the sky, reminding me of all that I had seen in the Dead One's den. This wasn't just a sleepover—I had an agenda. I had to play it cool.

"Hey," I said, pointing with my lips toward the boombox, "can you get *Brave New Waves* on CBC?"

He shook his head. "Radio never worked. Dropped it. Tape player works though." He pressed play and Bon Jovi's "You Give Love a Bad Name" came on. "My cousins made me this mix. They told me to play it when I missed them. They have a cool drum group called Your PA Cousins. Do you drum?"

I shook my head. "No."

He looked sleepy.

"Don't you fall asleep," I said. "It's party time."

"Party time? Yeah right. Why don't you tell me what happened to your eye," he said. "And be honest. Crees can always tell when someone's fibbing."

*How far will I let him in on what happened?*

"Terry Fox Run," I said and then realized I'd whispered it. I cleared my throat and tried again. "Sorry. It happened at the Terry Fox Run."

"Who hit you?" he asked.

"Silver Cranes and his brother Stanley," I said. "But it wasn't Stanley's fault."

"Mom's already warned us about Silver." He leaned forward. "He stole all that Terry Fox money, hey?"

I took a big breath. "After the Terry Fox Run, the organizers asked me to bring some stew to the Elders at the old folks' home."

"And?"

"I surprised him—while he was committing the B and E."

"You caught him?" Isaiah asked excitedly.

I nodded. "Yeah."

"Did you go to the cops?"

I shook my head. "They caught him on video."

"Holy. Okay, tell me everything."

He'd know if I left anything out, so I told him mostly everything. I told him about discovering Silver and Stanley trying to break into the Legion, about charging Silver because I knew I was going to lose if he struck first, about the fight, about Silver looking for their half-brother. I glanced up to see Isaiah reading the lyrics inside a cassette case.

"Am I boring you?" I asked.

"Nah," he said. "Keep going."

Not now. This wasn't the time. Isaiah was distracted and kept rubbing his neck. I could hear Isaiah's brothers laughing downstairs with Roxanne. Mrs. Valentine was in her room. This was not the time to tell him the whole truth. They were still unpacking their life in their new house—without their father here. I'd have to look for the signs Shari had mentioned and make sure that this was done properly.

"So, yeah," I said, "that's basically what happened. The end."

Isaiah reached into his dresser and pulled out a butterfly knife.

"So let me get this straight. Silver Cranes was going to steal all that money raised by the Terry Fox Run?"

"Yup," I said.

"And you jabbed his nose with a screwdriver?"

I nodded and felt the swelling under my eye. It had gone down, but it still hurt if I pressed on it.

"Something doesn't feel right about this," he said.

Robert Palmer's "Addicted to Love" started. I must have watched that video a thousand times—every chance I got. I really didn't understand why all five women never smiled. They were all glorious, but they danced like cyborgs. What was the message?

"Why?" I asked.

"Silver has a third brother?" Isaiah asked. "What's his name again?"

"Cody," I said.

"And he wasn't there?"

I shook my head. "He ran away."

"How come?"

"Cody's gay, and Silver hates him for that."

"So what?"

"We all knew Cody was gay in grade school."

"I'd run away." Isaiah shrugged.

I looked at him. "What?"

"If I was gay and my family hated me," he said. "I'd find a new family and live with them." Then he thought carefully before asking me, "So you really did and said all those things, huh, even though you knew you were going to catch a beating?"

I flexed both of my math arms and gave each one a kiss before doing an imitation of Dusty Rhodes from the NWA.

"God hates a coward, and that's the kiss of the Fort Simmer sting, Daddy!"

Isaiah laughed. He sat up and did this figure eight with his hands that flashed the blade out of the winged butterfly knife, before closing it, revealing it, vanishing it, pinwheeling it. I was hypnotized.

"Well, screw Silver Cranes if he hurt you," Isaiah said. "Welcome to our family."

"*Pfft.*" I gave him the hairy eyeball. "Only for a year." I reached for the knife. He handed it to me. I held it. It was still warm.

"I told you," he said, "if we like it here, we can stay longer."

"Well frickin' love it and stay forever, you," I said, and tried to close his butterfly knife. I'd seen this in the movie *Sharky's Machine* with Burt Reynolds, but this knife was quite heavy. I went slow and heard the clack of the blade finding its home in the handle. I was clumsy, but I'd get this in no time.

"I don't know about Simmer," he said. "B and Es and gay haters. Plus some dink knocked my new buddy out."

I started doing slow figure eights with the knife, then I started flipping the blade open and shut, open and shut. I clicked the butterfly knife shut perfectly.

"Tradesies, or nah?" I asked.

"No way," he said. "My dad got me this knife from the States for my fourteenth."

"So where is your dad?"

"Who knows?" He shrugged and lay back down. "Manitoba? South Dakota?"

"How long is he gone for?" I asked. "Like, how many days a year?"

He shrugged. "Depends on how much he and Mom are fighting."

"Oh," I said. "Sorry."

"Well, they're off and on. My dad has something called white line fever."

I frowned. "What's that?"

Isaiah shook his head. "He gets into a truck, and he can't stop. He makes good money. Holy cow, when he comes back to town, his wallet is just fat, boy, and he brings home at least two buckets of KFC. He pays the bills, and then we get to go shopping, and we eat out for a few days, and then the phone rings, and he and mom fight, and then he's gone again."

Isaiah went quiet, then continued, "It's a lonely life for you and for the family you leave behind."

I put the butterfly knife on Isaiah's dresser. Beside it, in his closet, were a folded foamy mattress that already had blankets on it, a few T-shirts and long-sleeved shirts—but farther in hung the regalia of a traditional Cree grass dancer, like I'd seen in his grandfather's photograph.

"Holy," I said and stopped.

"What?"

I wanted to reach out and touch it. This was Cree medicine. This was the flash that Shari had seen. "Is this . . . yours?"

"What?" he asked again.

"The regalia."

"Yup," he said.

It sparkled with emeralds, tassels and beadwork. There was a big suitcase with the number 2837 pinned to the side of it, maybe from his last competition. The beadwork must have taken years—blood reds, orangey yellows, blue, turquoise. Isaiah's regalia smelled like smoked deer hide.

"Your culture is so incredible," I said.

He nodded. "Thanks."

"Who made it for you?"

"My aunties. My kookum. My mom. Roxanne made my moccasins."

"Tell me more. You're so lucky."

"We're not supposed to talk about it."

I wanted to reach out and touch his arm, assure him that his secrets were safe with me, but I grew shy. But seeing this regalia was like being welcomed into something important. I could feel it. Shari was right.

Isaiah stood and went to the closet. He touched the regalia. "My mushom—when I was four—he rolled out two rain barrels and kept them on their sides. He propped them up with rocks so they wouldn't budge, and he got a two-by-four and made a bridge. This was at our last family reunion before he passed. He hopped up and did a dance that made everyone stop. He was so heartbroken that my dad and his brothers were drinking at what should have been a dry event."

I watched Isaiah. His chin started to tremble. "My mushom hopped up there in his moccasins, with his braids, and he did a dance that was so powerful that the women started to weep. A grass dancer clears the earth for the widows, the mothers, the children, the veterans, the chiefs, the leaders. We bless the earth and all who watch us in a good way. When you're grass-dancing, you always think that you're on the ground. You're always praying for the land, dancing as an animal or an insect, and looking around. You're praying for everything, so everything is blessed."

This was so beautiful. It was the medicine power that we needed.

"Remember, what I told you," he said. "When you become a grass dancer, your life isn't your own. That phone can ring anytime, and you have to go."

"Really?" I asked. "Where do you go?

"Wherever you're called for ceremony."

"Whoa," I said. And there again was the key—I would offer him tobacco. *Or*—I could offer him the fireweed that my mom had gathered with Cody before she passed. Yes! The

Valentines were guests here, and they deserved an offering from the Northwest Territories. This was our way. This was what Mom would do. This felt right.

"So," I asked, "if I wanted you to dance for a ceremony, I would just offer you tobacco?"

Isaiah continued, "It would depend on the ceremony, but probably yes. You'd have to tell me why I was needed and what your intention was. When someone offers you tobacco, you accept it as a contract to dance for them, and once you open the circle, you have to close it. You close it like this."

Isaiah stood and began to bob up and down in his moccasins with his arms out, looking left and right like a war scout scanning the horizon. He raised his hands as if he were going to start spinning, and he began to step lightly on his feet, tap-tap-tapping. He started to bob and crouch, looking left and right. I could almost hear the drums. I was in complete soul awe. I wanted to hug him and shake his hand. He stopped and looked at me.

"You can't tell anyone you saw this," he said sternly.

"Crees rule," I whispered.

"Tapwe," he said. "But you gotta promise me."

"Not a word," I said. "Promise."

I bowed like a samurai to his master. "I had no idea about any of this. This is why you were such a great dancer at the fundraiser dance!"

"Maybe," he shrugged and then thought about it. "I was the only grandchild who danced like Mushom, so he started to teach me. In fact, on his deathbed he asked me to dance one last time for him." He swallowed hard. "And I did."

"You know," I said, "usually it's Cody Cranes who starts all our dances. I'm glad you're here to start them this year."

"No problem," he said. "I kept wondering why no one was dancing when they were playing cool tunes."

A new song started on Isaiah's boombox: "This Could Be the Night" by Loverboy—maybe the best Canadian song of 1986.

"You have to teach me some moves. Like, whatever you want. I'm starving for culture. Like, we go to church here and that's it."

He frowned. "What?"

I went right to town: "All our parents went to residential school. Like, we don't drum here. We don't have hand games. Like, okay, maybe when there's a conference, and they bring in outsider drummers, we drum dance. But look at us: we all have short hair. We're 'good Indians,'" I said, making air quotes with my fingers. "Town Indians. I bet if you danced traditional, it would inspire us culturally, you know? And it would get us asking, 'Well, what do we do? What's our dance? Who are we without the church?'"

He looked at me up and down. "I think I'm looking at a future leader, Lawson."

He fast-forwarded the tape to Heart's "These Dreams." I really loved that song. If I were to ask Shari to the dance, "These Dreams" would be my pick for best American song.

"Are Dogrib allowed to grass dance?" he asked.

"Who knows?" I shrugged. "Just teach me."

He came up to me and felt my shoulder joints, arm joints, knee joints.

"Too late. Your bones have set. Plus—and I hate to break this to you—you're not Cree."

"Watch this," I said. I dropped down halfway into the splits and howled with pain when my jeans suddenly tightened. "Oh god, I think I bruised my scrotum."

He laughed. "Keep all of my teachings to yourself. Got it?"

I fell sideways and went fetal. I remembered Mom's words about medicine power, but decided to prod.

"Shouldn't this be something to be proud of?" I asked with a grimace. "You should give a presentation at school when we open."

"Crees don't talk," he said. "We show." His face turned serious.

And then I had the best thought ever. "Hey, you should dance for K'aílaza."

"The old man? Nah. I'm out of practice."

"So practise," I said.

I crawled to my bed. He laid in his.

"Why do you want me to dance so bad?" he asked.

"Because we need a ceremony. I'll bring you fireweed from the North. That was our tobacco. And this is fireweed that my mother harvested with Cody Cranes out at Tsu Lake."

He nodded. "Well, I would be honoured to accept that."

"So come on," I urged. "Show us how to be Native. Look at all of us. We're frickin' town Indians wearing clothes from the Bay."

"What do you want to wear—moosehide?"

I thought about it. "No, but show us something. Remind us who we are."

"You do it," he said suddenly. "This is your town. I just got here."

"Well, maybe you just got here so you could help us."

"Yeah, right," he said. But I could tell he was thinking about it.

"Think of that eagle feather that chose your mom's hand. Isn't that a perfect sign for what's happening here?"

"Maybe it is, but all I see is me grass-dancing while you're . . . wait . . . what *are* you doing to honour this peacekeeper?"

"I will make him moose nose soup."

He looked at me. "Do you know how?"

I shook my head. "No, but my uncle knows. I'll learn from him. I think it is what my mom would have wanted."

"Tapwe," he said in Cree.

"What?"

"It means 'truth,'" Isaiah explained. "My mushom would always say that when the truth was spoken. I just felt your words."

"He's an Elder and a peacekeeper. We have to honour him. I'll cook, you'll dance, Roxanne said she'd make him moccasins."

"You can be my oskâpêwis." he said.

"What's that?"

"My helper," he said. "I need to practise. My Prince Albert cousins usually drummed for me. I have a tape they made me before we came here."

"Then we can crank it on my dad's sound system in the Green Death."

"That's what you call your dad's truck?"

"Yeah," I said. "So we're agreed? I'll offer you my mom and Cody's fireweed, then you can't say no?"

He grinned. "Using my words against me, hey?"

I smiled. "That's my dad's first attack: use what they gave you against them."

"What's the second?"

"Kiss the knuckles that'll drive you into tomorrow," I said and flexed my little Dene Hawk muscles. "Pity the fool who tangles with me. They'll be picking up their teeth with broken fingers."

# Ride the Lightning

I WENT HOME MIDDAY TO SEE DAD, TELL HIM ABOUT MY night with the Valentines and bring up the idea of renaming the Friendship Centre in Mom's memory, but there was no Dad. I was surprised that he wasn't home. His truck was there. I found a note in the kitchen: *My boy, please start a fire at Sonny's. Four p.m. should be good to get things toasty. Take the truck but don't go crazy cruising, you. Singing starts about seven. See you there if you want. Love you.*

This meant that I could cruise—at least a bit!

I had a quick shower, brushed my teeth and took his keys from the key rack. *Should I call Shari? Nah. Not yet.* Maybe I was sort of using Isaiah by not telling him the whole truth, but I was waiting for signs to tell me it was the right time to come clean about what really happened to me in the twisted forest with the Dead One.

Above Mom's moccasins was her caribou medicine bag filled with the fireweed that she and Cody had collected out at Tsu Lake. I would prepare a pouch of fireweed for Isaiah, a pouch for the Valentines and a pouch for Sonny, for teaching me how to make moose nose soup. That felt so right even just thinking about it. Cody was here in spirit with that fireweed in Mom's medicine bag. That had to mean something good. Things were lining up.

I grabbed my tennis racquet just in case Slitter the slug came crawling back and I had to lob it across town. I went through the back door and locked it before taking Dad's truck for a cruise. It was the best. I waved at everyone who passed by, and everyone waved back. I put in Shari's cassette and "Talk to Me" by Stevie Nicks came on. I loved that song.

Fort Simmer is a figure eight: you go to the airport and make your way along the banks, then you wheel back around once you hit the yellow house and you weave past the cop shop. You can go to the town campsite, but it's pretty Alcatraz and needs a major upgrade. Mostly the stoners go there to smoke the devil's lettuce. I still didn't know how I felt about the Friendship Centre. I parked for a bit and looked at it. The service door was open. I could have gone in and seen Mom's words stencilled in the foyer. I could have gone in to get her jacket. I could have picked up Mom's boxes from her old office. I could have gone to the graveyard and prayed. But I felt a lurch in my heart, and I sped out of there. It was still overwhelming, and I was pretty good at just pushing it away, pushing it away, pushing it away, every time grief tried to invade me.

Shari's mix was pretty cool. She'd used a red pen for the band names and a blue pen for the song titles.

Side A ("The Ghost in You"):
"Call Me" by Blondie
"Don't You (Forget About Me)" by Simple Minds
"Touch Me (I Want Your Body)" by Samantha Fox
"Against All Odds" by Phil Collins

"(I Just) Died in Your Arms" by Cutting Crew
"Relax" by Frankie Goes to Hollywood
"Live to Tell" by Madonna
"Take Hold of the Flame" by Queensrÿche
"I Want You to Want Me" by Cheap Trick
"(You're a) Strange Animal" by Gowan
"Cast a Shadow" by Platinum Blonde
"Talk to Me" by Stevie Nicks

Side B ("Night Moves"):
"Sad Waters" by Nick Cave and the Bad Seeds
"Wasteland" by the Mission UK
"And the Dance Goes On" by the Mission UK
"Rain from Heaven" by the Sisterhood
"Colours" by the Sisterhood
"Bury Me Deep" by the Sisters of Mercy
"The Sweetest Chill" by Siouxsie and the Banshees
"Running up That Hill" by Kate Bush
"The Caterpillar" by the Cure

My heart sparkled when I saw Platinum Blonde on there. "Cast a Shadow" was such a haunting song, and I was never sure what it was about. I had no idea who most of the bands were on side B, but they were deep-voiced and mysterious. Some bands were heavy. Some used computers and synthesizers. I loved the wash of guitars in many of the songs, and how they blurred together. I was fascinated by Shari. How had she discovered all of these bands? I hit the gas station for a hoagie, all heated up, and a cherry Coke. While I was there I also bought ten leather pouches for Mom and Cody's fireweed offerings, and I knew I'd need to make more for anyone else who'd help me, like Shari and K'aílaza.

I went home to my room and filled each of the pouches with fireweed. *Mahsi cho, Cody. I hope you are safe. Mahsi cho, Mom. Thank you for protecting me. Both of you are here in spirit, and we need your help.*

I left the pouches in my room and grabbed Silver's nunchucks from my gym bag. It was time to burn them. They simply did not need to exist anymore. I returned Mom's medicine bag to its place above her moccasins, then I hopped back in Dad's truck and took off for Sonny's. It was a beautiful day despite the overcast sky. But it was getting colder. Trees were dropping their leaves. A few geese honked above, and I waved. Were the pelicans still here? I hadn't been down to the rocks in forever.

I'd loaded up the wood stove in Sonny's garage before. If I could get the fire going nice and hot, the garage would be warm for all the men who gathered to sing. When I got there I prepared the wood. As soon as I opened the garage door, I was hit with the smell of old cigarette smoke, beer, a few open bottles of wine. I made a small teepee in the wood stove and cut more kindling for later. There were old copies of the *Slave River Journal* and the *Edmonton Journal* that I could use to crumple up and put in the heart of my one-match-lucky construction. I lit a match, and it went right to work. "Still got it," I said to myself, and did a little jig.

As the fire got going, I opened the damper and filled the woodbox. Once the fire was nezi, I tossed Silver's nunchucks in and said, "Silver, you and I were never friends, and I'm saying this the best way I can: I hope the Crees pull Slitter out of you and throw it in a fire hotter than this one."

That was kind of gross, but I meant it. I made sure the damper was closed and I looked around. Sonny Nets was a Fleetwood Mac fan—there were posters. There was a dartboard and there were pictures of good times: pictures of my dad hugging my mom, pictures of townies, pictures of past hunts, past trapping expeditions. There was a piano in the middle of the garage that everyone leaned on when they sang, and there was his mighty tape deck surrounded by a pile of cassettes.

I tapped each picture of my mom three times. "I. Love. You," I whispered. "I. Love. You."

There was a picture of Sonny leading the Canada Day parade in his truck, Ragged Glory. The coolest truck in Fort Simmer. His war pony.

And there were pictures of three boys. Two looked like identical twins. These were Sonny's boys. I had been told that a terrible fire had claimed them all when I was around four or five. This story haunted our town and people whispered that it was the reason Sonny drank. I didn't know the whole story. It was just so sad. Sonny was a father, he had his own family, and one night all of it was taken from him.

"Cousins," I heard myself say as I tapped the pictures with my finger, "I'm sorry I never got to grow up with you."

Once everything was tidied up and ready for a singing, I closed the damper on the wood stove and drove to the drugstore, where I parked and sat at a picnic bench in the shade to eat my hoagie and sip my pop. The church was across from me. To my right was the old folks' home. To my left was the Legion, where it had all begun. Then I saw it, on my shoes: the faded dribbles of dried blood from Silver. Blood was power, Mom would say. I needed to chuck these and get new shoes at the Northern Store.

—

AS I MADE MY WAY TOWARD OUR HOUSE WEARING MY NEW Nike high-tops, tennis racquet in one hand, jingling truck keys in the other, Shari pulled up in her dad's big truck, heavy metal pumping from her rolled-down windows. She was crying.

I rushed over and she motioned for me to get in.

"What happened?" I asked.

"God," she said. Her face was wet with tears. "God. Oh my god. God."

"What?" I buckled up as Shari cried more. I braced myself for what was coming. We sped to the banks, where Shari parked and slammed her hands against the steering wheel.

"I can't believe it. He's gone!"

My eyes bugged and my mind raced. "Who, Shari?"

I was terrified. Cody? Was it Stanley? Was it Silver? Silver may have been a psychopath with my name on his kill list, but he didn't deserve to die.

Shari turned off the truck and rested her head on the steering wheel.

"Cliff Burton," she said, sobbing.

"Who?"

"Cliff Burton, you asshole!"

"Cliff who . . . from Hay River?"

"Cliff Burton from Metallica!"

I sank back into my seat.

"Their tour bus flipped. He's gone."

"Oh my god," I said. Everyone at PWS was obsessed with *Master of Puppets*, especially "Battery."

"He was the best," she said. "So young. He was only twenty-four. Why?"

I looked at her, astonished. She got out of the truck. I did the same.

"Shari," I said, "I'm so sorry."

"Are you? Do you even know one song?"

"'Battery'?"

"Everyone knows 'Battery'! Even my gran knew 'Battery.'"

I had no idea Shari loved Metallica so much. She came around and held on to me. She was shaking. The Slave River was loud, but not loud enough to drown out her weeping. I rested my head on hers. Luckily, no one was cruising by. We would have been town gossip by suppertime. I sank into her hug and surprised myself by kissing the top of her head.

"What's with the racquet?" She sniffed. "And did you just kiss me?"

"For Slitter the slug," I said. "And, yes, I just kissed you."

"Well, thank you. That's very sweet. Slitter's not here. I'd sense it. Can we go lie down?" she asked. "Like, could you cuddle me?"

"Sure." I nodded and felt relief wash over me—she wasn't mad about the kiss, and she'd called me sweet. But then I thought of her dad. "Where?"

"My house," she said. "My folks are gone to Hay River for the day. No hanky-panky, okay?"

I nodded. Her folks were gone. "Okay." *Hanky-panky?*

"I'm trusting you," she said. "I just need to cry with someone. Can you drive?"

"Yeah," I said.

She widened her eyes and looked at me. "Why do you smell like smoke?"

Her mascara was all over the place. I got into her dad's big truck, and she buckled her seat belt.

"I had to start a fire for Sonny," I said as I put the truck in gear, carefully backed up.

"Sonny Nets?" she asked.

"Yup," I said. "He's kind of my uncle."

She nodded and pointed to the stereo.

"I can't believe it. Listen to this. That's Cliff Burton right there. How can he be gone?"

The song built and built.

"Nice," I said. "What is this?"

"'Welcome Home (Sanitarium),'" she said. "The whole world is listening, and he's gone."

I shook my head. A truck with Alberta plates was headed our way. To my horror, my dad was on the passenger side, laughing. A woman I had never seen before was driving. She was also smiling. My heart imploded. Dad was with another woman.

"Oh no," Shari said. "Was that your dad?"

"Nope," I said. My black eye started to hum.

"As if," she said, and pushed me. "Don't frickin' fib. Who was that woman?"

My face burned. "I don't know."

"Alberta plates," she noted. "Sorry, Lawson. Do you think he's having an affair?"

No wonder he wasn't coming home much. "I don't know."

"Did you know about this?" she asked, brushing my hair back.

I shook my head. "No."

"You can just go home," she said.

"Why?" I asked. "For what? Who's there for me?"

I was in shock. I was stunned. "Let's go to your house," I said. My entire face was burning with outrage and shock.

"Okay," she said, placing her hand over my chest. "Your heart," she said. "I'm sorry."

I drove and said nothing. *So this is why my dad lets me run wild. It frees up more time for him and whoever that woman is.*

"Frick sakes," I said, and let my breath out.

"Wait," she said, "is it still an affair if your mom's passed away?"

"What? Yes, because they didn't get a divorce."

She looked at me and started laughing.

"I'm so sorry. It's . . . Did you just hear what you said?"

I started laughing, too. "My dad's cheating on my mom!"

She wiped her eyes. "Your secret's safe with me. I thought *I* was having a bad day."

I squeezed the steering wheel as hard as I could. If I saw Silver Cranes right now, I would frickin' drop-kick him, even though I wasn't supposed to. *My dad has a girlfriend!*

We pulled up to Shari's and got out. I handed her the truck keys. We didn't say a word as we entered the back porch. As soon as I followed her into her house, my head cleared. It smelled great here: cinnamon, something fried, baking, pepper.

Shari took my hand, and we walked down the hall after kicking off our shoes.

"Remember," she said, and pointed her finger at me. "No hanky-panky, and definitely don't be handsy."

"Got it," I nodded.

She stopped and pointed directly at me. "And definitely no hickeys."

"I promise," I said.

We pinkied on it.

She led me down the stairs to her room. Her jigging dress was displayed proudly on the family wall, along with portraits of decorated veterans and Shari's school photos through the years. Man, she was pretty. To my surprise, there was a picture of Shari standing with her parents while being presented with a certificate from the RCMP. The RCMP officer was wearing a red serge and hat. The NWT flag was behind her, and she wore her Métis dress proudly, while her dad wore his capote and her mom wore a dress and Métis shawl.

Shari walked into her room and lay on her side on the bed, pulling her pillow closer so she could rest her face looking left. On her nightstand was the book *Flowers in the Attic*. There was a circle of white powder on the carpet around the perimeter of her room.

"Whoa," I said. "What is that? Do you have ants?"

She laughed. "No. It's salt. To keep bad spirits out."

"Oh," I said. "May I come in?"

"You may. Welcome to my room. I spend a lot of time in here."

She had rock posters all over her walls: Killing Joke, Skinny Puppy, the Mission UK, Sisters of Mercy, Siouxsie and the Banshees, the Smiths, Nick Cave and the Bad Seeds, Metallica, Metallica, Metallica.

"Where did you get all these posters?"

"Megatunes in Calgary. Come lie with me, Lawson," she said.

I didn't hesitate, but wasn't sure what to do with my arm. If I placed it over her, I might brush my hand over her chest, and I didn't want to be a Merv the Perv.

"Put your hand under my pillow," she said as lifted her head.

I did. I slid my arm under her pillow, and she rested her head on the pillow on top of my arm, and then she backed into me. We were so snug. This felt amazing. She took my other arm and pulled it over her side. My hand tucked around her shoulder. She flicked her hair back so it wouldn't tickle my nose.

"Hold me," she whispered. Her neck smelled like peppermint and strawberry bubble gum.

She backed into me again, and we were immediately enveloped in warmth.

"Do you see?" she asked me. "How we were led?"

"What?" Gosh, she smelled so good, and she was so warm.

"Do you see how me showing up with the news of Cliff Burton led us to see your dad with his girlfriend?"

I thought about it. "Yes," I replied.

"That's my whole life, Lawson. I am led to see what I am meant to see so I can help others."

I was sinking into her humming warmth. My entire body started to thaw, and I wanted to let it all melt away. I realized I hadn't taken a full breath since I went to the den. I took one and pulled her closer.

"Are we safe, Shari? Can I let my guard down?"

She held her palm up and moved it in a circle. "Warm. The Dead One and his slaves are nowhere near here."

I was getting sleepy. *What about the red wolf? Is she safe?*

"You're safe," Shari said. "I promise."

I held Shari and I could feel her entire body against mine. It felt great. I wanted to kiss the back of her neck to see what would happen, but she started to fade in my arms. Her foot gave a gentle kick. She was out.

I smiled. For someone who didn't sleep, she was doing a good job of pretending.

I closed my eyes and pulled her even closer. As I was drifting off, I couldn't tell if I was holding Shari or the red wolf. This was a marvellous, cozy heaven, and soon I slept too.

# Black Magic

SILVER WOKE TO FIND HIMSELF LOOKING DOWN UPON A room full of men, the Chipewyan warriors he'd met in jail. He was standing upside down, barefoot, on the wooden ceiling of a room in a house they'd broken into in Edmonton.

He gazed down at the bound body of Cree Elder Charlie Snow, who appeared terrified. Charlie was praying in Cree and begging to be let go. He was crying. His hands were turning purple and swelling from the duct tape used to bind his ankles and wrists and throat. Silver recognized in Charlie's features those he remembered of Cody—the sharp nose, the same hands, the slender frame, the eyes.

Silver's gang of warriors looked up to him with reverence and fear. Each warrior held his palms up and out. They were chanting the prayer he'd taught them, each time louder than the last: "ʔetao t'ası neba serástthën sį̨. Neba hẽ́snąu sénaolnı. Sedarıyéne beghą k'ohıldhër. Neghą́nıtą́h."

The Dead One's medicine throttled through him. Silver could see his bloody footprints on the walls, on the ceiling, on the shards of a broken window. Defying natural laws, he had run laps around the room above Charlie and the gang members when they had questioned what they were doing to this Elder.

They had dared to doubt him.

But Nark, Sado, Vip, Pyro, Sid, Rancid and Ronny didn't doubt him anymore. They worshipped and feared him, having witnessed what his father's power could do.

Silver hovered over the bound body of Cody's father. He could feel Slitter watching the old man through his eyes. Slitter was preparing itself, swelling, perching.

Silver held his hands out like an upside-down Jesus on the cross as his father spoke through him: "Charlie Snow, where is your son?"

"Whoa," said Vip. "Silver, he's an Elder. Go easy."

Silver lowered himself until he could feel the heat and panic coming off Charlie's body. "Where is Cody?" he demanded.

The Elder stopped praying and spat at him. "Never. Whatever you are, I'll never—"

At that instant, Slitter shot from Silver's mouth into Charlie's. The Elder's head shot back as Slitter snaked its way down his throat. Charlie gagged and choked, his body bucked, his eyes rolled back and his lips turned blue as he twisted and rolled on the wooden floor. The gang grew quiet as they heard Slitter crawl deeper inside their captive. Charlie's windpipe gurgled wetly as he kicked and struggled.

The men sat in a circle around him and awaited their orders. Silver watched himself from afar as his father spoke through him to each of the men individually. Each of the warriors nodded in acceptance. Each now understood more clearly who they served. They understood how much they were needed. The power they craved in their own lives was on its way to them, but it would take time, sacrifice.

Silver could not hear his father's words when he channelled them. He did not need to. He only had to trust that his father's wisdom was beyond his understanding and that his purpose would be revealed through what happened next.

Charlie's body then sat up and looked to Silver before nodding.

"Masterrr," Charlie whispered. "Masterrr."

Silver looked to Charlie Snow, whose eyes were glazed over.

"Where is your son? Where is Cody?"

Charlie's throat swelled as Slitter moved inside of him.

"Astum, Master," Charlie said. "Let me show you where we hid him."

Each warrior nodded and smiled. More power was on its way to them. Their dreams were about to come true.

Charlie stood and began leading the men down the stairs and outside. When they had surrounded Charlie in the parking lot of his workplace, Charlie had a cane. Silver noted that Charlie didn't reach for it or ask for it now. He looked strong, younger, freer. He had the power of the father inside of him, and Cody would soon be theirs.

If Cody resisted, they would use Stanley as bait. Oh, the master's plan was brilliant.

"Yes, Father," Silver whispered. "We're so close. Thank you for choosing me. I serve only you." And he repeated his prayer: "ʔetao t'ası neba serástthën sį́. Neba hḗsnąu sénaolnı. Sedarıyéne beghą k'ohılddhër. Neghą́nıtą́h."

A warm, loving wind filled him, and he heard his father's voice speak to him of more power, more rewards. His father's glory. His glory. The Craneses' glory. For eternity.

# Even If You Dream

WHEN I WOKE, SHARI WAS ENTERING THE ROOM WITH TWO coffee mugs. She smiled.

"Well, well," she said. "Lawson Sauren snores."

I sat up. "What? Sorry."

*Oh god, was her dad home?*

She sat on the bed beside me and handed me a mug.

"My folks called from Hay. They'll be back in an hour, so let's have coffee and then you gotta skedaddle, okay?"

I nodded. "Okay. What's in Hay?"

She sipped her coffee and looked out the window. It was already starting to get dark.

"Dad's office is gearing up for K'aílaza's visit. They had to buy a ton of pickerel for a fish fry."

"K'aílaza," I said. "Do they know when he's coming?"

"Any time now."

She tapped my mug with hers and we both sipped.

"Wow," I said. "This is great." It had cream and sugar in it, and something else.

"I sprinkle cinnamon in it," she said and looked me

over. "You okay? How do you feel about your dad and his . . . special friend?"

"I don't know." I shrugged.

"You're in shock."

I frowned and shook my head. My dad was seeing someone.

"Yeah . . ." And then I wanted to talk about us. "Hey, you slept."

She smiled. "I sure did. That's the best nap I've had in years. Can we do more of that?"

I nodded like a puppy. "Yes. Yes, please. Anytime. I'll sneak through your window."

"Uh." She shook her head. "Have you met my dad?"

I thought of the intense eyes in his author photo in the paper every time he wrote an editorial. "Yeah. Okay. Just call me when you know the coast is clear."

"Deal," she said, and I caught her looking at my hands.

"What?" I looked at them, too.

"You have gorgeous hands. Did you know that?"

I looked at them again. I could see features from both Mom and Dad's hands in mine. "Thanks."

"And," she said, "did you know you're very handsome and pretty at the same time? You're kind of gorgeous, you know."

My face got hot. "Thank you."

We grew quiet and I realized that we had the whole house and this whole moment together. I wondered if I could kiss Shari on the lips this time. We had just cuddled, and I really wanted to kiss her and hold her. If Dad had someone special, maybe I should have someone special too. I looked around Shari's room. There were books, and her walls were a feast of graphics and band names on smaller posters of the Smiths, the Cure, Voivod, Danzig, Skinny Puppy, Ministry, Siouxsie and the Banshees, Depeche Mode.

I looked up and saw a poster of Rambo on her ceiling. *Whoa*. Sylvester Stallone was carrying a bazooka, and you could see his abs.

"Nice room. How did you get so cool?"

"Thanks."

She pointed to her bedroom window. It was bright, with pink curtains. "That's where your mom came to me as a chickadee. She looked right at me and would not stop chirping and calling me. When I went outside to see what was wrong, she was on my dad's truck. She would not stop, and when I started the truck, she flew from tree to tree to lead me to you."

I believed her. "Have birds or animals led you to places and people before?"

"That was the first time. Usually people come to me in dreams. It's like the dead and the dying can see me."

I wanted to ask more but decided not to. I would only accept if she offered. I looked at the salt circle around her room.

"So no spirits have ever walked over that?"

"Not yet," she said.

She rubbed my arm. "Are you okay?"

"I think so. Are you okay?" I looked at her, then I looked away shyly. I reached out and where we had lain it was still warm.

"I am now," she said, and squeezed my arm.

I could see her various jigging contest awards, and there was her red and yellow Métis sash hanging off the side of the mirror.

"Can I ask you about that photo of you and your family with the RCMP dude? Was that for helping find that German kayaker guy who passed away?"

She nodded.

"Why wasn't that in the paper?"

"I asked them to keep it private, but my dad insists on keeping that photo up. My gran had this gift too. He says she passed it along to me."

"Well, I'm proud of you. Think of the peace you helped bring to his family."

I suddenly had a flashback of when the phone rang, and it was the RCMP calling to tell us about Mom, but I pushed the image away. This wasn't the time or the place.

"How's Operation Cree Love coming along?" she asked.

"Good," I said. "Isaiah and I are hanging out, and he's agreed to make me his helper for his grass-dancing."

"Did you tell him about Silver and your vision?"

"I'm waiting for the right moment."

I saw her green eyes flash with concern. "K'aílaza is coming. Do you think Silver is bringing up his so-called warriors to fight him and his family? That's what the gang is for. Think about all the medicine power K'aílaza has. Isaiah needs to know this, too, so he can prepare himself in whatever way he needs to."

"How do we take on a gang without fighting?" I asked.

"Isaiah is the key. That's my message, over and over."

"I will offer him fireweed to grass-dance for us, to help us."

"Fireweed?" Shari asked.

I smacked my forehead. "I'm so sorry. I have some for you, too, to honour you, but when you showed up upset, I completely forgot about it. It's fireweed that my mom gathered with Cody out at Tsu Lake before her accident. I want to thank you and honour you for your help and guidance."

"Thank you." She smiled.

And then I felt it: her loneliness. It struck me how hard it must be for her to go anywhere.

"When school opens, are you coming to class?"

I'd thought about this a lot and wanted to talk to her to see if I could sway her decision.

"We're not sure yet." She stiffened. "I have certain anxieties. Like, I can't go some places because spirits can see me before I see them. That's scary. At the same time, if there's loud music and a lot of people, it deafens everything. They become blurry somehow."

This was definitely creepy. What a curse it was to have her powers.

"So," I said, "this is why you could go to the dance."

"Yeah. That was fun. I could just lose myself and be free. Do you know how long it's been since I could just be me? Everything has a price, and, for whatever reason, I can see things and spirits can see me, but with music and my headphones and my room and our home, I'm free here." Then she reached out and touched my arm. "And when you're with me, Lawson, that helps, too."

We were quiet for a bit.

"I'll tell you what," I offered. "It's our grade twelve year and the thought of you doing correspondence school all by yourself here just makes me sad. What if we sat next to each other in class?"

"Like a Seeing Eye dog?" she asked.

"I'd sit next to you and help you. Just please think about it. I'd love to sit next to you and help you in any way that I could. I'm sure Isaiah would, too."

She beamed. "Oh, I like this. Two gorgeous men beside me all day. I think my grandma would approve. Oh yup." She nodded. "She does."

"Hi, Grandma," I said, and waved. "Your granddaughter is incredible and is carrying on your family gifts in your name, and me and my buddy Isaiah Valentine would be so proud to help her with her final year at high school because she deserves to just be seventeen and free."

Shari placed her hand gently on my shoulder. "Thank you, Lawson. Mahsi cho. You are so sweet. I hope you know that."

"Well, we're only going to be seventeen once. We might as well make the most of it, right?"

She nodded. "I need more fun in my life."

"Me too," I said. And then I thought of Isaiah sitting with us, the three of us as a team, and of Shari saying Isaiah was the key. We had bigger issues than deciding where we would sit in class.

"Shari, can I ask you for some advice? I'm not asking you to channel or borrow from the grace, as you call it, but how do you think I get back to the forest? You said 'the Beneath,' and I still don't know what that is. We need Stanley turned back to full Stanley. He could help us. Remember how strong he used to be? There must be a way for him to help us in the forest."

She stood, closed her eyes and started to trance out. She held one hand up and pointed at me with the other.

I sat back and watched her. I remembered that Cody had told me Silver used to bury himself when he was left out in the bush. Maybe that was also how he returned to the forest to feed Stanley? I could do that. But what if it didn't work?

Shari was quiet for some time, and I started to worry about her folks coming home. When she opened her eyes, they looked glazed.

"The Dead One does not know about Isaiah," she said. "That's how we'll save Stanley. Let's keep asking for signs and work together when we need to."

I heard myself let my breath out. Shari was definitely in Body Finder mode.

"We'll show Silver's gang that he serves the Dead One. They'll flee when they see the truth—but they have to see it for themselves." She took three deep breaths. With each breath she seemed to get closer to returning to the Shari I knew. When she was done, she looked at me with a gentle smile. "Whew," she said. "I went deep."

I looked at her in awe. It was like she could reach into the future.

"How do you do this?" I asked. "Like, how do you know so much and—"

"I guess I just see and trust the world differently. I see things in flashes, or other times it's like a slow-motion dive, and I can reach through the foggy bubbles. I don't know if that makes sense."

I wanted to reach out and comfort her somehow but wasn't sure if that was appropriate.

"Remember what I told you," she said. "You were born for this. I was born for this. So was Isaiah. If we don't face it, this thing will only grow—like a cancer. But we need to face it together. It's getting stronger. Imagine if it kept spreading. Imagine our leaders under its spell. It feeds on the spirit of war that's in all of us. It's the hate that brews from revenge. Do you understand?"

I nodded. "I understand."

"Okay." She grinned, suddenly returning to herself. "In the meantime, is there something you'd like to ask me about the grad dance?"

That was a switch. *Oh lord.* My face started to burn. I looked at her alarm clock and it said 4:45. "I need time," I said. "Let's face this first. We have lots of time after."

"Time for what?" she asked. "Lawson, I'm just putting this out there, but I want you to know that I wouldn't say no to you if you asked me to the grad dance."

"Hey," I said, "can we get through freeing Stanley first? Oh, and then those warriors that Silver is mobilizing? And I saw my dad with another woman. Honestly, I can't even think about the grad dance right now."

"Trust me, okay? Your medicine is the earth."

"Earth?" I asked. "What does that mean?"

"That's all I was told. 'His medicine is the earth.'"

*So does this mean I have to bury myself?*

She stood on her tippytoes and hugged me as she glanced at the clock.

"Okay, you have to go now. I have to start cooking."

"Okay," I said. "Call me later?"

"You can call me, too, you know."

She motioned that she'd walk me out. I followed her.

"Is me being me too much?" she asked as we climbed the stairs. "I can try to cut back, even though I can't control what I see or who visits me."

"No," I fibbed. "You are definitely the most fascinating person I know."

When we got to the porch where we'd left our shoes, Shari looked at me intently.

"We can kiss if you want to," she said.

And we did. I kissed her and felt her bottom lip tremble. She pulled herself into me and we fit so perfectly. I loved that she had to stand on her toes to reach me. We kissed and kissed and kissed. I could taste coffee, and there was a smell of mint mixed with heat.

"Oh hello, luscious lips," she said, and pushed me away. She was blushing! "You gotta go. You do not want my dad to catch you here. Also, I may just get handsy with you."

"I wouldn't get mad if you did."

"Okay gorgeous, simmer down. Find a way to tell Isaiah about what we have to do together. That's your next mission. Got it? Take some dough gods with you," she said. "Tell everyone I baked them—because I did, and I'm really proud of them."

She popped the lid on a huge Tupperware tub, revealing dozens of pan-fried dough gods sprinkled with cinnamon and sugar. She then grabbed some paper towels from a roll, scooped up about ten dough gods, set them aside and handed me the Tupperware filled with the rest.

"Take a few for your dad and—"

"His girlfriend?" I asked.

"Yes, for his special someone. Maybe your dad just needs to be held the way you do." Then she said quietly, "Like I do."

"Can we do this again?" I asked.

"Cuddle?" she asked, and smiled. "Anytime."

I made my way down the hall to the porch and pulled on my brand-new shoes.

"Wait," she said, "did you come up with the best Canadian song not on my tape?"

"'This Could Be the Night' by Loverboy."

"Best American song?"

"'Welcome Home (Sanitarium),'" I said. "Metallica."

She made devil horns with her hand. "Agreed. Best international?"

I stepped outside and it was still nice out, not too cold.

"'Tenderness,'" I said, "by General Public." *Thank you, Cody, for introducing me to General Public!*

She smiled. "Holy, Lawson, you've been doing your homework. Can I ask you something?"

"Sure."

"When K'aílaza arrives, you're going to make moose nose soup, and Isaiah, hopefully, is going to grass-dance, but what do you think I can do?"

"You can be my spiritual bodyguard," I said.

She looked at me and smiled. "Oh, I like that. Yes, I can do that."

"And if Stanley is somehow ordered to attack us, can you distract him?"

"Yes. Yes, I can. Okay, deal."

Then, suddenly, I felt a presence looming in front of us. Standing on her lawn was the giant Stanley Cranes. He looked at me and raised his hands like a grizzly.

"Hi, Stanley," I said, putting the dough gods down slowly and putting on my biggest grin. "Want to play Grandpa and the Grizzly?"

He nodded slowly. I pretended I had a long stick. I smiled really big to show him this was only a game. "Okay, come at me slowly and I'll fake that I'm going to jab you in the heart. When I do, stand straight back."

He did exactly what I asked him to do when I fake-jabbed. He then pretended to walk around with a huge spear in his heart. His mouth was wide open. He was smiling, as if the old Stanley was coming back.

"Your whole family is made up of heroes because your grandpa saved all those kids. They call you 'the Arm,' Stanley. Do you remember why?"

He looked at me blankly. I felt like I was trying to talk down a Kodiak bear.

"Because you never miss, bud," I said and smiled. "You make our town so proud when you compete."

Stanley looked behind me and lowered his arms.

"Hi, Stanley," Shari said with her warmest smile. "Are you hungry? I'm so happy to see you. You know that Lawson Sauren and I are safe friends who will never hurt you and only want to feed you and see you happy, right?"

Stanley reached up to his throat and arched his head back as if he could still feel the burning coals scorching his throat. "Help me," he gurgled. He held out his hand to her.

Oh my god, he spoke. But the look that Shari gave me was not good at all.

"Lawson, listen to me: you need to tell Isaiah everything as soon as you can."

"Shari, what's happening?"

"I told you, the dead and dying can see me." She looked to me quickly before focusing on Stanley. "He's starting his journey."

Stanley let out a long groan from the back of his throat. Stanley was dying right in front of us—slowly, and without a soul.

"It's because Silver hasn't fed him," I said. "How long does he have?"

"He's fading," she said. "He only has days left. I'll drive him to his foster family, but you need to get Isaiah ready. Things are speeding up. Everything has changed. K'aílaza is on his way, and Silver and his warrior gang are gathering power somehow. They're closing in on Cody. I can feel them. They are getting closer by the second. We need Isaiah's family medicine to help us."

Stanley looked at me with foggy eyes. He blinked, and his eyes rolled back as if he were trying to see his past.

I looked to Shari and announced loudly, so that Stanley would hear me clearly: "Stanley's grandpa was a hero. He saved a pile of kids from a grizzly at a culture camp with only a sharp pole and what his Elders told him. When we save you, Stanley—and I promise you that we will—I need you to do the same thing your grandpa did to anyone who attacks us, okay? Put the spear right there." I pointed to where his ribs met.

I picked up the container of dough gods. Stanley looked right through me—he was back to his ghost trance—but we'd shared something. He had remembered that story about his grandfather. He had remembered. And Silver and his gang were getting closer to Cody by the second. They were closing in, Shari had said. I had to tell Isaiah everything.

# Cool Rider

"HELLO," PATRICK CALLED OUT. "LAWSON?"

I shut the door behind me, kicked off my shoes and peeked around the corner. Linus and Patrick were watching *Video Hits*. They had a pile of Garbage Pail Kids cards and the crumpled-up wrappers were all over the couch.

"Is Isaiah home?

"He and mom are at the Friendship Centre," said Linus.

"The pipes burst last night," Patrick said. "There was water everywhere."

"Oh shoot," I said. "Sorry to hear that."

"They came back with some boxes and stuff," Linus said. "And they went right back with Isaiah's grass-dancing stuff."

"So is the centre okay?" I asked.

Both boys shrugged and looked at the Tupperware I was holding. They smelled the dough gods.

Linus looked at me with the biggest smile. "What do you have there?"

"Yeah, what do you have there, bud?" Patrick rubbed his hands together so fast he could have started a fire.

I held the dough gods up and said, "By the power of Grayskull, I have dough gods! Save some for your family."

Patrick snatched four, Linus snatched three, and they went back to watching *Degrassi*.

I put the rest of the dough gods on the kitchen table.

"So Isaiah's grass-dancing?" I asked.

"Yup," Linus said. "Practising."

"What'd you say to him?" Patrick asked. "He said you got him motivated." He had sugar and cinnamon all over his face.

I was overjoyed with this news.

"Your brother's going to honour this Elder who's on the way."

"Yeah, we heard all about it. Can you cook us supper?" Linus asked. "Know how to fry fish? My mom and dad got into an argument on the phone last night, so Mom probably doesn't want to cook. Come on. Cheer her up."

"Please, Lawson?" Patrick asked.

"I'm really sorry to hear that. What do you got for groceries?"

"Pickerel," Patrick said. "We thawed it this morning and it's ready. We're just not allowed to cook anything in grease when Mom's not around."

Pickerel was my mom's favourite.

"Roxanne's sleeping," Linus said, pointing upstairs. "Can you cook supper?"

To cook for Mrs. Valentine and Roxanne and the boys would be a joy, especially if there'd been an argument in the house last night—and if I was going to share a brutal story with Isaiah. What better way to butter him up than to feed him and his family my mom's favourite recipe?

I made my way to the kitchen and looked around. There was a big bag of yellow potatoes on the counter. I saw the two huge fish fillets thawed in the fridge. They had two cans of yellow corn and a dozen eggs. I washed my hands and put water on for the spuds. I cracked three eggs and mixed them, spilled them into a smaller pot, turned it on low, and put flour, salt and pepper on a plate. I only knew how to do a pickerel fry with the fish cut up, so I went to work. I twirled the diced pickerel in the eggs with a pair of long tongs. I then traced each cube back and forth in the flour until they were coated. I remembered that Dad said canola oil was best because it didn't overpower the natural richness of the fish. The oil started to heat. I put it on six. With the water on high, I started to dice up the spuds. Mom always said to leave the skins on for nutrients, so that's what I did. I decided to put on some tea for Isaiah and his mom for when they got home.

Before I knew it, I had everything going. I had to turn the fan on because the grease started spitting. That fan was so loud I had to turn off CBC.

"How do you guys want your spuds?" I called out. "Just boiled with butter dripping down or what?"

Roxanne walked into the room and put the phone back in its place. That phone had the longest cord you could buy. She came up to me and picked off a piece of freshly cooked pickerel.

"Wow, Lawson. Look at you."

I looked at her and immediately looked away. "Oh, hi."

She was standing so close that I could feel her body heat. I wondered who she was calling: her loser ex, Joey, or her dad.

"Did you see those dough gods?" I asked.

Roxanne went and grabbed one. "Who made these?"

"Um, a friend."

"Oh," she teased, "a special friend?"

I shrugged and focused on cooking.

"Uh, you know, just a friend." Why was I blushing?

"I'm impressed," she said. "She's a great baker."

She gave me a gentle push. "What did you say to Isaiah?"

I shrugged and played dumb. "What do you mean?"

She gave me another gentle push. "Come on. He said you wanted him to dance for that Elder when he comes here. How did you get him to agree?"

I shook my head and checked the temperature on the corn. I gave it a stir with a fork. "I just asked him to honour your grandfather's memory. I'm about to offer him fireweed that my mom collected before she passed."

"You really are something, you know that?" Roxanne smiled and brushed her hair back. "Seriously, we had a rough night here. Mom was yelling at Dad on the phone last night, and it got pretty ugly, so thank you." She was going to lean in to kiss my cheek when she stopped cold. "Whoa." She wrinkled her nose.

"What?"

"I smell perfume. What is that smell—apples? Who were you making out with? Your special friend?"

And that's when Isaiah and his mom walked in. Mrs. Valentine gave me the biggest smile and said, "Holy! What's for supper?"

Isaiah looked at me with flushed cheeks and smiled. "That smells great."

"Welcome home. I heard you had a long night—at the Friendship Centre."

"Yeah," Isaiah said. "Lots of mopping. But I danced in the gym, and it felt so good. I gotta shower. Wait. What are those?"

"The Métis here call them dough gods," I said.

He devoured one and grabbed another.

"These are incredible. And thanks for cooking. Who made these?"

"Lawson's girlfriend," Roxanne called out. "She's trying to fatten him up so he can walrus her."

Isaiah, Mrs. Valentine, Patrick and Linus all exploded with laughter. I could not believe what she had just said.

"You have to join us, Lawson," Mrs. Valentine said. "You cooked and brought us dessert."

"Yeah," Linus said. "Thanks again, Lawson Bear. Hai hai."

I knew the family had had a rough night. I wasn't sure if I should stay to eat or just serve the food, talk to Isaiah and go. It was hard to know. I timed the pickerel with the boiling spuds. I didn't want to burn anything.

"So, can I ask—How is the centre?"

"Oh lord. The pipes burst, and we had a lot of cleaning to do. Thank God for Isaiah. Once the gym was clear, he came home for his regalia. My girl," Mrs. Valentine called to Roxanne, "we need you to mend a few things for your brother."

"Sure," she said.

Roxanne got up, and Mrs. Valentine handed her Isaiah's regalia in a large garment bag.

"You'll see where the stitching's come loose. I marked it with masking tape. You boys!" The boys turned off the TV. "Your brother—I am so proud of him—it took him one practice run with the tape your cousins made him. You should see Isaiah dance, boy. I couldn't believe it."

Mrs. Valentine started to cry. She covered her eyes. The boys and Roxanne immediately surrounded her.

"I just wish Mushom was here to see it."

"And Dad," Roxanne added.

They hugged, and Linus said, "Mom, don't cry."

Mrs. Valentine took such a big breath that it felt like a big wave washing over her family.

"What a tough night." She looked at me. "Lawson, thank you for cooking and thank you for getting Isaiah to dance again. You should see him. Oh my goodness, he is so beautiful."

Supper was just about done. I was using the tongs to fry the pickerel and, so far, was doing great with not burning anything. Yay for Fort Simmer magic! I couldn't wait to gift Mrs. Valentine with a pouch of fireweed to properly welcome them to town.

"So Isaiah's going to dance for that peacemaker, or what?" Patrick asked.

"He sure is," she said. "And your sister's making the Elder some moccasins."

"As soon as someone traces his feet," Roxanne said.

Mrs. Valentine mixed butter and milk with the boiled potatoes after she drained them. She saved the day, because I think I would have burned the fish otherwise and that would have been a crime.

I placed the pickerel—and there was so much—on paper napkins to absorb the grease, and grabbed the salt and pepper.

"You boys set the table. Make sure to set a plate for our champion bush cook."

"Aw," I said. "Thanks. Do you have a lemon, some mayonnaise and relish?"

"Yup," Mrs. Valentine said. "It's all in the fridge."

I grabbed all three and went to work on making homemade tartar sauce. I was never given an official recipe for this. I just jerry-rigged it.

"Look at you go," Mrs. Valentine said. "Where did you learn to do that?"

"My mom," I said. "She loved pickerel."

"Well, we are honoured. Hai hai, Lawson's mom. Tonight, we feast in your honour."

I got quiet and smiled.

"Lawson, your mother is so very proud of you. I can feel it."

"Thank you," I said.

I looked away and blushed. Mrs. Valentine hugged me.

"Thank you, my boy. Wait till you see Isaiah dance. I swear Mushom was here today. I could smell sweetgrass, and he always said that when I smell sweetgrass, it means he's checking up on me and our family."

She looked to her bundle of eagle feathers. "My girl, can you please pick a feather for Lawson?"

Roxanne got up slowly and made her way to the bundle of feathers. She closed her eyes and held her hand over the fifty or so eagle feathers. She picked one and gently pulled it out of the collection, like an arrow out of a quiver. She then came to me in a slow march. She didn't look at me. Not directly. Linus and Patrick and Mrs. Valentine all smiled with pride as she approached me.

"Lawson Sauren," Roxanne said, "thank you for honouring our family today." And then she looked at me. Into me. She smiled and nodded before handing me my first eagle feather. "Mahsi cho."

I accepted it. She was so radiant, so beautiful, so strong. She did a little bow and turned away. The feather hummed in my hand. Mrs. Valentine hugged me again.

"Did you boys show Lawson the portraits we saved?" she asked.

They looked at each other. "No."

"Lawson," said Mrs. Valentine, "we managed to save all those portraits you told me about. From the centre. They're downstairs. After we eat, I'll show you."

We sat and ate.

"I'm in mouth-love," Linus said.

"Me too," Mrs. Valentine said. "Wow, Lawson. Mahsi cho."

Roxanne's shoulders dropped and her eyelashes fluttered. "How did you do this, Lawson? Oh my god."

So this was how you could kiss someone from across the room. Cook for them with love in your heart.

We followed Mrs. Valentine downstairs and stood together in the basement. There, beside stacks of boxes yet to be unpacked, stood the portraits Mom had commissioned for our Elders years ago. There were twenty framed black and white portraits leaning against the wall, portraits of Fort Simmer royalty, our Fort Simmer Elders. I went through the portraits slowly—all those wrinkles, all that wisdom, all that dignity.

There were even portraits of Mr. and Mrs. Cranes. Mrs. Cranes looked kind and patient. Mr. Cranes had let his guard down for the photographer and almost had a smile, but his eyes were so fierce. I could see the warrior in him. I could feel it. What a shame he'd given in to his bitterness for the world.

There was a photograph of Grandpa Cranes—the old man, they called him—with his wife. He had his arm around her, and they were smiling. This was the Cranes Elder who killed the grizzly with a sharp pole and saved the children at that camp.

There was a portrait of Therese Cranes with her three sons. They had been helping Grandma and Grandpa Cranes that day and I guess there was time for a photo of them too. Stanley—with his full, radiant spirit—was standing between Silver and Cody. They all seemed so happy, like they were laughing at the same joke. Who would ever believe me if I told them I saw Silver pouring burning coals down Stanley's throat to keep him alive?

And there, behind his framed portrait, was a photo I didn't know existed and wasn't prepared to see at all: a portrait of my mother.

"She's so beautiful," Roxanne said.

My mother *was* so beautiful. I had her cheekbones. I had her eyes. Her hair used to be so black and so long, just like Roxanne's.

"My mom," I said. "That's my mom." I felt hands on my shoulders. "I never saw this photo of her before. Thank you so much." I started crying softly and couldn't stop.

"I miss Dad," Linus said suddenly to his mom. "I don't want you guys to break up."

"Me too," Roxanne said.

"What?" Mrs. Valentine turned to face her kids. "Where did you ever get that idea?"

"We heard you last night on the phone." Patrick sniffled.

"What if it's not a hickey and it's just from his electric razor?" Linus said. "Did you ever think of that?"

"My boys," Mrs. Valentine said. "Now's not the time. Let's—"

"When are we gonna be a family again?" Patrick asked.

To my surprise, everyone around me started crying: Mrs. Valentine, Roxanne, Linus and Patrick. It was a wail. Man, the tears were just falling.

"Holy!" Isaiah came down the stairs. "What happened? How come you guys are all crying?"

"That's a picture of Lawson's mom," Patrick cried and pointed. "And he never even saw it before."

"Oh my god," Isaiah said. "That's your mom?"

The portrait would just devastate Dad. There was no hiding from the strength in Mom's eyes in this portrait.

I wiped more tears away. "Thank you so much. Seriously. Thank you."

"Okay," Mrs. Valentine said and stood up slowly. "Lawson, these are here, and they're safe. You can gift them out to the families they belong to, or you can donate them back to the centre when it's ready. Your choice."

I would bring these to K'aílaza when he came to Simmer. These would remind him *and* Silver about happier times.

"Mahsi cho," I said. "I can't thank you enough."

Mrs. Valentine wiped the last of her tears from her eyes and let out her breath. "Man, we needed that."

"Dad just needs to come home now," Patrick said, and it was the way he said it: we could all feel how lonely he was without his father.

Mom would have loved that moment. I kept thinking of her portrait. It was a portrait of Mom's endless beauty and strength, but we'd never get over our grief if I took it home. We would never move on if that photo was in our house every single day, because it showed the full and terrible cost of losing Mom. Our sorrow would never leave. The framed portrait would have to stay at the centre, and I knew, deep down, that she deserved to have the centre renamed in her honour.

# Tell No Lies

I MADE MY WAY UP THE STAIRS THINKING OF STANLEY, AND how he had only days left on this planet if we did not do this right.

Isaiah wore a blue T-shirt and jeans, his hair still wet from the shower. He sat on his bed and suddenly seemed so sad.

"Hey," I asked, "what's up?"

"My mom thinks my dad's got a girlfriend."

"No way," I said. *What the eff? Our parents are like teenagers. Everyone's on the keemooch.*

"What's the point of catching eagle feathers if we can't even be a family?"

This wasn't the conversation I had planned.

"Like, how does she know?"

"Her sisters are keeping tabs," he sighed. "My dad couldn't handle my mom being sick. That's when things weren't fun anymore."

"I'm sorry," I said.

"My dad says he's scared of losing Mom but keeps blowing it every time they try to talk, so that's why he stays away. Try and figure that one out. One of my aunties saw my dad with a hickey."

"Frick sakes," I said. I hoped Linus was right, that it was his electric razor and not true at all about him having a hickey.

"That's the real reason we're here," said Isaiah. "Simmer is our escape plan. Mom survived chemo and radiation. You'd think now would be the time to be a husband and a dad. Who lets their family set up a new house all alone?"

"I'm sorry," I said.

"Her cancer could come back, too," he said. His voice cracked as he lay down. "So what's the point of all of these eagle gifts if she's going to pass away before we all graduate?"

I sat down on my bed. "I'm so sorry, Isaiah. No fair. Your mom rules—"

"My mom's my hero. She's my Terry Fox."

"Your mom is so proud of you. She's over the moon that you're grass-dancing again. She said she can feel her father around her when you dance."

He looked at me, stood up and went to the window.

This was my moment. I took a big breath.

"Look, Isaiah, I've come to you today to ask you to grass-dance for K'aílaza when he comes to town. Please. We need your help. We can't do this without you, and there's stuff I probably should have told you earlier."

"Stuff?" he asked, sounding worried.

"Okay," I said. "This is the real deal. A long time ago, here in the North, there were tribal wars. The Dogrib against the Chipewyan."

"Okay," Isaiah said. "You already told me this."

"There's more. I have to tell you more, okay? The leader of the Dogrib was Edzo. The leader of the Chipewyan was Akaitcho."

"Got it," he said.

"The Dogrib and the Chipewyan battled each other for decades. It was massacre after massacre."

"Sounds like us and the Blackfoot."

I took a big breath and shared my truth: "I'm a descendant of Edzo. The Cranes are descendants of Akaitcho. K'aílaza will want to meet with Silver Cranes and me when he gets here so he can see that we've honoured the peace treaty between the Dogrib and Chipewyan."

Isaiah motioned to my bruise. "The second Silver choked you, he broke it."

This was my moment to finally tell the whole truth: "I physically broke it first, but Silver psychically broke it, too, so we're both to blame."

"What do you mean?" Isaiah asked. "Slow down. *Psychically?* Is that even a word? Back up and start from the beginning."

I looked him in the eye. I had to be honest. "Do you remember when I asked you if you believed in mind reading? Silver read my mind."

"What are you talking about?"

I let my breath out and told him everything: about the fight, about the vision I had in the forest, about Silver gathering his gang of warriors and returning home. I even told him about Slitter and the wolf, about the bird attack, about Mom and Cody braiding medicine power together to protect me, but I did not tell him about the wolves. That still seemed separate, and I wasn't sure why. I told him about Stanley visiting me and Shari. I told him about Shari's abilities. I got it all out. Isaiah listened with such respect that he made it easy.

"Isaiah," I said, "there's something else, something that could help us."

"*Help* us?" Isaiah asked with a challenging tone. "You just told me about an ancient spirit called the Dead One, a little devil named Slitter that dove into Silver Cranes' mouth—and now you're throwing me a bone with a little something that could *help* us?" He threw his hands up in disbelief. "What could possibly help?"

I nodded. "I know it's a lot, but just hear me out—and thank you for listening this far. I know it sounds crazy, but it's not."

"Okay, what?" he asked.

"Silver begged me to help him."

"How? Was this before or after he gave you a choke job and you stabbed him in the nose with a screwdriver?"

"After. And I didn't stab him. I jabbed him with the handle."

"Okay." Isaiah rolled his eyes. "So what's the good news?"

"When I was in the Dead One's den, I think I figured out what it wants."

"Okay," he said. "What does it want?"

"It wants the end of all of us," I said, "and it's eating our medicine power to devour us whole. Not just humans but animals, too."

"Holy, Lawson," he said. "Are you kidding me? Come on."

I held my hands up. "Don't freak out. K'aílaza is on his way. He's a respected peacemaker. I feel like he just needs to get here and then we'll figure out what we need to do—even though we're not allowed to ask him what to do because he's an adult."

Isaiah grew quiet. Too quiet. I panicked and added, "Shari Burns feels that we need you to grass-dance because we need your family's medicine power to defend our treaty and free Stanley and Silver so we can face the Dead One together. We can't do this without you. Just please think about it."

Isaiah watched me for a long time. "I'm thinking. Shari said that?"

"Yes. And don't forget that the dead and the roaming can see her."

"How does this help us?" he asked.

I remembered the fireweed I'd brought. This was the perfect time to offer it to him.

"Isaiah Valentine, you said that when the people call a grass dancer for help, you have to go for ceremony. Stanley Cranes came to me and asked for help. Even Silver Cranes—my worst enemy—begged me for help. Cody Cranes is in the city being hunted right now. We can face this Dead One together—but we need your medicine."

I got down on my knees and offered the pouch of fireweed to Isaiah.

"Isaiah Valentine, my mom told me that before the white man came here, we offered fireweed to the land and to the water before we travelled, in the hope of ensuring safety. It was our version of tobacco offering. I am proud to offer you this fireweed, gathered by my mother and Cody Cranes, to dance for K'aílaza, the law keeper, to protect him when he comes to our community. Mahsi cho."

Isaiah looked at me and then at the pouch of fireweed in my hand. He stood and hugged me hard. "Thank you," he said. "Nobody's . . . ever . . . offered me anything before. This is fireweed from your mom and Cody Cranes?"

"Yes." I nodded. "So . . . do you accept? Please say yes, Isaiah. I can't face this without you. You moved here for a reason."

Isaiah held that pouch with pride.

"You're right," Isaiah said. "You know what I think?"

"What?" I asked.

"I think this Dead One is bugger all," he said quietly but angrily.

I was still on my knees but floored by his response.

"Do you know what my grandfather and uncles did back in their day?" he asked.

"What?"

"They hunted the wheetago. They were trained to hunt wheetago and face them together."

"The what?"

Isaiah gestured toward the window. "There's no snow on the ground, so we're not allowed to talk about them, but I will tell you everything I know when it does snow."

*The wheetago?*

Isaiah continued: "My mushom told me that if evil isn't faced early, it grows. I knew you were holding something back."

"How?" I asked.

He shrugged. "I just did. And I think that eagle feather led us here. I think it was my mushom showing us that we were needed here, to face the evil with you. I think we have no choice but to face this as one, because this thing—this soul parasite or whatever it is—it won't just stop with the Dogrib and the Chipewyan. It'll come for the Cree and our peace treaties. My mushom always said, 'An enemy of peace is my enemy.' So this thing, this Dead One, is my enemy now. Did you see it eat anything when you encountered it?"

"Yes. Well, I guess I didn't *see* it, but I heard it." I remembered the gross sounds behind me in the den.

"Then it can be starved and killed," he said. "So let's kill it."

I felt light enter my entire being as he spoke. I marvelled at his inkwo and grinned.

"You are amazing," I said.

"I'm a grass dancer," Isaiah replied, and held my fireweed offering over his heart. "We break trail for others to do what they were born to do. You can count me in."

My heart was pounding and filled with hope. My soul was doing backflips.

"Thank you, Isaiah. Thank you."

"My pleasure," he said. "It's time to honour my mushom. My mushom would have been the first to welcome a great peacemaker to any community." He smiled with pride. "Remember what I told you? Crees don't talk. They show. I just have one condition."

"Anything."

"We have to involve Linus and Patrick."

"I don't know, man." I frowned. "They're kids."

"This is their inheritance," Isaiah said. "They need to learn how to push through fear and to help out when called upon. This is good training for them, and for me."

"What about Roxanne?"

"No." He shook his head. "She has other medicines."

"Can women be wheetago hunters?" I asked.

"Of course," he said. "They're way more powerful than we are. But, for this fight, it's us and the boys, okay?"

"We need Shari. She's psychic and she can see spirits—and spirits can see her.

"Okay," he said.

"Oh, I forgot to tell you," I said, "that if we fail, it gets to suck my eyeballs out of my skull while I scream my head off."

He laughed but stopped when he could see that I wasn't joking.

"Yup. I had to make a deal with it," I said. "It had me tied up, man."

"Suck your eyeballs out of your skull? Are you frickin' kidding me?"

"Don't forget the 'while I scream my head off' part."

He shrugged. "Talk's cheap. Let's see how tough this thing is when you show up with ceremony and Cree backup."

Those were the words I needed to hear.

# The Dead Next Door

I COULDN'T SEE THE MOON, BUT I COULD SEE HALLEY'S Comet. It looked dimmer than the last time I saw it. Orion wasn't out yet. *It would be nice to—*

Before I could finish my thought, I saw them playing at the edge of the forest by the willows down the street from our house. A boy raced into the ditch and dodged two acorns that flew past him. Two other boys laughed as they chased after the first, occasionally stopping to toss more acorns up in the air and expertly strike them using long sticks like baseball bats, aiming the acorns toward the fleeing boy—but, to my supreme confusion, I realized the acorns were passing through the running boy without hitting him.

The boy raced toward me. I gasped in surprise as another acorn shot through his chest without bouncing off or slowing down.

"Hey!" I called out.

The boy stopped and crouched. The other two who'd been chasing him paused when they saw me, then turned around and ran back into the forest. They looked Dene, with gorgeous brown skin and freckles on their noses and cheekbones. Now that I could process what I had seen, I realized the two in the forest appeared to be identical twins, maybe two years older than the boy crouching near me. All three boys were wearing baseball uniforms.

I raised the tennis racquet and looked around for Slitter or Stanley or anyone or anything that could hurt me. *Is this a trick?* There was no stench of rot. This strange encounter felt different than the others.

“Hey, you kids!” I called out again. “What you’re doing, you?”

One of the two older ones stepped out to the willows to look at me. He was holding an egg in each hand. He motioned for the younger boy to return to the forest. The younger boy did, but he walked backwards toward his older brother, never taking his eyes off of me. Standing beside each other, the boys tilted their heads together and watched me.

“Hey,” I called again, raising the eagle feather with my other hand so they could see I had something sacred with me. “Time to go home,” I called, and pointed at the street lights on the side of the road. They were on. That was the signal for all the kids to head home for supper.

The older boy raised his hand. Then younger one did, too.

“He can see us?” the younger one asked.

“He called us,” said the older one.

“No way,” the younger one said. “Ray-Ray, what did you take? That chicken is gonna stop laying if you keep taking from her.”

“Maybe he’s sleepwalking,” the third boy said as he came out of the forest and stood beside his brothers.

The boy with the eggs looked at the street light and then looked at me. He crouched and started pawing the earth. He buried the eggs. “Scrambled,” he said. “My favourite.”

The other boys crouched beside him. They all started patting the earth like a drum—or like they were feeling for land mines. It looked like they were laughing.

"Are you okay?" I called. I wanted to start walking toward them, but something stopped me. "You kids better—"

It was then that I realized I could see through them.

"Oh my god," I heard myself whisper. "Who are you? Are you ghosts, or what?"

This youngest boy turned his chest toward me and held his hand up as if to ask a question or get me to hold up my eagle feather.

I held up my eagle feather to echo what he was doing.

He opened his hand.

I shrugged. "What?"

He pointed at my eagle feather, pointed to his hand and then pointed to our house.

*What?* "Give the feather to my dad?" I asked.

"You want our help?" the tallest of the boys called out to me. "Prove it. Give that eagle feather to our dad and tell him to stop drinking."

"Your dad?" I asked. "Who is your dad—Sonny? Are you his sons?"

I looked in the direction of our house. When I looked back to where the boys should have been, all three boys—human, spirit or both—were gone.

Holy, this was freaky. I raced home and took comfort in seeing Dad's truck as I came up the driveway. Parked beside it was Sonny's black '49 Ford F1.

*What the hell did I just see? Sonny's boys?*

I needed to get inside and figure out what had just happened. This was most definitely weird. I thought of Shari. If this was my daily life, I'd never leave my room either.

# Who's That Guy?

WHEN I ENTERED THE PORCH, I SAW SONNY'S COWBOY BOOTS toppled over on their sides. I could smell him. The smell of hot fuel meant hard drinking.

*Frick sakes, Sonny. So much for learning how to make moose nose soup today.*

Whatever Sonny had been sipping smelled like exhaust from a space shuttle. *Eeesh.* I closed the door and snuck the eagle feather inside the arm of my jacket so they wouldn't see it. I didn't want Sonny's drunk grubby hands touching it.

Sonny sat at our supper table looking down. His face was purple and puffy, and his hair looked like grey straw. He hadn't shaved, so his face looked like it had woken up in frost. Perfect little white hairs grew in patches around his cheeks and chin. His jacket and cap were on the table.

"Hello, nephew!" Sonny smiled and clapped his hands. His aim was off, so he slapped his wrist. Then he started laughing at nothing.

"Welcome home," my dad said dryly.

I untied my new runners and hung up my jacket. My dad shot me a look and shook his head. He'd started the pizza prep and wasn't happy. I could see green peppers, a huge block of cheese, the grater, a package of ham and a can of pineapple slices ready to be diced. The radio was on. Someone was playing the fiddle and it sounded great.

"Hey!" Sonny beamed and clapped his hands again. "Nephew. Edanat'e. Edanat'e."

He started laughing at nothing again.

"Come here, nephew," Sonny smiled.

I glanced at Dad and he gave me an apologetic look.

"Ahh," Sonny said, and scratched at his stubble. "I missed your birthday."

My birthday wasn't until September 20. Sonny reached into his pocket and pulled out a hundred-dollar bill.

"Here you go, my boy. You're turning into a real Geronimo."

I looked at my dad again and he shrugged. "If a drunk wants to give you money, take it. It'll save him from buying more booze."

I walked over to Sonny and held out my hand. He shook it and placed the money gently in my palm. He tapped it three times and let me be.

"That's for being such a good boy. It's payday. You better take it before Shirley does."

"Sonny," my dad warned.

"Thank you," I said. The air smelled like some chemical had caught fire. What had he been drinking? Then my eyes started to water from Sonny's cigarette smoke.

"Let me help cook," I said, putting the money in my pocket and going to wash up so I could start helping.

"I remember being young," Sonny said. "Best days of my life. Best days of your life, hey?"

I nodded. "Yeah."

He smiled. "And the queens! Who's your queen now?"

I thought of Shari and Roxanne. "No one," I replied.

Sonny had a special glass mug that had been awarded to him by the Town of Fort Simmer. Only he could drink from it. Nobody touched it. In fact, even if it was the only clean mug left, I'd wash all the others out of respect. Every year Sonny insisted on helping to decorate the big Christmas tree by the library. If you could guess the exact number of lights, you'd win a turkey. Dad was always after him, teasing him, offering him trades for the secret number, which only Sonny and one other person would know.

"Halloween soon. What you're going as?" Sonny asked.

I shrugged. "A ninja."

"Ninja?" He held his fists up. "Like Bruce Lee in long johns?" He broke into a huge cackle. My dad and I started laughing too, only because he was laughing so hard.

"We had our fighters, boy," he said and wiped his chin. "Warriors. Holy cow, they had to train all the time. Practise shooting arrows into the wind, the sleet. Tough, boy. Yabati. That's what you are. You defend with honour."

"I defend with honour," I repeated, and felt something like pride.

Sonny was Dogrib, and he was raised by his grandmother who didn't speak a word of English. She spoke Dogrib, but could also speak Slavey and a little bit of French.

He pointed at me. "You gotta train in this life. You gotta train and always look for the signs. A long time ago, you were allowed three arrows into the heart when you were hunting moose. Three arrows. That was the fall hide. Any more than three arrows, you were taking away from the hide that was needed for clothing and teepees—the aunties would get mad at you."

I could tell Dad was listening.

"Imagine running alongside a moose and shooting just three perfect arrows. Now that is a warrior," said Sonny.

Dad's wedding ring was on the counter by the dish soap. He always took it off when he cooked.

"I love your dad," Sonny announced to the room, then he looked to me. "Love you, too, nephew." He raised his glass of water, sipped it and frowned. "*Mah*! Water, no less. Holy, I'm Noah, er nah?"

"Sorry," Dad said as he stretched out the pizza dough with his knuckles. "One of his crushes just got engaged."

Sonny waved at something in the air and shook his head. I nodded that I understood and got to work shredding the cheese.

"So your dad was telling me that Silver Cranes gave you a lickin'," Sonny said.

I didn't want Sonny to know about Silver. Sonny would go after Silver if he saw him while he was drinking, and that was exactly what the Dead One wanted. I'd have to tell the story to Sonny while my dad listened, and I knew my dad would be looking for any slip-ups in my story. I'd tell the truth—I'd just tell it my way.

"Silver was going to kill me," I said. "I caught him trying to steal the money we raised for the Terry Fox Run."

"That little bastard," Sonny said through gritted teeth. "We raised thousands. And then I hear he hopped on the bus and was gone that night."

"Before I knew it, Silver had me in a chokehold and I could hardly breathe, so I jabbed him in the nose with his screwdriver."

"With the sharp end?" Sonny asked.

"I could have. As I was getting ready to pass out, I made the decision to only use the handle. I'm a Yabati, aren't I? It was to stun him or make him stop. He was going to break my neck. He even told me he was going to break my neck."

"That's my boy," Dad said with pride.

"He then ordered Stanley to knock me out, so Stanley did."

"Frick sakes." Sonny shook his head. "Frickin' wolf's head."

Dad and I looked at him.

"What?" I think I said it first.

"Silver," Sonny said. "He's part wolf. Look at that ugly smile of his. Just like his dad. Every few years that blood fever of his rises up. First it was the Gwich'in. His dad ran them out of town. Then it was the Inuit. Then it was the North Slavey. Remember all those house fires?"

Dad nodded.

"Now it's the Dogrib," Sonny said. "That's us, nephew. Silver's just mad cuz he's ugly. Even his tapeworms are ugly."

He started laughing at his own joke so hard that Dad and I started laughing too. Sonny laughed so hard that he spilled water on his legs. He held his hands up and looked to my dad.

"Oh. Oh. Oh. Sorry, your royal highness."

Dad shook his head with clear disappointment about this whole situation. Sonny did a bow from his seated position, and he gave me a salute.

"I miss her. Smarty, you know how much I miss Roberta." He hung his head.

"I do," Dad said, but there was an edge in his voice.

"Roberta. I'm grateful to have known her. She was a great woman. Strong woman," Sonny said and nodded with his eyes closed.

My dad relaxed and washed his hands. I looked for hickeys on Dad's neck but couldn't spot any. I leaned in for a sniff of perfume but couldn't sense any. We do-si-doed around each other, slicing and dicing up our pizza toppings.

"All that killing," Sonny said in a low voice. "Long time ago, my grandma said, how they killed you was—"

"Sonny," Dad said. "Not now. Please."

*Where did that come from? We were happy just seconds ago.* Sonny could be hard to follow when he'd been drinking.

"Sorry," said Sonny, and he wiped his eyes. "I can't imagine it. I apologize. You know we lost three, hey?"

I looked at Dad, who looked down. He wiped something off the counter.

"Three boys. We lost my beautiful boys."

He started to cry. The faded scar under his left eye held some of the tears before he could wipe them away. I looked at Dad again. He kept looking down and shook his head.

"Sonny," he said. "I'm sorry."

"You do everything you can," said Sonny. "You . . ." He used his knuckles to rub a tear sliding down the ridge of his nose.

I felt tears rush to my eyes. I went to Sonny and sat beside him.

"Sorry, Uncle. I didn't know."

I placed my hand on Sonny's shoulder, and he placed his hand over mine. It was warm and strong.

"Long time ago," he said. "House fire."

"It was nobody's fault, Sonny," Dad said. "It was an accident."

Sonny let out his breath.

"I'll see them on the other side," he said. "I will see them. 'Dad,' they're going to say. 'Daddy.' Most beautiful word you're ever going to hear. *Daddy*."

My heart ached for him, and I just had to honour Sonny for what he'd gone through. I wanted to tell him that I thought I'd just seen his boys and that they'd wanted me to give the eagle feather that had been gifted to me to their dad. I would tell Sonny everything about what I had just seen when the time was right, but, for now, the feather. I wiped my eyes and went to my jacket. I reached into my sleeve and pulled out the feather that had never touched the ground.

"Uncle, I have a gift for you."

He looked up at me, confused.

"I can't explain it, but I was just given this by the Valentine family for getting their son Isaiah to grass-dance."

Sonny frowned. "Grass-dance? They're Cree?"

I nodded. "I think they gave this to me so I could give it to you."

"Wow, son," Dad said. "What a tribute."

"Inle," Sonny said gently. He pointed with his lips for me to place the eagle feather on the table. "I can't touch it. Not when I'm drinking."

"This has never touched the ground," I said. "Mrs. Valentine caught it in the air."

Dad whistled in astonishment.

"Feather catcher," Sonny said. "I've heard about them. Their boy is a grass dancer?"

I nodded.

"That's who you're hanging around with these days?" Dad asked.

*And who are you hanging around with these days?* I wanted to ask him.

Sonny held out his hand. "Mahsi cho, nephew. Mahsi. That's the third feather I've ever been given. Your mother gave me my first one. Your father gave me my second." He thought about it. "One for each of my boys, I guess." He sniffed and smiled and nodded. Dad brought him a box of Kleenex. He placed it by the feather and leaned over and squeezed Sonny's shoulder.

Sonny looked at Dad. "It was my fault," he said.

"Sonny," Dad said swiftly, "she was supposed to be watching the kids. It wasn't your fault."

Sonny nodded. "I need a drink."

"Inle," Dad said. "You need some sleep. Go sleep at your home, you."

Sonny shook his head. "I'm okay." He reached for the feather but stopped himself. "I'm okay."

I stood and gave Sonny's shoulder a squeeze as well.

"So what're you gonna do when Silver comes back, nephew?" Sonny asked me. "With or without K'aílaza, that peace treaty is broken. We're now back to the real possibility of open war once word spreads to the other communities."

"He's right," Dad said.

*Who would believe me if I told them Silver read my mind as I tackled him to save Cody?*

"I have a plan," I said, "but first I need you to teach me how to make moose nose soup for the Elder."

Sonny stood and looked out the window. *Did he even hear what I just said?*

"You know, my wife was a nurse," said Sonny. "Sorry, my ex was a nurse. So you know Stanley?"

"Yeah," Dad and I said at the same time.

"He and Silver used to compete all the time when they were kids. Stanley whooped him every time without even trying. Remember how everyone would cheer for Stanley before he did anything? I used to watch Silver's face when we were all cheering. Silver hated it. He hated his own brother for making people happy and proud to be from Simmer."

"Sad," I said.

Sonny nodded. "Yup. Pretty frickin' sad." Then he continued. "He poisoned his father, too. Once they brought his dad in, and it was rat poison. You could never prove it. But you tell me how Stanley got the way he is today. Nearly mute? Dumb? Simple? He wasn't born that way. Remember his smile? Holy cow, Stanley's smile would light up the school at the Christmas concert. He was everyone's favourite kid—and that devil, Silver, did this to him somehow." He raised his fist in anger. "I know he did."

And I knew how, but said nothing.

The fear I felt in the forest was still inside of me. I knew where Stanley's spirit was. I had to get it back for him. *How can I return there without someone knocking me out?*

"When the cops find Silver—and they will—he'll head right back to the clink."

*If the cops find him and I can't figure out a way to return to the hell forest, Stanley will die without his soul.*

"Love and war," Sonny said, and took the last sip of his water. "She's all the same. Funny how life goes, hey, Smarty? You turn sixteen and you're like, 'I'm gonna buy an eight ball of hash.'"

"Christ," Dad said under his breath. "Sonny."

Sonny waved him away. "Then you turn forty and you're like, 'Tupperware with lids. We need more Tupperware with lids.' Then you get up there in age and you just try not to sit on your own balls."

Dad laughed, then half-jokingly said, "That's enough." He pointed a kitchen knife at Sonny. "I'm warning you."

"Okay, okay, okay." Sonny held up his hands in surrender, then looked down and to his left. "Hey, what's this?"

"What's what?" Dad asked in a tired voice.

"Roberta's moccasins and medicine bag?" Sonny asked. "Why didn't you burn those?"

"Leave it," Dad warned.

Sonny looked right at my dad. "I bet you never burned anything of hers."

"Nope," Dad said, putting his hands firmly on the counter.

"Her clothes are still hanging in her room?"

"You're damn right," said Dad.

"We talked about this," Sonny said. "The Dogrib burn everything to let their loved ones rest. I frickin' told you a year ago to burn everything."

I thought of Mom's sleeping bag, her scratchy HBC blanket and her three long hairs in my room. I don't think I could bring myself to burn those.

"Well, I ain't," Dad said, "so shut up about it."

"This ain't about you, Smarty," Sonny said, sounding suddenly sober, suddenly serious. "It's about her. Roberta needs to rest so she can move on."

"Well, maybe I don't want her to move on," Dad said.

"You're being selfish," Sonny said. "She can't rest, my brother. That's all I'm saying. When you're ready."

"I'm not ready," Dad said. He looked down.

"Okay," Sonny said. "I'm sorry. I'm sorry. I'll go home."

"Leave the key," Dad said. "You're not driving drunk."

I was surprised that Dad didn't ask Sonny to stay—but honestly, Sonny, when he was drinking, was exhausting.

I held up my hand. "Wait," I said. "I understand about burning everything, but Mom's medicine bag, she gave it to me, and I want it. I need it. As a Yabati. As her son." There was no debate in my voice. I wanted Mom's bag. It was the only thing of hers that I'd be willing to fight for.

Dad looked at Sonny. Sonny looked to him and then to me. He nodded.

"I like that. When you're ready, Smarty, I'll help you. Nephew, you can keep your mother's medicine bag. If she gave it to you, it's yours."

Sonny warily made his way to his boots.

"I am sorry for my mouth," he said.

"Go home," Dad announced to the room. "I'll drive your truck back tomorrow, or Lawson will."

"I'm going," he said as he made his way to the porch. "Nephew, bring me that eagle feather when you bring Ragged Glory home, and I'll teach you how to make moose nose soup the way my granny loved it, okay? It's the same recipe that I boiled up for you and your dad. I have a moose nose in my freezer. It's yours in the name of peace."

"Promise me," I said.

"I promise. Shake my hand," Sonny said. Then he added, "Smarty, shake my hand."

"Christ sakes," Dad muttered, giving me a gentle elbow.

We both walked over and shook Sonny's hand.

"I love you, Smarty. I love you, my nephew. I promise I'll thaw that moose nose."

"We love you, too," Dad said. "Just quit your goddamned drinking." They hugged.

"Nephew," Sonny said, "do you know what true love is?"

I watched him suspiciously. "Tell me."

"True love . . ." He took a big breath and thought about it. "True love is just wanting the best for someone. That's it. Plain and simple. Your mother just wanted the best for everyone and this town. Even the Cranes. Most of all, she just wanted the best for you and your dad."

My heart melted in my chest. *I will never forget this.* "Mahsi cho, Uncle."

He placed a long, thick stick of rat root in my palm and was about to offer it, but then stopped.

"I'm sorry. Not with booze. I can't offer this while drunk." He put it back in his pocket. "I can teach you how to gather rat root next year. I'll teach you how to make soup for K'aílaza. I'm sorry. I shouldn't even talk about any of this while I'm still high. We can't do this when I've been drinking. Always look for those signs, nephew. God, I need a drink." He grabbed his face.

"Aren't you tired of hiding?" I heard myself ask.

Sonny and Dad both looked at me with astonishment.

"Aren't you tired of being a lost king?" I asked him.

Sonny looked shocked.

"Sonny," I said. "I need you to quit drinking. I need an uncle and my dad needs a brother he can count on."

Sonny's mouth opened a little as if to say something, but nothing came out.

"I'm a Yabati and so are you. We're Dogrib. I need you strong and healthy. I'm tired of you being my drunk uncle. I want to believe everything you tell me. You're a Yabati. Teach me all that you know. Teach me everything you ever wanted to teach your sons. They would have been Yabati too, right?"

He pressed his fingers into his eyeballs and slumped against the wall.

"Smarty, did you put him up to this?"

"Not me," Dad said with a proud grin. "He's got his mother's courage."

I looked to Dad, who told me, "Say it now, son. Don't back down and don't stop now. Say what you have to say."

"I never thought of that," Sonny said softly. "Yes, they would have been Yabati, too."

"They are Yabati," I said, "in the spirit world."

I walked to Sonny and hugged him.

"Uncle, I need your help. Please stop drinking. Thaw that moose nose and teach me how to make soup. I want to present it to K'aílaza and his family when he gets here. I need your help and blessing. We have to do this right."

I backed up and smiled through tears. "We can do this together."

"Okay, okay," Sonny said, and ran his hands through his hair. He looked so suddenly tired.

"Will you be okay?" Dad asked Sonny.

Sonny nodded. "Yeah. Holy. Nephew's words just hit me like the Dene Hawk. I'll go home and pour out all my bottles."

"Thank you, Uncle."

"The Dene Hawk soars again," Dad said and kissed his flexed right arm.

Sonny did the same, and I joined them. We all laughed, fighting back tears.

And with that, Sonny Nets turned and left the house, closing the door gently behind him. I saw him look up at the sky. He said a few words that I could not decipher before making his way down the road that led to his house.

---

"CAN I ASK ABOUT WHAT HAPPENED TO SONNY'S SONS?"

Dad thought about it. "You were a baby. Thank God you don't remember this."

I waited for him to find the words.

"Sonny's wife was supposed to be home watching the boys," he said. "She left to drink and go to the dance. They think she vacuumed an ember by the fireplace and once it settled into the lint, it smouldered for a while before . . ." He made a *poof* gesture with his hands.

I felt cold enter me, and my heart started to squeeze itself. "God," I said. I could not imagine the guilt of both Sonny and the mother of those children.

"This whole town was so sad for so long after. Sonny lost everything."

"That was his first wife?" I asked cautiously.

He nodded. "She hung herself a month later."

Good lord. How horrible. How sad. I would never, ever drink. Ever.

"Sonny never used to drink, but it was just too much. Too much pain for one lifetime."

I thought of that picture of his sons at the Wallow Pit.

"Did they all have freckles?" I asked Dad.

He looked at me with surprise. "Yeah. All of them. Why?"

*I have to tell him the truth. This isn't about the Dead One. This isn't breaking our agreement.*

"I may have seen them," I said.

"What?"

"On my way home," I said, "I saw three kids playing in the willows."

Dad leaned against the sink. "Go on."

"The Valentines gave me the feather, and then I saw three young boys playing down the street in the willows by where that old man used to keep his dog team. They were wearing baseball uniforms."

"They loved that game and were good at it, too. But—"

"One of them waved at me to follow him," I said. "I think they were spirits. I . . . could see through them."

Dad shook his head. "And?"

"One of the boys told me to give my eagle feather to Sonny," I said.

Dad thought for a while before saying, "Two were twins. One was younger . . . Your mom saw spirits all the time. Christ, it scared me. She had nightmares, too, when I met her. Smudging with rat root helps. Prayer, too."

"Do you see spirits?" I asked. "Have you?"

He shook his head. "Felt them. Your blood turns to—"

"Slush," I said.

He looked at me. "Yeah."

"What kind of nightmares did she have?" I asked.

"She never told me, but she'd go to a certain place to break the bad dreams."

"A place?" I asked. "What place?"

"She called the place 'the Border.' When she'd sense something bad was about to happen or she'd had a nightmare, she'd go for a walk out to the canal."

*This is important. Maybe this is how I can get back to the twisted forest.*

"And? How did she get to the Border?"

He shrugged. "That was her medicine, and I thought one day she'd tell me about it, but—I should have asked her more about it. You always think you have more time together, hey? You just assume you're going to grow old together forever. Every time she'd come back, she'd have pine needles in her hair, and she'd be covered in dirt. She'd sleep for a day after. Your mom had her own medicine. That's one of the many reasons I fell in love with her."

*Why didn't I know that? How do I not remember my own mom returning home like that?*

"The other thing was, your mom could smell evil."

"What?"

"Oh yes. She could smell it just like she could feel it. She called it 'the rot.' She could smell it the second someone evil came to town. She'd back up from where she stood, bring her elbow up and try and breathe only in that small space in the crook of her elbow."

"Really?"

I was stunned. That was me. I could smell Silver and Slitter and the Dead One. I could smell the rot and feel it at the same time. But with the boys outside, they didn't feel or smell evil. They were just . . . eerie and see-through.

Dad walked over to the cupboard above the fridge and came back with a piece of charred rat root.

"Your mom smudged with this after seeing a spirit once." He handed it to me. "It's yours now. You should smudge with this. Singe the tip. Use the smoke." He demonstrated, motioning with his hands as if he were slowly fanning mist over himself.

I held it. *Mom . . .*

"Learn all you can from Sonny," Dad said. "He was a great dad. He really was."

*A lost king, I called him.*

"An eagle feather *and* spirits. You've had a big day."

I sniffed the rat root. It smelled a little bit like cork.

"Why does Sonny call Silver the Wolf's Head?"

"Sonny told me that when he was watching Silver at the courthouse being sentenced for shooting that teacher, he could see a wolf's head on him. It was the head of a wolf sent to destroy its own pack."

I thought of the wolf being torn to pieces after the Dead One's command. It wanted to go back to its family. That meant that it once had a home. My heart and mind were full with all that had happened.

Dad put our pizzas in the oven. I handed him the eagle feather.

"Can I talk to you about something else?"

He ran the feather over his fingers. "Sure."

"Mrs. Valentine, the new director at the Friendship Centre . . . Isaiah's mom . . ."

He handed the feather back to me. “Mm-hmm?”

I held the feather for courage.

“She suggested that when the new Friendship Centre opens . . .” The feather started to hum.

“Go on.”

I gave Mom’s rat root a squeeze. *Why do I feel like I’m going to get in trouble?* I took a big breath and closed my eyes.

“She’s suggesting that the centre be renamed after Mom.”

I could not meet his eyes.

“What? I don’t know what to say. What do *you* think?”

I shrugged. “Honestly, I couldn’t even think about it for a few days, but it might be nice to see her name up. It’ll be hard, but everyone agrees she’s a hero.”

“That she is. When do they need our decision?”

“Next board meeting, I guess,” I said.

“How about this?” he said. “You’ve had a lot taken from you—so young, too young. How about *you* decide what to do, cuz I sure as hell can’t.”

“Also, there are two boxes of Mom’s writing and stuff at the centre, and they want to know if we want to pick them up or have them dropped off.”

“Boxes? What boxes?”

“From her desk, I guess.”

“I don’t think I’m ready.” I could see him look at the family photos on the wall and at the door.

He started fiddling with his finger where his wedding ring should have been. It was off. Of course it was: he’d been on a date.

“Sonny’s right. At some point,” I said, “we are going to have to burn her stuff.” I thought of her sleeping bag, her three hairs, her blanket.

I saw his lips quiver.

"I'm so sorry," he said. "I'm sorry this happened to you."

"I'm sorry it happened to you, too, Dad," I heard myself say.

He was reeling. To my surprise, Dad spoke so quietly that I knew it was going to be important. "You know, my boy, I have a theory about what happened out in that water. I wish your mom never went on that trip to Edzo," he sighed. "Storms rise so fast on the lake there. I blame myself for not going with her."

"It's not your fault."

Dad put his hand on mine. "I always thought I had forever with her. She made being a dad easy. She was my everything and, looking back, I think I took her for granted, because I just assumed she'd always be there for us."

"I know," I said with tears in my eyes. "I think she just wants us to be happy now."

Dad wiped his eyes. "My boy, you are the light of this family. I know you're going to honour us—and I know you're going to defend that treaty. It was self-defence. Just tell that to K'aílaza. He'll understand."

We hugged again, and I realized that I no longer stood alone. I had Isaiah and his brothers. I had Shari. I had my dad and Sonny. And I would learn how to make moose nose soup.

The timer went off on the stove, and we ate those pizzas as if we were starving.

# Evil Has No Boundaries

CODY CRANES WOKE SUDDENLY TO THE SOUND OF HIS FATHER calling his name.

"Cody!" yelled Charlie Snow from a distance.

Cody sat up in bed, relieved that he was safe in his father's house in Enoch, just outside of Edmonton. But why was his father calling to him from outside?

Cody got out of bed and looked around. He loved his new room, his new home, life with his real family. Tomorrow, they'd be feasting. His sister was having a birthday party and many relatives would be travelling to Enoch to celebrate the occasion—many of whom he'd be meeting for the first time.

"My boy!" his father called again. "Astum. Hurry!"

Cody made his way down the hall in his pyjamas. As always, he could smell sweetgrass and sage as he walked past his father's home office. His dad always greeted the day with a smudge. He followed the sound of his father's voice.

"Dad?" he replied.

"Cody!" his father called again.

Cody reached the back door and froze at what he saw. His father was kneeling in the backyard with Silver standing over him. There were two holes beside Silver: a small hole that looked like it had been freshly dug by hand, and a huge hole that looked like the dirt had been pushed up from underneath. It was fresh and gaping—something you'd see in a graveyard.

His father's head was bowed, and Silver was grinning. This was the fresh-out-of-jail Silver—the taller, stronger Silver, his bent leg miraculously healed. This was evil Silver. How had he found Cody here?

"My boy! Astum. Hurry!" Charlie called without looking up. Silver shoved him.

"Dad?" Cody asked. "Are you okay? Silver, what are you doing here? What do you want?"

Silver's grin turned into his familiar cruel smile.

"Hi, Cody. I missed you. Why'd you leave town?"

Cody looked around for something to defend himself with. *A bat.* He grabbed the bat his dad kept by the door in case anyone threatened him or his family.

"Get out of here, Silver," Cody said firmly. "Leave my dad alone. And where's Stanley? Who's watching Stanley?"

"Oh, you'll be seeing Stanley soon." Silver nodded. "Don't you worry about that." He raised an arm and began to pull his shirt sleeve down as he did so.

"Just go, Silver," Cody said, "and we won't call the cops. Let my dad go."

"You call your father. I'll call mine," Silver said. "Want to see something cool?"

Silver dropped slowly to his knees, reached into the small hole and began to whisper something, something Cody couldn't make out. Was he praying? Yes, Silver was praying his dark prayers. These were the same whispers Cody had heard from Silver's room back in the old house in Fort Simmer. Silver was calling the Dead One.

"Stop it, Silver!" Cody yelled. "Just stop it. Dad! Dad, come inside."

Cody gripped his father's bat and showed it to Silver. "I'm calling the cops."

As Silver stood, Cody could see that he was holding something. He showed it to Cody. It was shiny and moving. Cody's mouth dropped open in horror as he realized it was a human heart. It was a pumping human heart. His father collapsed face-first into the grass and started kicking as he convulsed. Charlie's body bucked, and Cody could hear the breath leaving his father's lungs.

"NO!" Cody yelled as he raced toward his father. "NO! DAD! Silver, stop it!"

"Cool, hey?" Silver asked.

Before Cody could reach his father, he was grabbed by men who'd been hiding in the shadow of the house. These men were all Native, and much stronger than him. Cody fought and kicked and bit and yelled as loud as he could for help. He looked at the men who held him. Their faces were twisted. There was something wrong with them. Their eyes were dim. Almost zombie eyes. *They all have dead eyes.*

"Put it back!" Cody begged. "Put his heart back!"

Silver looked to his men, then he looked to the sky. He was calling and chanting. Then he thrust his arm back into the hole in the earth before pulling it out slowly. He opened his hand and splayed his bloody fingers. The heart was gone.

Charlie Snow let out a groan as he tried to pull himself up.

"Dad?" Cody called. "Dad!?"

"My boy," Charlie mumbled. "Run."

"You're my offering to my father, Cody," Silver said. "I get to be a god because of you."

Silver's men pushed Cody into the huge hole. Cody fell. And fell. It was as if the hole had no bottom. He fell and slid and was pulled by something that had him by his ankles. It was diving into the earth and dragging Cody with it. The earth grew colder and colder the deeper he was pulled. Cody began to pray. He prayed and begged with everything he had to Lawson's mother. He prayed for her help. They'd made a deal. She'd had a vision that a great terror would come for Cody and his brothers, and that Lawson would help them all.

"Auntie!" Cody yelled as he clawed at the tunnel walls. But it was no use. "Help me! Dad! Help!"

Could Lawson's mother hear him? Could Charlie?

Could even the Creator hear his screams?

Could anyone?

# Time After Time

SHARI CALLED. "I NEED A CUDDLE."

"I'm on my way," I said. I grabbed the pouch of fireweed that I had set aside for Shari and put it in my front pocket, then grabbed Sonny's truck key. I'd drop the truck off on the way.

I had to pull myself into his war pony with my left hand holding the steering wheel. The angle of Sonny's custom bucket seats was so tight that once you got settled you felt like a pilot. I could never find the lever to adjust the seat—maybe it was broken. I loved the steering wheel—it was solid, just like the truck's frame. But the leather interior was so musty. I'd only driven Ragged Glory a few times and, each time, it was because Sonny had been drinking and left it at our house.

I always had this feeling Ragged Glory could take flight if it needed to. Or drive on the bottom of Slave River and come out the other side like it was just another Tuesday. The springs in the driver's seat strained as I placed the key in the ignition. It started like a motor in a muskox. It wasn't loud until you hit sixty—then *look out!*

Sonny had bought Ragged Glory from a hot rod shop in Edmonton. I loved this truck: it was all muscled and curved. I loved that it had running boards and spokes on the hubcaps. It looked so cool and sleek from far away, but as you got closer you could see that it was rusted, beat up, dented. For some reason, I loved Ragged Glory even more because of that. Sonny's muffaloose hood ornament looked fierce and a bit dangerous, like Stanley before a track meet. There was a .22 bullet hole in a rear panel. *Fort Simmer Pride* was stencilled on the back. The bucket seats looked like they had been chewed by squirrels. I saw an empty mickey on the floor.

I drove Ragged Glory directly to Sonny's, scanning the trees with the hope that I'd see his sons again, but I didn't. Sonny wasn't home yet. I left the key on his porch and made my way to Shari's with her fireweed offering. I practically sprinted most of the way. I wanted more time with her. I'd let her lead. I wanted to know more about Shari Burns and her life.

---

CYNDI LAUPER'S "TIME AFTER TIME" PLAYED AS WE SNUGgled. I was just so cozy and happy in Shari's room. She was spooning me. This was heaven.

"Did you tell Isaiah everything?" she asked. "Is he in?"

"Yup. He's in. He also wants Linus and Patrick to join us."

"What? How old are they?"

"They're young," I explained, "but Isaiah's relatives—even young warriors—hunted the wheetago."

"The wheetago?"

"Some evil spirit that Isaiah couldn't discuss," I said. "Isaiah wants his brothers to face this and work as one. He says this will be good training for them."

"Wow, I like that," she said. "I guess this is why I was told to reach out to them. They come from a long line of hunters. Silver's still not here. I keep looking for the signs. I just wish I knew when K'aílaza was going to arrive—I have a feeling he will help us."

"I know, right?" I said. "He'll help us. He'll know what to do."

In my heart I felt a lightness where before there'd been dread and fear. I wasn't carrying this weight alone. We had a team, and everything about it felt right.

To my surprise and delight, Shari started to blow air gently on the back of my neck. Then she reached over and slipped her hand inside my shirt. I shivered.

"Your skin is so soft. Lie on your back."

What was up with her today?

She laughed and started to drag her sharp fingernails across my stomach like a big cat. "Try to guess what I'm spelling."

ME

AND

YOU

She blew her warm breath where she'd scratched, and I started to blush.

"Lawson, why don't you ever ask about my mom?"

I opened my eyes. "What?"

"Haven't you noticed my mom isn't here?"

"Sorry." I sat up. She was right. "Is she okay?"

She sighed. “We’re not talking.”

“Oh,” I said. “Sorry.”

She leaned into me, and I held her.

“If I tell you something, you can never repeat it, okay?”

I frowned. “Okay.”

“Okay,” she said. “My mom’s been cheating on my dad, and she’s now in Edmonton with her boyfriend.”

Casualties of the keemooch were piling up. “Oh no. I’m sorry.”

“Calgary was supposed to fix us,” she said, shaking her head. “I am so mad at all of them.”

“Holy,” I said. “I had no idea.”

She nodded. “Yeah. Well, I don’t really have anyone to talk to. We keep saying she’s working on her master’s, but sooner or later someone’s going to see her and Steve together.”

I was the big spoon now, and Shari kept backing into me, wiggling her hips as she spoke. My whole body started to feel like purring velvet.

“Hey,” she said. “What’s happening back there?”

I gave her wrist a gentle squeeze.

“Oh my god,” she said, pulling away a little. “Lawson Sauren, are you getting turned on?”

“I’m sorry! It’s your hips.”

“What?”

“Your hips. The way you—”

“Frogs have hips, Lawson. So what?”

“It’s just . . . I don’t know!”

“This isn’t a horny house, Lawson, okay?”

“I know. I’m sorry. It’s my legs. They were cramping or something. Maybe I have diabetes?”

“Yeah right,” she said. “From now on when we snuggle, we’re putting a pillow between us.”

"It's just that you smell so good today."

"What do I usually smell like—cold baloney?"

"I don't know." I shook my head and let out all of my breath. I was getting shivery. "I'm so sorry."

"Okay," she said, and clapped her hands. "We just . . . we can dance your horniness away."

She pulled me up with surprising strength and, holding my hand, she led me to her basement living room. As we went, I saw her parka, her Métis sashes and a Métis shawl. There were mirrors everywhere, with bars along the wall for ballet. There was a disco ball and a karaoke machine. Her Casio keyboard, an electric guitar and a drum kit were all set up. All along one wood-panelled wall were school photos of Shari, from kindergarten to now. I remembered her on every single one of those days: from the dresses to her early punk phase to the ten different hairstyles. It hit me that I'd known Shari my entire life.

"Hey!" a voice called out as the lights went on. "Shari?"

"Dad, hi!" She gave me a look of fear.

Big dad steps stormed down the stairs. Mr. Burns, Métis president of Fort Simmer, studied us with bright-blue eyes. He surveyed the room before focusing on me.

"Lawson Sauren. What's going on here?"

"We were visiting," Shari said. "Lawson's my friend. We were only visiting."

Mr. Burns looked at her and then at me.

"Oh. Sorry. It's . . . I saw his runners and, uh, you don't usually have visitors."

"Sorry, sir," I said, and raised my hands. He held out his hand and I shook it. He practically broke my hand with his grip. "I'm making K'aílaza and his family moose nose soup and was hoping Shari could help me."

It hit me that Mr. Burns had the saddest eyes. I also remembered that he negotiated with unions for big contracts, so he could probably read me like nothing.

"I want to make my first pot for K'aílaza and his family and, when I'm gifted with another moose nose, sir, I'd like to make my second pot for you."

Mr. Burns scratched his chin and relaxed a little. Then he looked from Shari to me and from me to Shari.

"Why would you want to make me moose nose soup?"

I was relieved to suddenly be able to tell the truth.

"Mr. Burns," I said, "when I lost my mom, you told me a few things at the funeral. You said a sorrow shared is a sorrow halved, and to take it one hour at a time."

He nodded.

"You also told me that there was no wrong way to grieve, and that I should ask for help when I needed to."

He nodded again.

"I wanted to thank you. Your words carried me. I mean it." And I did.

"I'm sorry she's gone," he said. "You don't ever get over it. You just do your best every day. Try to. But family and friends, your work–it all keeps you going."

"I really missed your family these last two years. I'm happy to have Shari back. In fact, I have a gift for both of you."

I raced upstairs and grabbed the pouch of Mom's fireweed from my jacket. I had intended it for Shari, but it felt right to offer it to her dad. I came back and could tell Mr. Burns wasn't sure what to expect.

I offered the pouch of fireweed to him. "Mr. Burns, mahsi cho for giving me the words that helped me mourn my mom." My voice cracked and I started to tear up. "I, uh, my dad and I are just starting to come out of our sorrow. Your words really helped me every single day. The fireweed I offer you is the fireweed Mom gave me right before she passed."

"Oh," Mr. Burns said, and I heard the breath leave his lungs. "Wow, Lawson. Well, this is a pleasant surprise. I am honoured."

He was smiling. I saw his eyes sparkle with tears. He squeezed my shoulder, just like he'd done at Mom's funeral.

"Oh, Dad," Shari said, and pushed him. "Please don't cry." Then she hugged him. This family, too, was carrying so much sorrow. Shari wiped her eyes and looked at me with what seemed like love, even admiration. I decided to go for it.

"And, sir," I said, "I've come to ask your permission to ask Shari to the grad dance next June."

He looked at me and he looked at Shari. Shari started to jump and clap.

"Buttering me up, hey?" he smiled and winked. "My girl, what do you think of all of this?"

I held my breath. I think we all did.

"I say yes," she said.

"Okay," he said. "You have your answer."

I looked at Shari and held my hand out. "Thank you."

She shook it. I hoped that she wanted to kiss me. I wanted to kiss her.

"Tell your dad I said hi," said Mr. Burns.

I smiled. "Okay. Mahsi."

"Mahsi," he said. Mr. Burns was about to leave us, but stopped.

"Hey, did you hear? The old man K'aílaza just arrived," Mr. Burns said from the hallway leading to the stairs. "Big show tomorrow night in the elementary school gym. Are you two ready to meet a legend?" He looked at Shari. "We better get baking."

"And I better go get cooking," I said. "Do you know where they're staying?"

"Arnie's," he said. "Looks like they got the whole house to themselves, and that big backyard. Who got you the nose?"

"Sonny," I said.

"Sonny Nets?" he asked.

I nodded. Arnie's was a whole-house rental. I could bring K'aílaza and his family moose nose soup as an offering and introduce myself. In fact, I could bring Isaiah and Patrick and Linus with some of the portraits. Isaiah could grass-dance to welcome K'aílaza. Shari could use her psychic radar and warn us if the Dead One or Silver and his gang were near. I would not tell K'ailaza anything. We would go there and listen for clues about how to get back to the Beneath and release Stanley so we could face the Dead One together.

"Learn all you can from Sonny," Mr. Burns said. "He knows his stuff. Are you ready to honour a great peacemaker, my girl?"

"I'm ready," replied Shari. "Bye, Lawson. Thank you for asking my dad in front of me." Shari hugged me so hard I heard a rib pop back into place—probably from when Silver tackled me.

I wanted to give Shari a quick kiss and apologize for crossing over into Hornyville, but I had to go see Sonny. I left as quickly as I could, astonished and excited. This was it. K'aílaza and his daughters were here. I'd go to Sonny's and cook the moose nose. If we could get Stanley back and have him on our side, we could face the Dead One in his den. If we couldn't get Stanley back, we could use Mom's flare gun to distract him so he wouldn't knock me out again—or worse. My theory was he was drawn to fireworks and blinking lights. Why else would he be so drawn to watching the sunrise? I also needed Sonny's eagle feather, his fireweed offering and Mom's rat root. I made my way home and grabbed everything I could think of, including my tennis racquet—just in case Slitter showed up and tried anything. I also took an extra handful of fireweed and filled both my front pockets with it. Who knew when I'd need it? I had to be ready for anything.

# Take Hold of the Flame

I FOUND SONNY IN HIS BACKYARD CHOPPING WOOD BESIDE A big campfire. Behind him, to my surprise, Ragged Glory was washed and waxed. Man, did she ever look beautiful and wicked. I put down the flare gun kit where he wouldn't see it, and I held the eagle feather in front of me and the racquet beside me. It was amazing how light and heavy the feather was all at the same time, and how it caught the air when I walked with it. Sonny had set a chainsaw up on a stump beside a jerry can. I could smell the wood chips of spruce and pine. Oh, it smelled good. He had two big pots of water boiling on cooking grates: one for tea, the other just open and steaming over the firepit.

There was also a huge moose head on a small bench. The head was tilted and its eyes were closed. The antlers and ears had been cut off. I knew that this would have been done right after the moose was downed by whoever shot it. Sonny told me once that the Dogrib hang the ears up high in a young poplar so they won't ever hear you coming when you hunt the moose's family—the wind stays in the moose's ears. The

Dogrib also poke the eyes of a fallen caribou so it won't see itself being butchered. As a hunter, and as someone who prepares the meat, you always have to pray to give thanks. You even have to take special care of the bones and the hide afterwards. In Fort Rae, where Mom was born, people used to tie up the caribou bones in a bundle, take them out on the land, find a crack in a hill, and drop them down there, to return them to the land. It was always done with respect and gratitude.

This was the first time I'd seen a moose head up close. Beautiful brown everything. Eyes closed. Big nose.

Sonny pointed his lips at my racquet. "I didn't know you played."

I placed the racquet down on a stump and offered the eagle feather to him. "For you, Uncle."

He smiled and came toward me, taking his work gloves off. "Mahsi cho."

I looked at the moose head. "And thank you."

"So K'aílaza and his family are here," he said. "Are you ready to learn how to make some moose nose soup?"

"How did you know he was here?" I asked. "Did you see them?"

"I was at the car wash when he and his family pulled into town. He's with two other trucks. Man, does he look ancient."

"Did you say anything to him?" I asked.

"I sure did. I welcomed him to our town and told him you'd be cooking for him tonight, before all the hullabaloo tomorrow. I hope that's okay. This moose nose is ready. Let's do this."

"Thanks, Uncle," I said and looked again at Ragged Glory, all gussied up.

"It's amazing," he said, "what you can do in a day, when you're not drinking."

He winked and I smirked.

"Before I accept this feather," he asked, "have you looked for the signs?"

I nodded and looked to a branch where three little birds—sparrows—seemed to be watching us.

"I have, Uncle."

"Before I shake your hand, and before I accept this eagle feather," he said, "has everything you're doing been done in a good and honest way? I need to know this before I show you what I know."

"Uncle, I've been patient. I've looked for the signs, and I have everyone I need with me to help me move forward in the way of peacemaking as a Yabati."

He shook my hand. "Mahsi cho. Nezį. Good. I can feel that you have done all you can and that your protectors are with you, Yabati. Mahsi cho for your patience with me. I, uh, there's always anniversaries, you know, for my boys? I accept this sacred feather that has never touched the earth for my boys and for me and for their mother. I accept it and I thank you." Sonny accepted the eagle feather gently, with tears in his eyes, and held it over his heart. He closed his eyes and prayed quietly. I bowed my head and listened to him pray in Dogrib. I hoped his spirit sons were here so they could be proud of their dad.

"I want to thank you, Lawson. Everything you said was true. I was hiding. But no more. It's time to take care of all that I have, you know? And that includes Ragged Glory, you and your pops, and my spirit sons." He carefully held the eagle feather up to the sky.

"Today, I just want to say a huge mahsi cho, Creator. Mahsi cho. My nephew has brought me a sacred eagle feather,

Creator, and I am humbled. He drop-kicked me with the truth, Creator, and I am humbled."

He was being totally serious, so I closed my eyes and listened to him.

"I ask, Creator, that you watch over Lawson and his friends, our family, my boys, Linda—yes, even my ex. I just want to thank you for another beautiful day, and tell you how much I look forward to watching Lawson grow. I'm his adopted uncle, and I am so proud of him, Creator. I pray for his father and mother. I pray for our little town. A peacekeeper and his family are here. They're a long way from home. My wish today is that we can still make the perfect pot of moose nose soup for him and his family and for the Elders. Creator, I ask that you guide us so that when the law keeper feasts on what we are about to prepare, he remembers only happy days, only happy times. Mahsi cho, Creator. Mahsi for hearing me, and mahsi cho for my brother, Smarty, who has always been there for me, through the good times and through my years of sorrow."

He held the feather and again prayed quietly to himself. "Darrel, Sonny Junior and Ray, Daddy loves you." He broke down and wept.

So those were their names: Darrel, Sonny Junior and Ray.

I knew in a heartbeat that I needed their help. I would ask them to help me. I stood and dug into my pockets for fireweed and held the fireweed out to the fire.

"Uncle, is it okay if I offer this to the fire to honour them?"

"That would be sweet," he said.

"Can I say a few words to them as my cousins?" I asked.

"Sure, but don't you dare make me cry."

I offered the fireweed, tossing some into the fire, and prayed, "Darrel, Sonny Junior and Ray, my cousins, I hope you're happy in the spirit world and that you come back every once in a while to support your dad."

"I'm trying, boys," Sonny said and covered his eyes. "I just miss you so much."

"Come back to check up on us and help us when you can," I said, and dropped more of the fireweed into the fire.

If losing your mom felt like the hardest thing in the world to climb through, I just couldn't imagine losing your children.

After a while, as we watched the fire, Sonny stood and looked at me. "This is your feather," he said, and handed it back to me. "You need this for what you are about to do. Gift it to K'aílaza on behalf of our family and the town. He can't refuse you if you offer this to him in friendship and as a peace offering."

I took it and held it. It was humming again. "Really? But I gave it to you."

"Yes, you did," he said, "but it's yours. It was given to you, and it's telling me to gift it right back to you."

He walked up to his house to get something, and I felt someone watching me from the trees. "Mahsi cho for being here, whoever you are. Help us please for what we need to do." I felt the breeze and decided to really pray, now that I knew that this feather was for me and what I had to do next: "Creator, Mom, red wolf, little swallow spirit helpers, cousins, and to the mother of us all, mahsi cho for allowing me to see Sonny's sons. Mahsi cho for bringing the Valentines to Fort Simmer. I, too, would like to pray for K'aílaza and his family. I also want to pray for Cody Cranes, wherever he is. May he be safe. I also want to pray for Stanley, pray that he holds on until we can free him and return him whole to his own sweet self. And for Silver—I do want to pray for him. My wish for everyone is peace. Please give us strength and courage as we move forward to defend our treaty and stop escalating war and suffering. Mahsi cho."

Sonny came back carrying a plate filled with little chunks of meat. He held it out to me. "Nah," he said, which was Dogrib for *here*.

I took the plate. I placed the stem of my eagle feather in a wedge on the side of a stump so it was secured standing up. It could not touch the ground. I then focused on Sonny, who pointed with his lips.

"Offer this moose fat to those birds. Our little guides. Always feed the birds, my boy. Share what you have. They have power."

I knelt and tipped the plate, and all of the chunks of moose fat tumbled into the pine and spruce needles.

"Mahsi cho, bird people," I said. "Bless the winged ones."

Sonny pulled on his work gloves and returned to his axe and chopping block.

"I am proud to teach you my gran's recipe," he said. "It's the old way. The true way. The first time we make this together, you watch and help. The next time we make it, you make it and I'll help, okay?"

He pointed with his lips to a long knife to the right of the moose head.

"Grab that knife," he said. "I'll guide you."

He started squeezing the moose nose and found where the cartilage met bone.

"Feel here."

I did. He pointed. "Cut down to the bone, all the way. Slide the knife. She knows what to do."

He motioned for me to pinch the soft fur and cartilage and hold it while I sawed the knife down. The nose was heavy, solid. That had to be bone. I did as I was told. Dad told me that Sonny was such a good knife sharpener that if any of his knives ever cut you, you wouldn't feel it until it was too late. I dug the knife all the way until I felt solid bone.

"Cut around," he said. "Nah."

He motioned for me to pull the knife toward me.

I did. There was blood. A little bit.

"Peel it up," he said, motioning for me to pull up.

I angled the knife down and felt the meat and cartilage give way as I pulled and cut.

"Here," he said. "Pull up."

I did. I squeezed even harder with my left hand and sliced the nose up and away. I felt like I was holding a hairy football that was full of solid meat.

"We could singe the nose," Sonny said, "but my ehtsį loved it like this. I think K'aílaza will, too."

Sonny took a box of salt and dumped a bit in the boiling water. He pointed with his lips.

"Drop it in," he said. "Slowly. Don't get splashed."

I lowered the moose nose into the boiling water. It fit in the pot, nice and snug.

"For how long?"

"One hour," he said, taking the knife from me. He tapped the moose nose a few times to fully submerge it before putting the lid on. "Hour and a half."

I grabbed the fourth pouch of fireweed and offered it to him.

"Uncle," I said. "Mahsi cho for teaching me how to make something so special for K'aílaza and his family."

He looked at me and sniffed the pouch. "Tobacco?"

I shook my head. "Fireweed. From Mom. This was the last thing she gave me before she passed."

He held it to his chest. "Roberta," I heard him say.

This felt right. Everything we were doing felt right. Suddenly I remembered the Border. Was it the entryway to the same place, the Beneath, that Shari envisioned?

"Uncle," I asked, "did our people ever do sweat lodges or ceremonies where we'd become more spirit than human?"

"My ehtsį told me that when the Dogrib got really sick, they'd bury themselves in the earth with hot rocks and pray. Someone would add water to those rocks, and the steam would help them. But it was only one person doing this. Not a group, like the Cree in their sweat lodges."

So that's how Mom did it. That's how Mom returned at the Border. Maybe not with hot rocks, but it sounds like she buried herself. I could do that. Shari and Isaiah could help me.

"Okay. Let's feed the fire." Sonny sprinkled some of Mom's fireweed into the fire and then offered some to me. I did what he did, pinching a small bit and offering it gently into the fire.

"Nezį, Nephew. I am so proud of you. Always feed the fire and pay the land and the water, and do it, always, with respect. With this soup, that eagle feather, and all the signs lining up? You can't lose."

"Can I ask you . . . how someone gains power through evil ways?"

"Like in bad medicine?" he asked.

I nodded.

He was quiet for a while as he thought. And then he spoke: "Those evil spirits are very friendly when they start off with you. When you accept their terms. When you're offered įk'ǫ̀ǫ—medicine power—you have to do a certain thing or a series of things. You make a deal with the spirit, then you're under their power and all they do is steal from you. That's the nature of the beast, and there are no happy endings. Wait here."

He went into the house. I continued to stack wood. The wind picked up a little.

Sonny returned and handed me something wrapped in red fabric.

"Nah," he said. "Open it."

I did. It was a piece of a root. Curved. Tough. With it was a black lighter.

"The night your dad made up with me," he said. "He gave me that. Even though I was in the wrong, he gave that to me. I knew right then and there that I was in the presence of a great man. A better man than me, that's for sure. I deserved what I got. I regret every single day what I said about your mom. No more drinking for me, nephew. I have lost so much because of it. You're right: it's time to live a life me and my boys would be proud of."

"Mahsi cho, Uncle," I said. It was all coming together. Medicines were blooming around us.

"You give this to Silver," he said. "Give it to him in the name of peace. Honour the peacemaker and his family."

I started stacking a bunch of wood by the side of the house and then by the Wallow Pit. If the temperature really dropped, Sonny could just open the door real quick and help himself to a few pieces.

"You know how to say 'Creator' in our language?" Sonny asked me.

I shook my head.

"Nohtii," he said.

"Nohtii," I repeated.

That felt so much closer to my heart than *God*.

"How do you say 'red wolf'?" I asked.

"'Red wolf' is dìga dek'o."

It took the full hour and a half for us to stack all his wood. As I worked, I repeated *dìga dek'o* over and over in my mind. I was going to free her and her brother.

"Okay," he said, brushing his hands together. He took the lid off the pot, and, with tongs, gently lifted up the moose nose. It looked rubbery. He placed it on a long plate on the table.

The moose nose was steaming. The fur was soaked. He handed me two white cotton gloves. I put them on.

"Just like plucking ducks," he said. He demonstrated with his hands how I should pinch and pull the fur. I started tugging. The fur came off in patches. He motioned for me to drop the tufts on the cutting board that we had used to slice the nose. I was surprised to see that the flesh of the moose was white.

"Look at that," he said. "The pores are wide open. Start plucking and I'll change the water."

I pulled all the fur from the nose and enjoyed the heat from the fire. Sonny put a fresh batch of water on the grill.

"You always want to pluck the fur off when she's still hot," he said. "That's an old Indian trick."

Sonny went into his house and got a big bag of carrots, spuds, onions. He put them on another table he had. He returned to the house and came out with a measuring cup filled with rice. In his left hand he held two strawberries. He offered them to the swallows that had been watching us from the trees, putting them on the ground. The swallows flitted to the berries and began pecking gently.

He handed me his knife. "Cut that cartilage bone out from the middle." He showed me where it was.

I pinched the bone and cut around it until it gave.

"Good," he said. "Nezį."

"Nezi." I nodded.

He took it and threw it into the fire.

"For Bracken," he said. "Best hunting dog ever."

"Cut that cartilage up," he told me. "Small chunks. Dice 'em up."

He had another pot of warm water, and he motioned for me to put the chunks—about twenty of them—into the flushing water.

"Get all that gunk out," he said. "Clean them good."

I nodded and did what I was told. I grabbed a clean knife and got to work dicing up the carrots, spuds and onions. Holy cow, Sonny's knives were so sharp.

He put more salt in the fresh pot of water. It was boiling now.

"Put them all in and let it boil for forty minutes and then you're done. Sometimes you can throw in a handful of rice. This is your show. What do you think?"

I was starting to get hungry. This all smelled so good, even the smoke. I thought of K'aílaza. He was probably very traditional. If I was the last of the war chiefs and had to pick the best moose nose soup ever . . .

"So when you add the rice, does it thicken everything?"

Sonny smacked his lips. "Yup. I love it. Add some pepper and, holy cow, you're full for hours."

Even the chickadees were watching me.

"Okay," I said. "Fort Simmer 1986, we have the best of everything here."

"Nezį." He nodded.

"It seems to me that we always take the best of the traditional and the new."

"A-ho," he said.

"I think if I was an Elder taking a tour of the North under Halley's Comet, it would really be something to see how other communities celebrate their own ways."

"I'm loving what I'm hearing, nephew. What do you think, bosses?"

One swallow hopped toward us. It chirped. It chirped again.

"What's that?" Sonny asked. "One chirp for adding the rice and two for not?"

It chirped once.

I felt like I was on *The Price Is Right.*

I held the cup of rice over the bubbling moose nose soup.

The birds watched me, their little heads twitching.

"Do I add the rice for K'aílaza in the name of peace between the Dogrib and the Chipewyan?"

One swallow chirped.

I was about to pour when both birds started squawking and I stopped. One grain of rice fell in.

"One fell in," hissed Sonny.

Both birds were quiet.

"Is that good?" I asked.

Both birds chirped and flew away.

"Ho-ly!" he cheered. He took the measuring cup. "Did you see that? Did you see it? That's medicine power right there. That's it! These are the good signs, nephew!"

To see the one grain of rice roll with the onions, spuds, moose nose chunks, carrots—oh, it looked and smelled so good.

"Now we're protected," Sonny said, and closed the lid. "Don't ever tell anyone what happened here or we'll lose the įk'ǫ̀ǫ̀."

I nodded. *Inkwo.* There was so much power in secrets.

"I can't thank you enough." I smiled.

"Now," he said, "in forty minutes, this is going to be done. Let's drop tobacco in the fire for the moose who offered itself to the hunters, and for K'aílaza and his family. Let's also drop tobacco for Silver and his family. His late parents. Your mom. Your dad. You. Your buddies. Your sweethearts."

I looked at him. "Wah."

He winked and reached over to give my shoulder a squeeze. "And let's give thanks to our mothers." He handed me a bag of tobacco. I pinched some and dropped it into the fire.

"Mahsi cho, Creator."

He did the same before closing his eyes and praying in Dogrib. "SeNǫ̀htsı̨, dìı dzę̀ę̀ k'e gok'ènendì. Hazǫ̀ǫ̀ ha masì nets'ı̨ı̨whǫ, gozha, gokǫ̀, gonèk'e, hazǫ̀ǫ̀ ha wet'à ts'eenda. Hotı hǫt'e nı̨de. Mahsi cho, Creator. May this meal renew the peace between the Dogrib and the Chipewyan. May we honour the peace treaty in Roberta Sauren's name. I want to especially pray for my nephew, Lawson."

Sonny opened his eyes and squeezed my shoulder again. "I think my boys would have been a lot like you."

I nodded—I felt so honoured to hear that. "Thank you, Uncle. Mahsi cho."

In the forty minutes that it took for the final boil, I tidied up everything that I could of Sonny's. I raked all the smaller kindling into boxes for both his house and the Wallow Pit. I dusted off his old piano in the garage. And I had a good look at all of his pictures of past parties: pictures of my dad, my mom, dogs, old-timers, the rapids, pelicans, a bunch of firefighters, his three sons—a life lived laughing, singing, partying, and taking it easy.

Man, there were lots of bottles.

"Call the Scouts," I said. "They'll take these for their bottle drive."

"You do it," he said, and winked at me. "Someone might think I'm an alcoholic."

"I need to borrow your war pony," I said after I was done.

"Go for it," he said. "Key's in the ignition."

Sonny grabbed a few two-by-fours, a hammer, some nails. He started to build a little box frame. He grabbed some plywood so the pot wouldn't burn the floor of Ragged Glory.

Now that the moose nose soup was ready, I just had to assemble my peacekeepers. I carefully picked up the eagle feather and placed it on the passenger seat of Ragged Glory. I also grabbed the hidden flare gun kit and placed it in the truck.

"Good luck, nephew. Our ancestors are with you. Go in peace. The soup should stay hot for the next forty minutes. It can be reheated, but make sure they eat it tonight—and if you do reheat it, stir it slowly and continuously so you don't burn the bottom."

"Mahsi."

"Hey," he said, "isn't it your graduation year coming up?"

I nodded. "Yeah."

He pointed with his lips to Ragged Glory. "You can have her."

"What!?"

He nodded. "Consider her your graduation present."

I was stunned. Time slowed. "Are you serious?"

He nodded again. "We were blessed today. You and I both saw it. You go do what you have to do and honour K'aílaza and his family. They've come a long way. Once you've done what you have to do, you go soup up that war pony of yours and let Uncle borrow it every once in a while, okay?"

I shook my head in disbelief. "Okay. Thank you."

He hugged me and patted me on the back.

I was astonished. "Thank you for everything, Uncle. Mahsi cho."

Once everything was secured, I took a look at Sonny and his yard. He was ready for the winter. As I started up *my* truck, I was armed with nothing but goodness. Maybe K'aílaza would tell us what to do about the Dead One and Slitter. The key would be getting the information out of him without ever telling him about the Dead One. I bet he would know how to free Stanley and Silver, too. Holy cow, that moose nose soup smelled good.

Sonny waved and yelled, "Yabati power!"

I yelled it back and he returned to his fire.

Ragged Glory's dashboard lit with a glowing blue. I looked at the engine temperature gauge, the speedometer, the gas gauge and another one that I didn't recognize. It was like four octopus eyes looking back at me from underwater. I moved the flare gun kit behind the passenger seat so it wouldn't be seen if I got pulled over. I then made my way to Shari's house. We'd need her dad's truck for Isaiah's regalia. After that, we'd pick up Isaiah, Patrick and Linus. They all deserved to meet K'aílaza.

Maybe all this worry was for nothing. Maybe Cody's family had nuked Slitter in the city. Maybe those wolves had faced the Dead One in the forest.

I could not wait to meet K'aílaza and watch him and his daughters feast.

# Leaders in Danger

SHARI ANSWERED THE DOOR WITH PANIC IN HER EYES.

"They're here. Silver's back with his gang. I can feel them."

"What?" I asked, shocked. "I thought . . ."

She shook her head. "I'm sorry. It was like one second the town was warm, and the next it was ice-cold."

*Frick, I thought this would be easy, that we'd get K'aílaza on our side first. They must have caught the afternoon flight up to Simmer or arrived by bus.*

"Do they have Cody?" I asked.

Shari closed her eyes and shook her head. "I don't know. I'm sorry. We have to try to get to K'aílaza before they do."

That meant Slitter was back and Silver had assembled a gang.

"Nice ride," she said, looking at Ragged Glory.

"Thanks," I said. "Wait 'til you see what I have planned for our grad dance night." If we made it through this in one piece, I'd get Ragged Glory all spruced up for our grad ceremony and date.

"We need your dad's truck too, if that's okay," I said. "Can you give the Valentines a ride? I don't have room in my truck."

"Sure," she said as she grabbed her Ramones jean jacket from her porch.

"Follow me and we'll hatch a plan at Isaiah's as to how this is all going to go."

"Okay," she said.

I remembered that we might need Mom's flare gun to distract Stanley.

"Do you know how to use a flare gun?"

"If it has a trigger," she said, "I can fire it." She grabbed her dad's truck keys and shut the door. "Let's go."

*Let me repeat this to the universe: Shari Burns is a warrior goddess who can fire anything that has a trigger!* That line alone filled me with courage.

I got in Ragged Glory and turned the key. Shari got in the Midnight Toker, fired it up and tailed me to Isaiah's. I hadn't felt this alive in years. When I looked in my rear-view mirror, I saw her wave and smile, and I felt a love bomb go off in my heart.

We pulled up in front of the Valentines' house and knocked on the door. Roxanne answered and looked at our two vehicles before she focused on us.

"Hey," she said.

Shari stood beside me and took my hand.

"Uh, who's this?" Roxanne asked.

"Roxanne," I said, "this is Shari Burns, my girlfriend."

Roxanne appraised Shari and nodded. "Hello."

"Gosh, you're beautiful," Shari said, and held out her hand. "What a pleasure to meet you. Welcome to Fort Simmer."

This seemed to take Roxanne by surprise. She shook Shari's hand once, firmly.

"Well, thank you. I hear you're taking my brothers to meet K'aílaza?"

I nodded. "Yup."

She stepped back and called the boys. Shari squeezed my hand and I squeezed hers back. *My girlfriend.* Roxanne was gorgeous, but there was no doubt left in my mind that I wanted to be the boyfriend of Shari Burns.

Patrick and Linus came out and met Shari. Isaiah came down the stairs and gave us a nod.

"Is tonight the night?" he asked with a wink.

"It sure is," I said. "I made moose nose soup with my uncle Sonny." I said this with pride. I wanted the whole town to know it.

"Right on," Isaiah said. "So I guess I better keep my promise, hey?"

While Isaiah got dressed in his grass-dancing regalia, the younger boys and I went to the basement to choose which portraits to present to K'aílaza. I picked out two frames and handed them to Patrick. I hesitated before making my final choice.

"Are you sure about that?" asked Linus.

I nodded.

As we loaded the portraits in Shari's dad's truck, Isaiah walked out of his house wearing his regalia. His right hand held the handle of a black suitcase. In his left he held a cassette tape. He looked magnificent.

"Who's got the louder system?" he asked.

"Ragged Glory," I said, and tapped the dashboard gently.

He handed the tape to me. I popped it in and turned it up. The drums began, and the cry of Cree men singing was glorious! Holy wow. I felt my Dogrib and Mountain Dene blood wake up with a roar. Isaiah did a few moves, and I knew we had our A-team.

"You take care of my brothers," Roxanne called to me.

"I will. I promise."

"And take care of you, Lawson," she added.

Isaiah placed his suitcase in the back of Ragged Glory but realized that there was no room for him with his regalia on. He carried with him two fur-covered hoops with eagle feathers hanging from them. The cab was filled with the smell of moose nose soup. He took a big sniff.

"Nice ride," he said. "Holy, it smells great, too."

"You'll have to go with Shari."

"Your nicimos?" he asked me with a grin. "That's Cree for 'sweetheart.'"

I nodded. "You bet."

"No more keemooch for you?" he teased. "I'm happy for both of you. You got the flare gun?"

"I do."

"Holy," he said. "We're really doing this."

"Yup," I said. "We have to. It's time."

He looked at me. "You feel like a kamikaze?"

"Kamikazes don't come home," I replied. "I feel like a Yabati, and I'm adopting you as my brother and fellow Yabati."

"Mahsi cho." He tightened his belt and shook my hand. "Hai hai."

"You and your brothers are Cree. Shari's Métis. I'm Dogrib," I said. "Our ancestors are with us. If K'aílaza can see what we're doing, he'll help us send the Dead One back to whatever hell it crawled up from. We are there to stop Silver and free Stanley."

I looked in the rear-view. Linus and Patrick were waiting in Shari's truck. Shari gave me the nod and blew me a kiss.

"Protect, respect and defend with honour," I said. "Let's go."

Isaiah hurried to Shari's truck.

The moose nose soup sloshed as I sped up and slowed down, but it didn't spill. I held the stem of the eagle feather as I drove.

"Creator, Mom, ancestors, protect us please," I said. This was our night to face the Dead One. Enough was enough. I didn't want any more suffering for anyone.

# Eye of the Tiger

I KILLED RAGGED GLORY'S LIGHTS AND REVERSED AS CLOSE as I could to the backyard. Arnie's rental house was in the new part of town, surrounded by dirt roads and walls of spruce and pine trees, with an access road behind it. There was a huge bonfire in the backyard, and I could see people sitting in lawn chairs around it. I didn't recognize any of them—but then I saw Silver, holding a microphone.

I motioned for Shari to kill the lights on her truck as she pulled up beside me. When the time was right, I'd hit play, and Isaiah's PA cousins would start singing and drumming on the cassette. I wanted Ragged Glory's speakers cranked so everyone would hear the powwow songs loud and clear.

"We'll have to make this up as we go," I said to Shari as I got out of the truck. I was still holding the eagle feather for K'aílaza.

We could hear Silver making a speech through the loudspeaker. This was exactly what his dad used to do: spread hate in his speeches and get everyone fired up against his latest opponent.

Isaiah got out of The Midnight Toker, opened his suitcase and started pulling on the rest of his regalia. He looked incredible—ribbons, beadwork: he was the living image of his grandfather. The aromas of Sonny's soup and sweetgrass surrounded us as I felt all of my senses go on full alert.

"We feel cold," Patrick and Linus said.

"Good," Isaiah said. "You're sensing evil."

"What?" Patrick asked.

"Lawson, tell my brothers why we're here."

"I thought we were here to bring an Elder these pictures," Linus said.

"We are," I said as I handed Shari the flare gun kit. "It's just that there's a guy named Silver Cranes who made a deal with an ancient spirit. A bad one."

"Seriously?" asked Linus.

Shari, Isaiah and I all nodded.

"Seriously," said Shari.

"What we're going to do," I said, "is crank your PA cousins on my truck's tape player, and Isaiah is going to grass-dance. We're going to pretend we're the chefs and Silver Cranes hired us to cook for everyone."

Shari laughed and clapped quietly. "Brilliant!"

"Who would attack the chefs?" I asked. "These people deserve to be hosted as honoured guests—and we have fresh moose nose soup."

Everyone nodded in agreement with my logic.

I continued with my plan: "I'm going to bring this soup to the gathering over there and make a speech. Silver's not going to like what I say, but we are here to free him from the spirit—and this little frog-like thing that crawled into him through his mouth."

Linus and Patrick looked to me. Then they looked to Isaiah.

"Are you being frickin' serious, Lawson?" Linus asked.

"Like come on, eh? As if," Patrick said nervously.

"It's true," Isaiah said, standing tall. He was in full grass-dancing mode. "Brothers, remember when Dad told us that our family is different from other families because he, Mushom and our uncles are wheetago hunters?"

"Yeah," they both said.

"Well, this is our night to face something just as evil, just as brutal, just as starving. But this thing inside Silver doesn't want meat. It wants people's spirits. I won't let it anywhere near you, I promise. Look to Lawson and me, and trust your instincts."

I handed Patrick my racquet. "If that frickin' frog goblin comes anywhere near you two, you have my full permission to whack it and stomp it."

Patrick and Linus grinned at each other.

"I like this," said Patrick.

"I'm in," Linus agreed.

"Hold those portraits up, boys, and pass them to Elder K'aílaza when we ask you to," Isaiah said.

"But stay on guard," I said. "Shari, are you sensing anything?"

Shari closed her eyes, and we felt the air fill with something like static electricity, pushing against us. I could see the air shimmer around her.

"Uh," Patrick said, "what's happening with her?"

"Shari's psychic and is sensing everything around us," I said. "She's scanning for spirits."

"Is she doing a seance?" Linus whispered.

"She's channelling," I said. "She can see the dead and dying."

"Holy frick," Linus said.

"Frickin' cool, boy," Patrick said.

"Silver does have something inside of him," Shari said, opening her eyes. "The gang guys he's hired do not. They're still human, but they're under his spell."

"Ready?" I asked Isaiah.

"I prayed for Mushom's strength," Isaiah said, "and we're representing our family. I can smell sweetgrass. He's here with us. You boys ready? This thing we're about to face is nothing but good training for something bigger and far more ferocious. The wheetago take no prisoners and will eat you alive. All this thing takes are slaves and souls. Are you ready, my brothers?"

"We're ready," Patrick said.

"Let me at 'im," Linus said with a grin.

---

THROUGH THE LOUDSPEAKER, WE HEARD SILVER CRANES clear his throat and take a big breath.

"K'aílaza," Silver Cranes announced, "I come before you as a peacemaker. I have united enemies. Many of the men that I sit with used to be members of rival gangs. I have shown them a better way—our way."

Through the willows and trees, we could see the huge bonfire. There were maybe twenty people gathered: Silver, with Stanley standing beside him like a bodyguard, K'aílaza and his daughters, plus a bunch of huge leather- and jeans-wearing men who looked young and fierce.

To my right, I could hear Isaiah's jingles and smell the deer hide. I took a huge breath and drew strength from it.

I singed both Sonny's and Mom's rat roots with the lighter Dad had given Sonny when they made up, and I smudged with its smoke. Mom, Dad and Sonny were with us in spirit. I fanned the smoke over my hair, over my face, over my heart, in the name of my mother. I did the same to Isaiah. I walked around him and used Sonny's eagle feather to fan the smoke all over him. As Shari, Linus and Patrick walked up to me carrying the portraits, I smudged them, too.

"I dare anyone here to challenge my leadership," Silver's voice boomed. "Everyone tonight will feast upon the food we have prepared for you."

I looked at Isaiah and frowned. I didn't see that coming. *Can Silver cook?*

"And K'aílaza," Silver continued, "please know that the Dogrib who assaulted me and broke our peace treaty—Lawson Sauren—I have forgiven him, too, in the name of peace and to honour our friendship treaty. He is a coward who refused to join me tonight to meet with you."

I saw Stanley guarding Silver. We had to get Stanley away, and Shari was the key.

"I have prepared buffalo kidney," said Silver, "and I would love to eat this with you as your champion warrior, and with our warriors, and with your daughters."

K'aílaza listened with a bowed head.

I was puzzled. If Silver had prepared a feast, this was all honourable—

"Did you hear that?" Shari asked with alarm. "I promise you that everything Silver's prepared is poisoned."

"What?" we all asked simultaneously.

"Yes, it's poisoned. The Dead One wants K'aílaza dead."

"Lawson, let's get the cops," said Isaiah. "Silver's wanted, isn't he?"

"We don't have time," said Shari. "We have to stop him. This is exactly what the beast wants. What's inside Silver doesn't care who kills him after the job is done. I promise you. I swear on everything I am that this is an assassination."

This was what the Dead One meant when he told Silver, "Remember our plan."

We had to act now.

"Everyone," I said, "you are all Yabati tonight. You are all peacemakers. I need all of you to stay calm and do what I tell you, okay?"

Everyone nodded.

"Okay," I said. "That frog-like thing inside Silver is directing him. Silver is not our enemy. What's inside him is. Just be ready for anything."

Isaiah and Linus picked up the portraits of Grandpa and Grandma Cranes, Therese Cranes with her sons, and my beautiful mother, Roberta Sauren. They held them facing out for everyone to see as we appeared. The brothers looked to me and nodded. Shari wore her grandmother's Métis shawl. She placed her hand gently on my back as I helped Isaiah suit up. The bells on his ankles sounded every time he moved.

"Remember," I said, "we'll pretend *we're* the cooks for the feast, okay?"

Mom's flare gun kit had five shots. Shari loaded the first flare, popped the gun shut, cocked it, looked at me and nodded.

"Now would be the time for a quick speech, Lawson," Isaiah said, as he stretched in his grass-dancing regalia.

I looked at each of them. "Think of your families surrounding us," I said. "Now think of our ancestors working together to bring us strength." I looked at Isaiah and his brothers.

"Think of your grandfather, your mushom, and I'll think of my ancestor, Edzo, stealing into Akaitcho's camp to make peace with the Chipewyan. We have to save Silver and Stanley. If we do this, we break the grip of this thing that wishes to creep into our world and declare war on everyone."

"Holy, Lawson," Linus said. "No pressure."

"We can do this," Isaiah said. "We have to do this."

Shari looked at me, and I drew strength from her. I looked at the portraits Patrick and Linus held up. We had to save K'aílaza and his family from the poison they were being offered.

"Let's stop whatever this thing is—whatever this beast is—right now," I said.

I made sure the tape player in Ragged Glory was turned all the way up. I placed the two sticks of smouldering rat root on a small rock beside the truck so it would blow itself out. I took the eagle feather gently and held it up like a shield. It was already humming with ancient power.

"Do it," I said to Shari as I turned Ragged Glory's headlights back on.

Shari fired the orange plastic flare gun. *Boom!* It sounded like a shotgun. The flare arced high, a dazzlingly fierce ruby ball of fire.

"Crank it," said Isaiah, and I walked over to Ragged Glory and pressed play. Shari flicked the headlights on Midnight Toker. The drumbeat began, loud and immediate. The voices of Cree men singing together rang high in a tribal harmony. I heard Isaiah's jingles as he raised his hoops over his heart. I watched him pray.

Isaiah Valentine began to grass-dance. He started low and danced in front of the headlights of Sonny's truck, and what I saw was incredible. Isaiah Valentine was dancing, honouring, blessing, clearing the earth before him to make it safe. His movements were bigger than they ever were when he practised in his basement. He was free here. He arced his leg back behind him, searching the ground, searching for anything that would harm others. He hopped, turned, arced again, each time raising his fur-covered hoops, with the eagle feathers attached to them, parallel to his waist, praying all the while.

We made our way toward the gathering but soon saw Stanley lumbering in our direction with his war face on. Shari approached him, smiling, offering her hand to him.

He looked at her, stopped, looked at Isaiah and smiled dimly. He held out his hand to Shari. She led him away, past the music, past the dancing, past the reach of Silver's voice. She fired another flare. Stanley followed her, gazing into the sky at the bright-red flare that soared above us. She needed to keep him distracted until this was done.

I could hear the bells on Isaiah's belts jingle in unison with the drum music. I caught a flash of his shadow on the fire and light on the trees. As much as I wanted to watch him, now that we had the crowd's attention, I had to focus on my part of the plan. I held the feather that had been gifted to me, first by Mrs. Valentine and then by Sonny. I held it out and felt its hum.

"Hold those portraits high," I said to Patrick and Linus.

"Got 'em," Linus said.

"We're with you, Lawson," Patrick said.

"And Darrel, Sonny Junior and Ray," I said, "if you're here, watch everything that happens next because I'm going to need your help, cousins."

I didn't see them, but I prayed they'd been following me ever since my visit with their dad.

Patrick, Linus and I walked together slowly, in the same way Roxanne had when she first brought me the feather. It was a slow, dignified walk. I held the eagle feather high and made my way to Silver, who was still holding the microphone. He was surrounded by gang members who looked to him for direction. Silver's mouth dropped open when he saw us. He was stunned by our display of beauty. He kept looking for Stanley, but I could tell he didn't want to move from where he stood. He was a distance from K'aílaza, and I had to keep them separated. We didn't need Slitter to leap into K'aílaza's mouth.

"Oh wow," a gang member said, smiling at Isaiah's grass dance. "Did you arrange this, boss?"

"Cool!" another gang member said, and clapped.

Silver had no words. K'aílaza stood with his daughters, all with big smiles. They clearly thought this was part of their welcome to our town. K'aílaza's two daughters were my mom's age. They wore Ranger gear: red parkas with fingerless gloves. The gang members wore jeans, jean jackets, and black vests with patches on them. Some were tattooed. Others had scars on their faces from what might have been knife fights. They were fierce looking, but they made no movement to stop us. They too were in awe of Isaiah, disarmed by the beauty of all they were seeing.

K'aílaza looked to me and nodded. Like with my red wolf, I felt an immediate connection with him. I could see that two pots of stew had been prepared on a table to the far right. Bowls and cutlery were stacked, ready to go. The pots were covered, but I could see a large silver bowl filled with bannock. Beside it was jam and butter. It all smelled good.

"Stop them!" Silver commanded. But his gang ignored him, continuing to watch Isaiah.

"Let them pass," declared K'aílaza, and they did. They let us pass as Silver scrambled to find the right words.

"Stop them, you guys!" he yelled. "I'm paying you to stop them! They are the enemy!"

"Silver, that's enough," said K'aílaza. "Don't scare my daughters. Let us hear what these young people have to say. My goodness. What a reception, I tell you." He clapped. "This is how it's done."

K'aílaza's daughters stood beside him watching the show, but you could tell they were also on guard. They knew something bigger was happening than what they could see.

Isaiah must have spun quickly or done a flip because the crowd let out an *aah*. I had to trust that the medicine of Isaiah's grandfather, Harold Valentine, was blessing the earth and all who witnessed the grass dance. Linus and Patrick continued to hold the framed portraits. The flickering flames of the bonfire reflected in the glass.

I made my way forward in my mother's name, in my father's name and in the name of our ancient leader, Edzo. I was scared but I knew we had to do this.

Silver approached me. He looked sick. He was still holding the microphone but spoke well away from it.

"Lawson Sauren," he whispered to me, "turn around and go home or we will kill you and your friends tonight."

I could hear him grinding his molars. And there was that smell again: bad meat, tongue rot, a foulness so wrong that it filled my nostrils and I started mouth-breathing. Slitter was still inside him, controlling him. Silver motioned for the gang to surround us, but they did not approach while I held the eagle feather in front of me. Patrick and Linus tucked themselves closer to me. K'aílaza's daughters guarded him as I approached, but their eyes lit up when they saw my peace offering of an eagle feather and the portraits.

"Hello. Who is this?" K'aílaza asked the crowd. He meant me.

"I'm the cook, Uncle. Me and my uncle Sonny just made the most delicious moose nose soup for everyone here tonight because we heard it was your favourite." I remembered Mom's teachings and addressed the crowd the same way she always did.

"Hello, honoured guests," I said with a smile. "Welcome to Fort Simmer. I hope you're hungry."

"They're liars!" Silver yelled. "Anything they say—"

K'aílaza raised his hand in a way that silenced Silver. K'aílaza had the fiercest eyes I'd ever looked into. He looked like a kind older man—but those eyes . . . There would be no lying to him.

Silver then made a show of presenting me to K'aílaza.

"This is Lawson Sauren," he announced, "enemy of the Chipewyan and coward. Breaker of our treaty. This is the one who assaulted me. But I forgive him. I forgive him in the name of peace."

I ignored Silver and held my head high as the eagle feather I carried hummed in my hand. I raised the feather as an offering to K'aílaza and his daughters. I was shaking, but I used my voice to push through my fear. I had to be heard.

"I am Lawson Sauren, son of Lawson Sauren Senior and the late Roberta Sauren, who passed away saving Stanley's life. I am a descendant of Edzo through my mother and her mother's mother."

"Sit, everyone," K'aílaza instructed the crowd. "I want to hear this young man and welcome him to our circle. May no harm come to him or his friends."

"What the hell is this?" Silver asked even though he did as he was told. He looked to where Stanley walked with Shari and called out frantically, "Stanley! Stanley!"

Stanley couldn't hear him over the drums, the dancing and the firing of the flare gun. To be certain, Shari fired again, while continuing to hold Stanley's hand. Stanley stood spellbound, looking up at both the flare and at Halley's Comet.

"Stop yelling!" K'aílaza commanded Silver. "Let this young man speak. I'm hungry. I know we all are."

I glanced around quickly and saw each of the gang members nodding in agreement. They were hungry. Good! Silver sat down, furious. This was not part of his, Slitter's or the Dead One's plan at all. I picked up the microphone that Silver had put down. I felt my father's cockiness fly into me as I held it.

"Uncle, welcome to Fort Simmer. Mahsi cho for bringing your daughters with you." I then looked to Silver's gang. "Welcome, new friends, to Fort Simmer. You are all honoured guests here, and we mean you no harm or disrespect. We are your cooks and servers this evening. We have prepared moose nose soup for all of you, and we cannot wait to feed you and honour you all. My name is Lawson Sauren. I am Dogrib with Mountain Dene blood. Dogrib through my late mother and Mountain Dene through my father. I am a descendant of Edzo, and I am here today in the name of peacemaking and honouring our friendship treaty, and to welcome you to our community. My Cree brother Isaiah Valentine dances to honour you and your families. These are his brothers, Patrick and Linus. And honouring the Métis here, my nicimos, Shari

Burns, welcomes you on behalf of her father, the president of the Métis Association."

Shari must have smiled and waved at them because several of the gang members smiled back and two of them waved. They looked like young boys sitting there, completely charmed by Shari and everything that was happening.

"Lawson," K'aílaza repeated my name. "This is wonderful. Mahsi. Go on, chef. You have the floor, but make it quick. We're hungry."

The gang members slowly began to grumble and gesture to one another and gave the stink eye to Silver. If I was a good guy in the eyes of this Elder, they had all been tricked. Whatever they had been told about us was clearly a lie: we were harmless and only wanted to feed and honour them as guests.

"Uncle," I said, "we have come here today in the name of peace. We bring to you an eagle feather that has never touched the ground, and portraits our community's own descendants of Akaitcho and Edzo, as a gift to you and your family—as a peacemaker. May I gift these to honour you and your family and to welcome you to Fort Simmer?"

I felt a quiet pass through the crowd. The gang members were now glaring at Silver. Even though they were city Natives, they clearly understood that they had been welcomed into an honouring.

K'aílaza motioned for me to approach.

"Don't do it, Grandpa," Silver called out. "It's a trick! Do not believe him. I have shown you that I can unite enemies. I have prepared a feast in your honour. I have shown you I am a peacemaker—"

"Shut up, Silver!" the biggest gang member shouted.

"Yeah," another said. "You hired us to fight these kids? Why? They're Native—like us. And they cooked for us, too."

K'aílaza held up his hand before Silver could respond. I passed the eagle feather to him. K'aílaza accepted it and shook my hand.

"You are now touching the sky, Uncle," I continued. "And the sky is now touching you. This eagle feather has never touched the ground. It was caught by Betty Valentine, mother of Isaiah, Roxanne, Patrick and Linus. They are Cree from Saskatchewan."

K'aílaza held the eagle feather up for everyone to see and then offered it to the gang member on his left.

"I want everyone here to hold this feather and feel the blessings of the Creator," said K'aílaza. "Give thanks for all that you have before our feast. Hold this feather and ask yourself, What is my purpose in life? Why am I here? Do this, our relations, and then pass it along to the one on your left to make a circle." He made the motion of a circle growing.

The first gang member with the feather stood, closed his eyes and bowed his head. Immediately, we could see the muscles in his face soften. It was like he became younger and then we could see the little boy in him: innocent. He prayed for a bit before nodding and passing the feather to the gang member on his left. The same thing happened again and again as each gang member stood and prayed while holding the eagle feather tenderly. It was like we were witnessing a miracle under the bright-red flare lingering in the sky.

Then K'aílaza looked at me to continue. "Go on, nephew."

Like my father and Sonny, I used my free hand to make my speech more eloquent. I pointed to Isaiah, presenting him like I was a magician.

"My friend and adopted brother, Isaiah Valentine of the Plains Cree from Prince Albert, Saskatchewan, dances to honour you, Uncle. He dances to honour you as a great leader. He dances in the name of his mushom, Harold Valentine. He does this to honour you and your family. He also dances to honour everyone here as our relations."

I bet the Dead One never saw this coming. These gang members, as warlike as they looked, had a deep respect for the spirit of the eagle. Again, I saw them as boys. They were boys before they got into gangs, and we were reaching them by honouring them in the right way, with a good welcome, kind words and great food.

K'aílaza watched Isaiah dance and smiled.

"I have always wanted to see a grass dancer in real life," he said. "Mahsi cho."

"It is our pleasure to honour you and our honoured guests, Uncle," I continued. "Before we feed everyone, we also bring photographs that my late mother Roberta Sauren commissioned. They are of Silver's family, who are Dene Sorulthren, and this one is of my mother, a Yabati, who drowned while defending the treaty and saving Stanley Cranes. These are gifts for you and your family on behalf of our town and Friendship Centre, which my late mother used to run."

I motioned for Patrick and Linus to come forward holding the portraits. K'aílaza's chin started to quiver as he looked at them.

"Look, my girls. Yahbati and Dene Sorulthren," he said, and looked to his daughters. "Living in peace. How beautiful." he said, and looked to his daughters.

His daughters nodded as they admired the portraits.

"These are yours, Uncle," I continued—but I wanted to make sure I addressed the gang members with the promise of food. "Uncle, we have fresh moose nose soup that my uncle Sonny Nets and I prepared for all of you. It's still hot, made with respect for you and your family, who are so far away from your home."

Silver leapt to his feet and yelled, "Grandpa, I have made you the most wonderful food! This is all a Dogrib trick!"

"Quiet," K'aílaza said. "Let this descendant of Edzo speak."

I could not see the buffalo kidneys that he'd prepared, so I gestured toward Silver's two pots of stew.

"Uncle," I said calmly, "I have reason to believe the feast of buffalo kidneys that Silver has prepared for you is poisoned."

"What?" The gang members and K'aílaza's daughters gasped.

A roar of confusion and anger erupted from the gang members. Silver yelled for everyone to shut up and listen.

K'aílaza glared at Silver. "Is this true?"

"Dogrib lies!" Silver spat and looked at me. "If it is poisoned, it's because the Dogrib want you dead. They want to break the treaty so we can keep fighting. This one, Lawson"—he pointed at his nose—"attacked me. He knowingly broke our peace treaty and now comes here to lie. I bet what *he's* made you is poisoned."

"Silver," I said, "you have always been tougher than me. Do you really think me and my little math arms and my one little chest hair could ever hurt you?"

The gang members burst out laughing, as they could all see that I was no match for anyone, really. I had them now in good spirits, so I continued: "I'm a cook, not a fighter. I have no muscles. I am straight nuts and ribs, but I have a good heart, and I can't wait to feed you all moose nose soup."

K'aílaza smiled. "A chef and a comedian. Go on."

"I have lived my life never really thinking much about the Dogrib and Chipewyan peace treaty," I said. "I was told that

I was a Yabati, a defender of that promise of friendship and partnership. Honestly, I never believed in that until I caught Silver breaking into the Legion here in town to steal the money that we'd raised from the Terry Fox Run—money for anyone fighting cancer. I'm talking *anyone*. It was for anyone with cancer who needed it."

The crowd focused on Silver in disgust.

"Silver and I did fight, and I may have landed the first blow, but everything I did to Silver was out of straight-up fear and self-defence." I pointed to Silver. "Silver, you told me that you were going to kill me when you were choking me after you stole all the money. You told me that you were going to paralyze me." I looked to the gang members. "My friends, I am sure that none of you knew Silver was paying with money stolen from a Terry Fox Run. I swear this on my mother's name and on the eagle feather you have all held. I speak to you with a good heart and in truth."

"Lawson Sauren is a liar!" Silver yelled.

K'aílaza shook his head. I had to move quickly.

"Silver," I challenged, "how about you eat what you've prepared for our guests, and I'll happily eat the moose nose soup I just made with my uncle today, right here and right now? You go first."

Silver shook his head. "I made this for K'aílaza and for my warriors."

"It's poisoned," I announced. I looked at the gang members. "This means he would have killed you all, too."

Silver's gang looked at each other in horror and disbelief.

K'aílaza looked at me and looked at Silver.

"Is this true, Silver? Did you call this meeting to kill us? You stole money from the Terry Fox Run? How low can somebody go?"

"My sister has cancer, you asshole!" an outraged gang member yelled.

Silver pointed at me and yelled, "It's all one big Dogrib lie!"

"So eat then," I challenged him. "Eat from the food you brought. I will eat from a bowl that someone prepares for me from the soup I brought. It's in my truck. I'll sit here and eat it. You sit there and eat what you've made. We'll see who dies first. I swear by everything holy on this Earth that I did not poison my soup. My soup was made the old way, the traditional way. With moose nose, an onion, spuds and carrots."

"Mmm," said K'aílaza. "I'll try yours."

He was smiling. His daughters laughed. I noticed a long rifle by one of his daughters and a shotgun by his other daughter. A gang member—the tallest and toughest looking of them all—stood and handed the eagle feather to one of K'aílaza's daughters. He said something to her and she nodded. She took the eagle feather and motioned for her sister to stand next to Silver. I looked to the gang members and could see regret and embarrassment on every single face.

I'd done it. I'd made the group doubt their leader. In fact, I'd made each of them despise Silver for what he'd done. Now I had to expose Slitter. They needed to see who and what was directing Silver.

"All of you sit," one of K'aílaza's daughters ordered. The gang members did as they were told. I could see they were worried. It hit them that I had just saved all of their lives.

The taller of K'aílaza's daughters came to me with a woven necklace made of sinew. She motioned for me to bow my head and I did. She placed it over me and let it fall over my neck.

"Keep going," she whispered. "We believe you."

"Mahsi," I said.

"Give him a necklace too," K'aílaza said, nodding at Silver.

"No," Silver said. "What is this?"

"Do it," K'aílaza said. "They made one for each of you."

Whatever medicine was braided into the necklaces, it was ancient: it smelled of smoke and earth and rat root and spruce. Silver tried to stand from his chair but when K'aílaza's daughter placed the lasso around his neck, he slumped and grew quiet.

"What have you done to me?" he gasped.

K'aílaza let his breath all the way out, then he bowed his head and began to pray. His daughters did the same. I watched Silver as the wind picked up. It was so cold. The prayer was ancient—a chant, a calling, a wish. I could hear the drums from Isaiah's cousins. I could hear another flare being fired, but I felt this prayer. I felt hands pulling smoke through my body, cleansing smoke, life. I felt lifted. I felt calm. As they prayed, Silver struggled in his chair, but he was growing weaker, weaker.

After they were done praying, K'aílaza's daughters placed braided necklaces around Silver's hands and ankles. He was powerless. He was muttering. Drool spilled from his mouth onto his shirt and moosehide vest.

I looked at Patrick and made a motion for him to get ready. He nodded and pulled out the racquet.

K'aílaza spoke with the most serious face. "Anyone who has done so much to receive us"—he gestured to Patrick and Linus, to Isaiah and to Shari—"has a good heart." He then looked at Silver. "Silver, you have been touched by something. Something stealing from your soul. We could see it the moment we met you. You're not you, Silver. There's something claiming your spirit right now. These men that you surround yourself with, they do not know who or what they're working for right now." He looked to each of them and pointed at the night sky. "What Silver serves is without pity, and feeds on suffering. It has a thousand names and answers to every single one of them. The Dead One. The Twisted One. The Medicine Eater."

The gang members looked to each other with worry and fear.

"Why don't you tell them who you serve, Silver?" K'aílaza asked.

We all watched Silver carefully. His features started to change. He was slumped in his chair but his legs started to shake. He started twitching. Then he started to laugh. Silver Cranes' leg started to bend back to the way it used to be when the town had called him Banana Leg. We all saw it. He screamed from the back of his throat.

"No! Don't! Please!"

The gang members watched Silver with horror.

Silver glared at me. "Dog scum! You're wrecking everything." It was his voice—but lower, angrier, full of hate.

"So it's true," K'aílaza said to him. "You would poison me, my family and everyone here to bring war back to the North."

"No," said Silver. "It's a lie. I promise you. Please take off these ties."

"You said the food was ready," K'aílaza spoke so calmly to him. "You told us the feast was ready. It smells ready."

Silver tried to stand to defend himself, but K'aílaza's daughter put her hands on his shoulders and told him to sit. His other daughter lit a piece of rat root and started fanning it over Silver. Silver immediately started to groan with agony.

"Stop it. Please stop. No. No. NO!"

K'aílaza looked at me. He came toward me and stood. He held out his hand and I shook it. I didn't realize how strong and huge he was.

"Keep talking. Whatever is feeding on Silver needs to hear and see us in peace together."

"Uncle, help me!" Silver called out, but K'aílaza held up his hand.

"That's enough," his daughter said.

"I should have killed you," Silver said. And when he spoke, it was pure hatred, pure evil.

"What was that?" K'aílaza asked Silver.

"I want to kill you all," Silver said, looking at all of us, his eyes darting back and forth.

We all looked at him in horror. Isaiah guided his brothers to stand behind him, so he could face Silver as a protector and defender.

Silver began chanting in mumbles and cries.

K'aílaza's daughters remained completely calm. It was as though they had been expecting this all along. The gang members were less calm. You could feel their outrage at learning Silver's plan.

"You serve the Medicine Eater," said K'aílaza. "Take my words because I have seen your eyes before. A long time ago, when I was a young man, the Medicine Eater came to us with promises under the light of the comet. It wanted to eat the dead of our enemies for power. Then it wanted to eat our dead for their medicine. It wanted to help us raise an army to kill the Inuit and then to kill the Cree. The one thing your master keeps forgetting is we have a long memory in the North. You and your kind are just a whisper compared to all we know and remember. These necklaces are braided with strong medicine and will expose any poison within."

Silver let out a powerful cry and his throat started to bulge. As Silver yelled, Slitter crawled out of his mouth and landed on the ground with a wet plop. It spun in a daze, looking around at the crowd. It blinked and bared its yellow teeth to hiss at everyone, then jumped out of the circle. Patrick rushed in and walloped it back in with the racquet. It landed with a splat in front of K'aílaza. Patrick was about to hack at it again with the racquet, but K'aílaza motioned him back.

"Nésken bésken ka bekanaídél ha sį́," Slitter said.

"Séskene béskene nekayéʔıu nuwe bá k'a thekéh ha sį́," K'aílaza said calmly.

"Dene Dedline yaį́łtí-u?" Slitter asked K'aílaza, confused.

K'aílaza nodded. "ʔę́h Dene·yasti. Sésken beskéne Dene Dedline dáyałti tth'í sį́."

Slitter did not like K'aílaza's response. It planted its knuckles and looked ready to leap toward K'aílaza and possess him—but then we heard a *boom* from his daughter's shotgun. Slitter's body exploded into meat and mist in front of all of us. The stench from its body was overpowering. Linus kicked Slitter's skull into the fire, where it started to bubble and pop.

"This," said K'aílaza, pointing at Slitter's carcass, "is just a scout. The beast this scout served would eat your tongues and hang each of your faces off the branches in its den."

There was stunned silence.

"There are rocks already set aside for slaves to pound your brains into berries for the one who wants to crawl into our world and feast on every single one of us," he said grimly.

*That was it! That was the Dead One's plan all along: to eat our medicines and grow so it could enter our world and take it over!*

"Is that how he was able to read our minds in jail?" a gang member asked.

"Yes, but the kind of power that you were promised was a lie," K'aílaza explained to Silver and his gang. "The Dead One would have you eating your own children for more power—and it would not stop there."

The gang members all looked like scared boys now.

"Every time the Dead One returns"—K'aílaza pointed to Halley's Comet—"a peacemaker like me has to witness other peacemakers facing it together. This one is different. It feeds on medicine power. We need a Yabati and a Dene Sorulthen to face the Dead One, and to send it back so it can do no more harm to anyone."

He looked to me, "Lawson, you are a Yabati. Everything you have done, everything you have prepared has been done in a good way. Do you have a Dene Sorulthen to help you face the twisted one?"

"Yes," I nodded and pointed to Stanley. "I have Stanley. But I have to return to the Dead One's den and help Stanley get his soul back."

"Do you know how?" K'aílaza asked me curiously.

"I think so," I said. I knew Stanley's soul was hidden in the tree beside him.

"Good," he said. "The Dead One is wounded so he'll be out for blood."

"Mahsi." I nodded. I had to go. *Now*. I felt it. Isaiah, Patrick and Linus could serve soup to everyone. I needed Shari to drive me and bury me.

Silver glared at all of us. "My father knows you're coming!"

K'aílaza gestured toward the carcass of Slitter. "The one you serve can't hear you now."

"He promised me," Silver cried out. "My father promised me power!"

K'aílaza nodded. "That's all he does. He promises. But what he does in the end is take from you while you steal for him."

"Lawson?" a voice spoke in the darkness.

It was Isaiah, who had been standing with Shari and Stanley. I could hear the jingles of Isaiah's regalia with every step of his approach. I felt his hand on my shoulder as he extended his other hand in friendship to K'aílaza. Isaiah was covered in sweat. His headpiece was soaked. I glanced at Silver, who now appeared to be sleeping.

Isaiah bowed with respect to K'aílaza. I was surprised to see that in Isaiah's hand was another eagle feather.

"From my family to yours, Uncle. I dance in honour of our late mushom, Harold Valentine, and I dance to bless your family, bless our new friends here who have travelled so far to see the truth. I am proud to stand with my brothers. We come here in peace."

"What a pleasure to meet you," said K'aílaza. "Mahsi cho for honouring all of us."

"Sir." Shari walked up and held out her hand to K'aílaza. "Welcome."

She wrapped her arm around mine and leaned into me.

K'aílaza shook her hand and bowed. "A pleasure to meet you."

"I'm Shari Burns, daughter of Carlson Burns, Métis president."

K'aílaza smiled. "I remember your dad. Even as a kid, he was already leading. President, you say? He always wanted that. I'm happy for him."

I looked at K'aílaza and his daughters. They were watching for my next move.

"Okay," I said, "Shari and I have to go. I know how to save Stanley, but we've got to move quickly while the Dead One's hurt. Can you serve everyone here?"

Isaiah nodded. "Sure. The soup's ready to go?"

"Yup. There's lots. You can drive the truck home and I'll pick it up tomorrow." I looked to Shari. "Can you drive me to the canal?"

She nodded. "Sure."

"Okay." I looked to K'aílaza. "Uncle, we have to go. Isaiah and his brothers will take good care of you and your family."

K'aílaza nodded. "Come see us in a year. Mesa Lake. That's where we'll take Silver."

I shook his hand. "Deal, Uncle. It was an honour meeting you."

He looked at me and smiled. "Oh now," he said. "The honour was all mine."

He held his hand out to the portraits. "These belong in Fort Simmer. Take them. Hang your mother's high, somewhere that can be seen by everyone. She is a hero. A true Yahbati. And return the others to Silver, when he is ready."

"Mahsi cho. I will," I said, "and Uncle, may I please ask, what did that little imp say to you?"

K'aílaza looked to me. "It said it would be back for all of our grandchildren, including yours."

"No," I heard myself say in outrage. I wasn't scared. Now I was just mad.

K'aílaza looked to me and gripped my shoulder. "Unless you find a way to destroy it forever. Go do what you have to do, Lawson Sauren. Master chef. Yabati. Defender of the Edzo and Akaitcho peace treaty." K'aílaza held his arms out and I hugged him. He smelled like moosehide and smoke. "Go now. Save Stanley's soul. Face the Dead One and send him back to whatever hell he crawled up from—for all of our grandchildren."

# Fight Fire with Fire

WHILE SHARI CLOSED HER EYES AND SENSED ALL THAT SHE could, I drove the Midnight Toker and shared my plan with her.

"Oh, I like this," she said. "You're a genius."

"Yeah, a genius who forgot a shovel," I said. "Please tell me you have a shovel."

"Yup," she said. "You can thank my dad later. He's ready for just about anything."

As we got closer to the canal, Shari started to fidget in her seat. Then she went stiff as a board.

"Hey," I said. "Are you okay?

"Oh no," she said with eyes closed.

"What?" I asked.

"This place you're about to return to," she whispered, "it's not just the soul ghoul's den. It's a nest."

Fear juice shot through my heart. "A nest?"

"When you faced it before, did you actually see the Dead One?"

"No."

"But you heard it?"

"Yes," I said.

"What did it ask for—besides souls?" she asked.

"Twenty caribou," I said. "It asked to feed. It said it was hungry."

I had to be careful with how I answered. I did not want to lose any wolf medicine by mentioning the wolves.

"Caribou? To eat?"

"I guess so," I shrugged.

She thought. "Okay. I think I can understand how you're going to soul-dive there, but how will you return from its den?"

"Because I know you'll be waiting, babe," I said. "And that's all I need."

She looked to me to say something else but stopped. Then we started laughing.

"Holy, take it easy there, lover boy."

I gave her a wink and kissed the muscle on my right arm. "The Dene Hawk is gonna bring Sugar Bear home, babe. Don't you worry."

Man, I felt so cheeky, and I didn't know why. Maybe it was the adrenalin. We'd just watched Slitter get annihilated! No. I knew why I was getting goofy. I was gearing up to take on the Dead One, who'd threatened to kill all of our grandchildren.

"Look at you," she said, giving me a playful push. "Yabati. Protector, defender and warrior."

She kissed my cheek and held my hand.

"I am so proud of you, Lawson Sauren. Good spirits are with you."

I squeezed her hand gently and glanced at the framed portrait of my mother tucked safely behind the passenger seat.

"I know."

—

WHEN WE ARRIVED AT THE CANAL, WE FOUND A CLEARING off the road that looked soft enough for digging. I grabbed the shovel and, with the help of adrenalin, quickly scraped and dug a shallow trench that I could lie down in. Then I covered myself with soil and leaves. Shari topped me up, leaving my face free.

I thought of Mom and Cody and their bird medicine and wondered if they could help. I asked Shari if she could sense anything.

"I'm sorry, Lawson. I am not picking up your mom like I used to—or Cody. I think their work is done."

I nodded. As tough as that was to hear, I had my own plan.

She kissed my lips gently. "Good luck. Call for me when you return. You and I have a grad dance to go to together, right, babe?"

I heard the truck doors slam, engine start, and then the tires move away as Shari drove off. I was alone. I cleared my mind. I could see the fading light of Halley's Comet and our family constellation.

As the wind blew through the poplars, spruce and pine, I started to find the quiet inside of me. I had to get to the Beneath.

K'aílaza and his daughters would begin their journey home with Silver. We would see them in a year at Mesa Lake. I was still wearing the necklace of sinew given to me by K'aílaza's daughter. I still had fireweed in both pockets of my jeans. I was still Lawson Sauren.

I settled myself and let my soul dive with faith in all that I had done to be here. I decided to focus deeper into myself than I ever had before. I prayed to the mother of all Dogrib. I prayed to the mother who gave birth to the six pups who were our original ancestors. I prayed to the mother who was banished for her medicine power, the mother who had the gift of giving birth to shape-shifters, our ancestors. I prayed for her strength, and I prayed for my father's fearlessness. I also prayed to the red wolf and her brother for help upon my return to the Dead One.

"Cousins!" I called with a raised voice. "I need your help. Darrel Nets, Sonny Nets Junior, Ray Nets. Nah! Come."

I closed my eyes and called their names over and over, repeating them louder and louder until I felt them approach. When I opened my eyes, they were there sitting near me.

"What're you doing, you?" Darrel asked. I could tell it was Darrel because his face was a bit rounder than his twin's.

"Cousins," I said, "I am a Yabati and defender of the Dogrib and Chipewyan treaty. So is your dad. This means you are, too." They'd shown themselves to me for a reason and this, I believe, was why: to help their father forgive himself and to help me face the Dead One as part of a family of Yabati.

"I welcome you as Yabati," I said. "Help me, cousins. I need you."

They looked at each other with light in their eyes.

"Okay, boss," Darrel said. "How can we help you?"

"Bury my spirit," I said. "I need your help to fight a soul stealer. Do not look into its eyes. Everything it does is meant to trick us so that we can never leave its nest. We need to save a young Chipewyan man—Stanley Cranes. He's weak, so we need to move fast. Once we get his soul back inside him, we can all face the Dead One together. But how do I return to the living world? I don't know. Do you?"

The youngest, Ray, looked to Darrel. Darrel used his index finger to touch his right cheek below his eye until it started to smoke. He then touched my right cheek under my eye, and it started to scorch me. Grey smoke smouldered from my face.

"Ouch! That frickin' hurt, you know!"

Sonny Junior and Ray got the giggles.

Darrel cradled my head and whispered in my ear, "I marked you so we can find you. You're our anchor. Cross over now. Do what you need to do. We will help you, and we'll help you come back all the way."

"Okay," I nodded, as if this made sense.

"Can you please bring Stanley back, too?"

The boys looked to each other.

"We'll do our best, cousin," Sonny Junior said.

I was returning to the twisted forest so much stronger than the first time. I returned to my prayer, and I was angry. Slitter had threatened to come back for all of our grandchildren. We had to destroy the beast who started all of this suffering and warfare. We had to destroy it so it could not cross over and come to our living world. This was all that mattered now. I prayed hard. And as I prayed, I could feel my soul loosen, and I started to float upside down. I could feel my heartbeat: *Lub-dub, lub-dub, lub-dub.*

I heard a loud *whoosh* and experienced the sensation of sinking.

---

WHEN I AWAKE, I FIND MYSELF IN THE DEAD ONE'S NEST, THIS time standing and unbound. I am free, with my back against a huge push-up, facing Stanley and Cody.

*Cody! What is Cody doing here? How did he get here?*

Cody and Stanley stand together facing the tree with vacant eyes. The small fire is still smoking away. Beside the fire is the long, sharp stick that Silver had used to take down Stanley's spirit wrapped in cloth. And beside that is the rolled-up funnel he had used to feed Stanley hot coals.

The Dead One has all three of the Cranes brothers—and now he has me, too. This is a trap. I knew it—I've been tricked by Silver. Everything he told me, everything he begged me for was a lie.

Hanging from trees all around me are the death bundles decorated with jawbones, rib cages and wings, all tied together using long, dark hair. Some are wrapped in rotting skin and hide.

I can't be distracted. I will use everything here to destroy it. If I can free both Cody and Stanley, then we can face the Dead One together—but I need help.

I freeze when I hear something chewing on what sounds like a tree on the other side of the push-up behind me.

Now it sounds like something is raking its teeth back and forth over a tree stump.

I turn to watch a giant hairless bear-like figure sitting with its back to me beside a pile of antlers, near a field of caribou, all lying on their sides. So many caribou. All suffering. I can see the creature's muscles glisten as it works to pull the antlers off a caribou's head. I hear a pop, and the caribou cries out in pain. The creature tosses the antlers on the pile. I can hear the caribou's rasping breath. And on one of the beast's fingers is the silver ring of hair—Silver's hair.

The beast, like a bear born with hands, holds a hoof in its mouth as the caribou struggles, trying to get away. This caribou is one of twenty on their sides, tied down with red willows and ropes of hair. All are panting and terrified. The creature pauses its gnawing to wipe its face, and I notice that it's wearing a cape of maggots. It's infested. This is the Dead One. The rotting bear mask that I saw in the reflection of Stanley's eyes is hanging in a tree beside it. I'm seeing the beast's body for the first time. It stops eating and digs around its own face. I see its long claws reach into its skull and slap both of its shiny eyes on a log beside it with a wet *schlop*.

The eyes of the beast stare upward, and I move farther back behind the push-up. That liquid fear is shooting through my veins again. The Dead One places its lower jawbone on the log beside its eyes. It then thrusts knife-like claws under the caribou's fur. I hear something like carpet ripping and the caribou's cries. The Dead One moans and slurps as it smears crawling maggots in its eye sockets and mouth. All three openings started to chew.

"Cousins, are you here?" I call quietly.

The Dead One's body sways slowly back and forth as it eats, sucking and mashing up as much as it can hold. It swallows in stages, making *glut-glut-glut* sounds. Its throat balloons. Then, to my further horror, its back, a combination of meat, bone and gristle, starts to split—two rips below its shoulder blades as it expands.

This is why it eats our medicine. It needs our medicine to grow to its full power. And once it has consumed what it needs, it will come to our living world and do everything it can to take over.

The Dead One grips the snout of another caribou who lies on its side bucking and struggling on the snow. The caribou seems exhausted from trying to escape. The Dead One squeezes its muzzle and blows breath up its nostrils, causing the caribou to shake. Something moves like little knuckles under the caribou's hide. Soon the caribou's fur is crawling with parasites. There, to the left, are the two wolves: the black one and the red one. Their eyes are glazed over as they look up to the sky in the direction of Halley's Comet.

They must have looked into the Dead One's eyes.

I hear stumbling. Something is tangled in dry willows in the distance. Something off to the right is staggering in deep slush. Four caribou wander around eyeless. All around me, caribou are suffering. I look closer and can see things wriggling out of exposed cuts where it looks like they've been whipped.

Tiny Slitters. They are growing—in the hundreds—as they emerge. Slitter was born through another creature's suffering and fed on its pain. Shari was right: this isn't just the beast's den—it's a nest. The Slitters are its babies. *Gross!*

I start to pray: *Don't leave me, Creator. Please.*

"Darrel, Sonny Junior and Ray," I whisper again. "Cousins, are you with me?"

"Yes," Darrel says.

*Thank God. Okay.*

"Wow," he says, "this place is rank. It's gross here."

"I guess it's a good thing that we're already dead, hey?" Ray asks. "Like, there's no way we could die twice, right?"

"I frickin' hope not," Darrel says.

"Where are we?" Sonny Junior asks, looking around at all the suffering. "Who would do this?"

I point with my thumb in the direction of the creature on the other side of the tree. "That's the Dead One. Don't let it see you," I say quietly. "And don't look into its eyes."

The boys look at the beast.

"Holy frick," Sonny Junior says. "It's chewing with its eyes and mouth?"

"Gross," Darrel says.

"I need to free Stanley and Cody," I say, "and I need you to distract that thing if it comes for me. Grab some sticks. If it comes for you, aim for its head. Confuse it, okay, so it doesn't know where I am."

"Ray," Darrel and Sonny Junior whisper together. "What are you doing? Get back here."

The brothers are motioning for Ray to return to our hiding spot immediately. I peek around the tree to see where he has gone.

Ray Nets snuck up to the Dead One and is now returning with a smile as he squeezes something in his hands.

"Oh god," I say. "Did he just steal—"

"Yup," Ray says. "He just stole the Dead One's eyes."

"What a dweeb," Darrel says. "He never frickin' listens."

Ray walks past us and places his hands in the fire. We hear hissing as the Dead One's eyes begin to bubble and smoke.

"Frick yeah," he smiles proudly. "We don't have to worry about looking in his eyes if he doesn't have any."

I want to get angry and scold him but stop myself. He's right. This is awesome.

"Frickin' deadly, bro," Darrel says.

"Okay," says Ray, "what next?"

I tell them my plan, and the brothers fan out to look for long sticks or sharp poles. The land rises, falls and moans as we hear the Dead One chewing. The wind picks up, causing the death bundles to shiver and rattle.

I start to chant silently to myself: *It's blind, but it can hear us. It has no eyes, but it can still speak. God hates a coward. Protect.*

*Accept. Defend. Think through the fear. Push through the fear. Fear is a gift for focus.*

I cannot be a coward here. I close my eyes and invent my own prayer:

*The red wolf's trust,*
*My mother's hug.*
*My father's love.*
*God hates a coward.*
*Turn my fear into focus. Like Edzo. Like Akaitcho. Like Terry Fox.*
*You are a Yabati.*
*I am a Yabati standing with other Yabati.*
*You have to do this.*
*We have to do this.*
*Protect, respect, defend.*

We need to free Stanley and Cody. It's time. Stanley and that throwing arm of his will protect us once he knows the truth.

And there he is: standing motionless to the right of the tree where his spirit is held captive. Stanley is so still, and his skin is so grey. He's dying. I can see it. He stares with cloudy eyes up at his tree. Every once in a while, he shivers and twitches.

Cody looks fresher. He still has colour, but he has the same glazed eyes. He's been hypnotized by the Dead One.

I can see where I was crucified during my last visit. I can see the hair ropes that Silver used to tie me up. And behind that I can see blood slush where the Dead One drooled when it spoke Cody's name. I look up at the twisted forest's winter sky, and there's Halley's Comet, black and swirling, before it gets swallowed by clouds. Flakes of ash float through the air.

My youngest cousin, Ray, runs through the snow toward me. He carries a long, sharpened stick.

"Who're they?" Darrel asks.

"Stanley and Cody Cranes," I explain, "brothers and defenders of our treaty from the Chipewyan side. Dene Sorulthen."

Neither Stanley nor Cody look at me, even though they should have heard me whispering. They simply stare at the sky, frozen, suspended, gurgling when they struggle to breathe. I want to check if I can see the shelf of branches where Stanley's soul is hidden. I need to wake him up—now. *Where would Cody's soul be hidden?*

"What's wrong with them?" Ray asks.

"Stanley's spirit is up in that tree," I say. "We have to bring it down and get it back inside of him."

Ray gestures toward Cody. "Where's his?"

I shake my head. "I hope it's right beside Stanley's."

The fire pops to life as I near it, and the coals glow beside the spruce funnel that Silver had used to feed Stanley.

"Okay," I take a big breath. "Let's go."

I have to destroy anything that can be used as a tool or weapon in the future. I pick up the sharpened pole beside the fire and am about to nudge the spruce funnel into the fire with my foot when I realize that we can use the red-hot coals to start spot fires. What did Dad say about the fire that claimed the boys' lives? It was a spark from an ember that hit the lint in the vacuum bag. Underneath us, in those push-ups, is hair and fur.

"Darrel," I call quietly.

Darrel comes to me. "Yes, boss."

I point to where the land is split in front of us.

"Every place you see a push-up like that one, use this funnel as a shovel to drop a few of these hot coals in there, okay? We have to burn its nest out from under it."

"You got it," Ray says.

"Done," Darrel says. "Anything else?"

I point at another push-up not too far away.

"Surround the Dead One with fire so the heat pushes it toward us. I want so many root fires that it burns this whole forest down from under it. You hear me? Those poor caribou can't live. Their bodies are infested with its eggs." I look to the caribou, all suffering, and shake my head in pity. "It's too late for them. Everything here needs to die."

He takes the funnel from me and gets to work scooping up red-hot coals and dropping them like little grenades down the push-up closest to us before heading out to start fires farther away, to drive the beast toward us.

I walk through the snow to the tree where I had watched Silver hide Stanley's spirit. Way up high is a bundle of black cloth. I can see it. And right beside it, as I hoped, is a second bundle of black cloth. *That must be Cody's spirit.*

I grip the sharpened pole like a spear and hook the fabric. I lower the bundle gently onto the snow. I then hook Cody's and place it beside his brother's. I unfold both and look: inside each is a light that shines blue, bright blue, like the aurora when it is coldest outside. Stanley's is dimmer than Cody's, and I know Stanley is weaker than Cody, so I'll free him first. I make my way to Stanley and am about to use my own hands to do this, but I stop. I know in a heartbeat and with everything inside of me that if I hold Stanley's soul with my bare hands, I'll never leave here. *I knew it!* Silver had shown me where it was, but that was before he tried trading my soul for Stanley's.

This is a trap. What did the Dead One say? "Good luck getting it back inside him"? Why would it say that? It must have been baiting me. Dad said that with anyone he'd ever fought, he just used their own words against them.

The Dead One's words.

*They're all traps!*

This is what Dave Prince had shown Cody and me and everyone at Tsu Lake when he taught us how to set snares, traps and deadfalls for marten or wolverines. You have to show a prize to anything you want to catch so that instinct and caution are short-circuited by desire.

So if I were to touch Stanley's soul myself, I'd trade my soul for Stanley's. My soul would end up in that tree. That's why Cody's soul is placed beside Stanley's: to make it easy for me to get sloppy, to short-circuit logic with hope.

*How can I return Stanley and Cody's souls back to their bodies safely?*

I look around.

*Think. Think. Think.*

Then I realize that this would have to be done by a spirit. A spirit to return a spirit. That's the key. I look to Ray and point to Stanley's spirit.

"See that? That's Stanley's spirit. I can't touch it. Can you please pick it up and place it back into his body? Can you do that?"

"Sure." Ray nods. He scoops up the warm shimmering light with his bare hands before pressing it into Stanley's chest. I hear Stanley take what must have been the biggest breath of his life. Ray looks at me and smiles. "Well, that was easy. Want me to do Cody?"

"Yes, please."

He does. "Done."

"Thank you, cousin."

"You're welcome," Ray says. "I'll get back to work."

He picks up his sharp stick and uses it like a hockey stick to guide a hot, glowing coal down the push-up nearest to him.

Both Stanley and Cody vomit coals onto the snow. The coals hiss and steam.

"Stanley," I call with absolute relief. I want to cry, I'm so happy. "Cody!"

Both brothers look at me, confused, then look around, blinking their newly clear eyes.

"Lawson?" Cody asks. *There's his voice! Oh, I've missed him!* Cody holds my shoulders as he steadies himself and looks around. "Lawson, where are we? Is this real?" He waves his hand at the ash that's falling around us. "What is that? Snow?"

*Soul ash.*

"Cody," Stanley stammers. "Brother, what happened? Where are we? What the frick happened to me—and my body?" Then he sees Darrel, Ray and Sonny Junior. "Who's with you?" he asks. He squints into the forest as the boys pour more coals down more crevices.

"My cousins," I say. "They're here to help us."

I look up at Stanley. He still towers over me.

"Stanley," I say, "you're safe. You're back."

"Your mom"—he squeezes my shoulders—"she saved me. The last thing I remember was paddling the canoe with your mom when suddenly the water turned black and this wind came out of nowhere. Our boat flipped. My gumboots filled with water, and I couldn't kick them off. Your mom took her life jacket off and handed it to me. Is she safe? Did she make it to shore?"

I close my eyes and shake my head.

"No. She drowned. We lost her. But she did it to save you, and now I need your help."

Tears spring to his eyes, and he hugs me.

"Oh, Lawson. I'm so sorry. She saved me. Your mom gave her life for me. What can I do?"

"It's okay, Stanley. I'm going to help you, but you have to trust me—"

He lets me go and looks around.

"How did we get here?"

How can I begin to answer such a simple question from someone who'd vanished from their own life for the last two years?

Stanley's jaw drops as he stares at something behind me.

"What the hell is that?"

The Dead One is facing our direction and crouching in the snow. It has pulled its bear skull back on. Its maggot-cloaked body does look like a skinned bear with hands. It hunches its back and starts growing. Maggots spill from its body, wriggling and free.

"Silver," it calls. "Did you kill K'aílaza and his family? Did you kill your warriors? Where are my eyes and what are you cooking me? Come to me, my boy." It holds out its clawed hands. "Help me find my eyes."

Darrel is doing a great job of starting root fires. I can see plumes of smoke jetting up from four push-ups. One of the smaller push-ups that's pumping smoke up and out suddenly bursts with a radiant fire: pure orange and yellow. There's no way the Dead One or any of its Slitters will recover from this any time soon.

Darrel runs to me with the funnel. "Good enough, or what?"

"Great job," I reply.

"Who's this?" he asks.

"Darrel Nets, please meet Stanley Cranes and his brother Cody."

Cody shakes Darrel's hand quickly. "Hey."

Stanley nods at Darrel but says nothing. He's stunned by what he sees around him, but also by his body. He has changed so much and is trying to piece together how he ended up here.

"What now?" Darrel asks.

I motion for him to join his brothers.

"Aim for its face with anything you can fire at it, and do not listen to anything it says."

He races to his brothers. Ray hands him a long stick that would be perfect for target practice.

"Get ready," I say to Stanley. "I need you to spear this thing right through the heart, okay? Just like your grandpa and that bear."

"Lawson," Stanley whispers, and I can hear the fear in his voice, "Is this hell? Are we in hell?"

"Holy," Cody says, "this is where the Dead One lives? Wasn't I right, Lawson? Didn't I tell you?"

"Who's there?" the Dead One's voice hisses as he clicks his teeth together. "Wait, I know this scent. I smell you, Dogrib, and I smell—what do I smell? And where are my eyes?"

The Dead One takes a big breath and turns toward me. It holds its thumbs to its ears and spreads its fingers out like spider legs so it can hear better. Each cousin watches in horror as this thing we're about to face starts to grow. First it is as tall and wide as Stanley. Then it grows taller and thicker. Its skin looks like it's bubbling. My cousins all look to me for direction. I motion for each of them to fan out and get ready to attack from a distance. I remind them to aim for its eye sockets and mouth.

"Who's here? Answer me!" the Dead One commands as its head sweeps back and forth, listening to the forest. "Stanley Cranes, Cody Cranes, I smell you, and . . . three burnt boys. Name yourselves."

I hold my finger to my lips to tell to the boys to not answer. I make another motion for them to get ready to attack. They nod that they're ready.

"Now!"

The boys grab skulls and bones and throw them up in the air with their left hands before skilfully blasting them at the Dead One's face with well-aimed swings. Each hit is a solid *crack*, and the boys keep launching at the beast from three different directions. The Dead One swings its head from side to side, clawing at the air and trying to locate where each blast is coming from.

"Take this," I whisper and hand Stanley the sharpened pole I'd just used to free his spirit from the tree. "Remember that story I told you about your grandpa—how he killed that silvertip grizzly out on the Barrenlands?"

He nods. "Yeah. Sort of. Why?"

"Because if this thing kills us here," I say, "it kills us in real life."

"No frickin' way," Stanley says. He grips the long, sharp pole, and I watch him jostle it from hand to hand just like a javelin, just like he used to.

"You have to kill that creature," I hear myself say. "That is the Dead One, and it's kept you here for two years."

"Are you serious?" He looks around. "That thing?"

"Yes," Cody says. "Lawson's right."

"This is not a nightmare," I say. "This is a killing place, and it's all real. You can't miss."

The Dead One is now standing in the snow, where it continues to grow and now produces chattering and clicking sounds.

"Where are my slaves?" it asks. "Stanley and Cody Cranes, defend me. Find my eyes."

*Chatter-chatter.*

*Chatter-chatter.*

*Click-click.*

*Click-click.*

The Dead One's feet curl inward. Its hands move in circles, unravelling something. Unravelling Silver's hair from around its finger. Unspooling it, drawing it out to create a whip.

Stanley positions himself like a warrior and grips the pole, this time not a javelin but a weapon—like Conan would.

"Now, Lawson? Do I kill it now?"

"Stanley!" the Dead One calls. "Come to me."

Darrel, Sonny Junior and Ray work ever faster, blasting the death bundles directly at the Dead One, striking it in the face and eye sockets. The Dead One spins in confused circles, snapping at them, lunging in the directions the boys are firing from. Where it spins, its clawed feet dig up the forest floor under the snow—where, instead of mud, there is only frozen animal fur and human hair. The fur and hair is starting to ignite from the coals dropped into the root systems of the twisted trees. This place is burning, and we can smell it: burning hair is so rank. *This should kill the baby Slitters and end the suffering of the caribou.*

The Dead One's head pops and twists all the way around like an owl's. Its skin is crawling with baby Slitters.

*Click-click.*

*Click-click-click.*

*Chatter-chatter-chatter.*

The clicking—it's clicking its tongue against the roof of its mouth. It's using echolocation like a bat to find us.

The chatter is to gather strength.

"Where are you, Stanley and Cody? And where are my eyes?" the Dead One calls as it continues unravelling the long whip made not only of Silver's hair but also of hair from others who must have trusted it.

"Lawson Sauren destroyed your peace treaty. If he kills me, you'll never leave here."

"That's a lie," I whisper to Stanley and Cody. "My cousins and I are going to bring you home."

Stanley looks at me and nods. "I believe you."

"Me too," Cody says.

The Dead One starts walking toward us, using the *chatter-chatter—click!* to find us. It can smell me. Then I realize that it's smelling the fireweed in my pockets and the necklace K'aílaza's daughter had given me. The Dead One sniffs the air and flicks its whip of human hair. The sound that whip makes when it shoots out shatters the air around us. It's a blast to all of our senses. Stanley, Cody and I all jump.

I yank the sinew necklace off my neck and toss it on the snow in front of us. Then I reach for the fireweed in my pockets, flinging a giant handful as far away from Stanley and me as I can.

"Lawson Sauren!" the Dead One calls out. Its empty eye sockets look for me. "You will be my new war chief. Work for me, and I will give you more power than you could ever imagine."

I look to Stanley and Cody and remind them to remain quiet.

"No?" the Dead One says. "You think you've won? Your people will forget, and I'll just take the North the next time I return."

*No. No. You threatened all of our grandchildren. I cannot let you return.*

I motion to Stanley to get ready.

The Dead One sniffs in the direction of the fireweed before marching toward it and raking at it with its sharp claws. As it stands to its full height, I can see that, though it does look like a bear born with hands and no fur, its skin is that thick moth-like skin that I saw on Slitter. Thousands of Slitter grubs warble under its skin as it moves. I motion to Stanley to spear the Dead One when it charges me.

"Two years," Stanley whispers. "Two years it stole from me."

He's angry now. He plants his feet and begins to focus.

"Show me what you can do, Stanley," I say.

The Dead One opens the slits of its bloody eye holes and calls, "We hear you. We smell you." It starts licking the blood from its cheeks.

"You can do this, Stanley."

"Yes, I can," Stanley says.

"Get ready," I warn.

"I can do this," he says. He nods. He's ready.

"Yes, you can, my brother!" Cody yells.

"I'm here!" I call, and start doing the YMCA dance. "Y-M-C-A!" I form the shapes of the letters with my arms, bending sideways to form the C. "I'm here! Cody, dance with me."

The Dead One changes direction and starts to come closer.

"Come to me, come to me, come to me," it says.

The smell of rot and burning hair blankets us, and my eyes are watering. Cody and I keep doing the YMCA as I breathe through my mouth and call out, "My name is Lawson Sauren and this is Stanley Cranes. I am a Dogrib Yabati. Stanley and Cody Cranes are Dene Sorulthen, and we stand in peace together to face you. With me are three other Yabati: Darrel, Sonny Junior and Ray."

The Dead One starts smacking its lips, widening its jaws until they pop and dislocate and hang crooked from its deformed face, its two tongues twirling like a thorned drill as it tastes the air in front of it.

As the Dead One is preparing to attack and maul me, Stanley pushes me out of the way and spears the sharp pole through the beast's heart. The Dead One staggers, suspended in the air for a few seconds as it struggles, then falls upon the sharp pole, impaling itself like the grizzly Stanley's grandfather killed out on the Barrenlands.

"Whoa," I hear myself say.

"Woo-hoo!" Cody cheers.

Darrel, Sonny Junior and Ray stand with Stanley, Cody and me as we watch the Dead One's face begin to bubble, flare, boil and dissolve. We cover our ears as its piercing scream splits and curls every tree.

We have to burn its body. I've seen enough Friday the 13th movies to know that nothing is officially dead until you cremate it.

"Help me," I say, and we roll its body over to the fire using thick broken branches as levers.

I can see that, like rings in a tree, its body is made of layers of mashed hair and fur. I bet each strand is from someone who'd trusted it. Its body begins to smoke right away, and soon the Dead One ignites. We all jump back. The stench is unbearable.

"That's deader than dead," Darrel says.

"Deader than us, anyway," Sonny Junior says.

Sonny's boys side-eye each other and laugh.

"Wait," Cody says, catching on. "You guys are dead?"

"Yup," Ray says. "Died in a house fire. But it's okay. You can see us, so we're still kind of alive."

"Does that mean we're dead, too?" Stanley asks.

"No," I say. "You're here in spirit form, and we're bringing you back to Fort Simmer."

I nudge the Dead One's braided whip into the fire with my foot, and it catches quickly. My hope is that if it burns here, it will release the grip the Dead One has on Silver and the rest of its spiritual hostages.

"May everyone who trusted the Dead One be released," I pray aloud.

Stanley looks at me. "What the hell was that thing?"

"A soul stealer," I say. "And we just killed it forever. Welcome back, Stanley. You just saved all of us." I look at my cousins. "Cousins, you just saved us, too. Mahsi cho."

Stanley and Cody have to get back to the living world.

"Sonny Junior and Ray," I say, "can you please take Stanley and Cody back? I have one more thing to do. Darrel, can you please wait here and take me back when I'm done?"

"Okay." He nods.

"Lawson." Stanley points. "Look."

We watch as the bodies of the caribou sink into the hollowed burning earth. The land moans. The willows and other trees around us start to melt slowly into the ground. The twisted forest and the nest of the Dead One are dying.

The wolves! I have to save them before they too are swallowed and burned.

I find them both frozen nearby, their eyes glazed over, and I immediately begin untying them from the red willows. I want to be the first thing my red wolf sees when she can see clearly again.

They both start when they come to and smell the smoke. They sit up quickly and look around. They can see the Dead One's body on fire and the trees and the push-ups smoking and burning now from the underground inferno that's still building.

"Hello," I smile. "I'm Lawson Sauren, Yabati and friend."

They both look at me before looking around again.

"I made you a promise and I kept it," I say proudly. "You're free."

"Lawson Sauren," the black wolf says. "Is it done? Did you kill it?"

"Yes," I say. "It's dead. You're free."

"Lawson Sauren," my red wolf says and looks deep into my eyes. "There you are."

"You can go home now," I say. "Go back to your families. Live in peace."

The black wolf nods. "We have to go. This place is burning."

I look to my red wolf, and even though she's panicked, I have to tell her: "I came back for you."

"I know," she says. "I kept calling you and calling you."

"Can you come with us?" I ask her. I'm afraid to look into her eyes because it might make me too shy to talk.

"No. I have to return to my family, but you can call on me when you need my power," she says.

"Sister," the black wolf urges, "we have to go now. Lawson Sauren, we are grateful to you, but we have to return to our homes."

"Can I hug you?" I ask the red wolf.

She nods.

I touch my nose to hers as I hug her. The fire is now surrounding us and the heat is unbearable. Their chance of escape is getting slimmer every second we delay.

"Lawson Sauren," she says, "you saved me, and now I offer my medicine power to you in both the living and spirit worlds. Call me when you need me. We can work together to help those who need it."

This is it. This is my medicine dream. This is exactly what Mom spoke about at Tsu Lake. This is ours together now: me and my red wolf.

"Dìga Dek'o," I say. "That is your name in our language. I want you to know you gave me courage. Mahsi cho."

"We need to go, Lawson. I'm taking you home," Darrel says, and holds me from behind until I can see and feel myself start to vanish. I can feel the forest fade, and I see the red wolf watch me leave. I hear a high-pitched whistle as I close my eyes and feel my soul soar. I am safe. I am held. My spirit cousin has me.

—

AND I RETURNED, STILL BURIED AT THE CANAL, WITH SHIVering stars above, greeting me, welcoming me back to the land of the living—and there was Mom's star, Dad's star and mine.

It was done. We did it. All three Cranes brothers were free. Our treaty had been defended and restored. Holy frickin' moly, we had killed the Dead One.

"Cousin," a voice spoke. It was Darrel. "We did it." All three brothers twirled slowly as their feet left the ground. They spun slowly in the air before sitting beside me and smiling. Each one took turns standing, raising their arms to gather starlight, and then they came to me and brought their armfuls down like they were spilling starlight upon me.

"You have three spirit cousins who are here when you need them," Darrel said.

"You called us. Now we can call you," said Sonny Junior.

"Take care of our dad," Ray said. "Learn everything he would have taught us so we can watch."

"Deal," I whispered. "Cousins." I was so tired.

---

WE ALWAYS HEAL FASTEST UNDER BLANKETS, MOM USED to say.

It took Shari a long time to dig me out of the hole I'd been buried in. I'd been there for two hours, she said, and it was like the earth had claimed me. I could smell the smoke that clung to my clothes and hair as I was dug up. My spirit cousins hooted and howled as I returned to the living.

I don't remember the ride back to my house.

I don't remember Shari brushing me off, taking my jacket, my shirt, my pants and socks off and tucking me in, lying with me.

All I remember is waking up in my room with Shari sleeping beside me, all curled up, holding my hand. I had pine needles in my hair, just like Mom when she returned from the Border. And I was changed forever.

# We Are the Champions

TWO DAYS LATER, AFTER I HAD RESTED COMPLETELY, I DROVE Ragged Glory to Benji's Body Shop. I told Benji what I wanted, and he called his mechanics in for a huddle. The mechanic with the handlebar moustache smiled and rubbed his palms together.

"Oh, man," he said. "Are you kidding me? Sonny's war pony? Do you know how long I have wanted to restore this classic beauty?"

They looked at each other and nodded in agreement.

"Have fun with it," I said. "Soup it up, please."

He blushed and eyed the hood. "You got it."

Benji was all business. "And who's paying? Your pops?"

"My mom," I said.

Benji looked at me with sudden tenderness. He had been at Mom's funeral, along with the whole town.

"After my mom passed, I got an inheritance," I said, and dry-swallowed. "This is her grad present to me."

"When's the grad dance?" asked Benji.

I thought about it. "June 29?"

"So, next year?" asked Benji.

The mechanics looked at each other again.

"We have some time," the darker one said. He looked Native. Maybe Chipewyan. Maybe Cree.

"Got a date for the prom?" the guy with the moustache asked.

"Yes, sir," I said.

They smiled.

"Okay," Benji said. "Leave 'er with us and we'll work out a deal. Cash is king on this one. Got it?"

"Got it," I nodded. "Can I ask a special favour?"

"What did you have in mind?" asked Benji.

I pointed to the hood ornament. "I'd like to return this muffaloose to Sonny. Do you know who made it for him?"

"Yeah," Benji nodded. "Casey's Customs in Edmonton."

"Can you work with them to make me something new?"

"Sure," he said, taking out his notepad. "What would you like?"

"I'd love a red wolf running into a storm," I said. "I want her to look fearless."

The men all looked to each other and howled.

"Ho-HO! Take it easy," said one of the mechanics.

"Fearless, no less," Benji grinned. "I like it. I like it."

I nodded with a grin. "Please."

"Casey loves a challenge, Lawson," Benji said, and we all shook hands. "Consider it done."

---

SHARI AND I WERE GETTING READY TO GO TO THE PINEBOUGH together. It was the fanciest restaurant in town. I wanted something nicer than just a burger, fries and gravy with her. I wanted to feast with her to celebrate what we'd faced together, how we worked as a team—and I wanted to show the town that we were a couple. I was nervous and excited, but it was time to enjoy being seventeen, about to start grade twelve.

Shari had already started walking and met me halfway. She reached out and touched gently where Darrel had marked the cheek beneath my eye in the spirit way.

"Hello, handsome," she said.

I looked around and made sure the coast was clear—no dads to spy on us—to sneak a kiss, then another, then another, each one longer and deeper.

This was fun, being teenagers on the keemooch who'd just stopped an ancient beast from enslaving the world.

I started shivering for her and she pulled me closer.

"I'm so yours," she said, then looked a bit embarrassed. She was flushed and leaned into me.

"Shari Burns," I said, "are you blushing?"

"Just a little."

We held hands and started walking to the Pinebough.

"You know," she said, "one day you should write about this and tell the world what happened."

"That we faced a soul stealer together and beat it?"

"Yeah," she said.

"No one would ever believe it," I said.

As we walked, I touched under my right eye where Darrel spirit-marked me. I had a light dent in my right cheek now. It was Darrel's fingerprint.

"I'll always have this spirit mark as a reminder of everything that happened and what we faced together," I said.

She stopped walking, turned to face me and touched it again.

"I like it," she said. "Um, and you know your three cousins are following us, hey?"

I turned and there they were: the speckled dead, my spirit cousins.

"Yes."

"So," Shari asked, "will they always be around?"

I shrugged and spoke politely: "Guys, can I please have a few hours alone with my girlfriend? I'm taking her on a date."

They looked at each other and nodded, then waved and walked away. I waved back and Shari did, too.

"Where do they go?" I asked her.

"Oh," she said, "probably to check up on their dad."

Darrel, Sonny Junior and Ray had told me they still had work to do here. I'd tell Sonny everything about his boys when the time felt right.

"You know what you are, Lawson?" she said with a smile. "You're an off-duty angel with the heart of your ancestors."

"Oh now, I think I'm just a proud Yabati," I replied.

"Yes, you are, but I'm serious," she said. "I have a feeling that if anything ever tries to destroy peace here in the North, you, me, Isaiah and our families—and others like us—will use our gifts to stop it."

*Others like us. Wow. Other Yabati, other Dene Sorulthen—other protectors defending peace.*

We would travel next year to Mesa Lake to visit K'aílaza and his family. I'd bring Cody and Stanley. We all needed to talk, and I looked forward to seeing Silver. I was rooting for him now that K'aílaza and his family had him. Hopefully he could reclaim his life in a good way.

The necklace that K'aílaza's daughter had given me did not return with me from the twisted forest. It must have burned along with the fireweed. And there was something new about me besides the spirit mark on my face. That morning I'd noticed that I didn't have just one chest hair anymore—I had two!

Speaking of change, Dad told me that he was having Starla over on Saturday to make proper introductions, and that I could bring Shari. We agreed that perhaps it was time to take Mom and Dad's wedding photos down, and I could have them when I left for my own home. Before I met Starla, he said, we should have a burning and return what Mom needed to her on the other side. After, he said, we could go to the graveyard and offer tobacco and fresh fireweed, and then we could plan a giveaway for the rest of her stuff. I told him that this all sounded good to me. Dad reminded me that Mom's medicine bag was already mine to claim, which was good, as I had already moved it into my room, hanging it high over the shelf filled with all of my Conan comics.

Sonny was stopping by later. He'd made dry meat and wanted us to try his new recipe. This was also the day I'd return the ZZ Top tape he'd left in his truck along with his muffaloose hood ornament.

Dad said we should donate Mom's jackets, sweaters, mitts, snowshoes and camping gear to the women's shelter in town. She would have loved that. I didn't know what to do with other things, like all the photos of her around the house, but Shari told me that I didn't need to have all the answers today. Whenever I missed Mom I would inhale the sweet aroma of fireweed or wave to a chickadee. She was everywhere now, and her name and legacy would soon be honoured in the renaming of the renovated Friendship Centre. Dad and I had made the decision together.

—

"HEY," SHARI SAID AND POINTED WITH HER CHIN. STANLEY Cranes was standing at the four-way stop. Cody was with him. They were holding two bouquets of flowers. They both turned to us, smiled and called out together, "Hey, lovebirds!"

Cody approached me first. He placed his hand on my shoulder, and I did the same to him.

"So, you're still alive," I said.

"So, *you're* still alive." He smiled and nodded.

"What you up to?" I asked them.

Cody looked to Stanley, who looked handsome with a fresh haircut.

"We're going to visit Mom and Dad," said Cody.

"Oh," I said, wondering if this would be the first time Stanley would visit his parents' gravesites. "I'm sorry," I said. "You two have my deepest condolences."

"Thanks," Stanley said. "Thank you."

"Thank you, Lawson," Cody said. "You saved my brothers. Did our spirit helpers come to you? Me and your mom's? The chickadee and the swallows?"

"They sure did, buddy. Mahsi cho."

Cody and I hugged. He looked at the dent in my face where Darrel had touched me.

"And this? Did Silver do this?"

"Oh," I said, "that's a longer story. For tomorrow? Lunchtime? Stop by the house. Right now, we're off to the Pinebough. Shari and I are on a date."

"Oh, we're officially on a date, are we?" Shari asked cheekily. "Does this mean we get to sit on the fancy side?"

It was the snazziest Fort Simmer tradition: when you were no longer on the keemooch with someone and you wanted to make it official, you took them from the café side of the Pinebough to the smorg side, where they had classier forks and knives, and cloth napkins.

"It would be my honour," I smiled.

Shari held out her hand and I took it, and together we walked in a sunbeam. I thought of Dìga Dek'o, my red wolf, and trusted that she was home with her pack and safe with her brother. I had a feeling that one day I'd ask for her help again and she would answer. My spiritual connection to her was something I would have the rest of my life to enjoy. I'd never tell anyone about my bond with Dìga Dek'o.

Speaking of bonds, I smiled as I remembered my talk with my dad that morning.

"Dad," I'd asked, "is Sonny your best friend?"

Dad had thought about it and then said, "Maybe."

"Everyone needs a best friend," I'd said, and then I thought about it too. "Wait. Am I your best friend?"

My dad had hugged me. "You're more than my best friend. You're my son."

Looking forward, I realized grade twelve was going to be so rad: Shari Burns as my nicimos, the Valentines, the Cranes—with our peace treaty renewed—my spirit cousins, my customized and super-modified Ragged Glory, and Dìga Dek'o by my side if I needed her. Who knew that after all our losses and battles, everything we'd faced and gone through together, life could be so sweet?

A MESSAGE TO YOU IF THE DEAD ONE EVER RETURNS:

Please don't let our peace treaties with each other fade.
Don't let the ways of the Yabati and the Dene Sorulthen die.
Protect, accept, respect and forgive.

Be the medicine the world needs.

Lead with love.

Sigha naxixè welè.

Peace be with you.

Mahsi cho.

# Acknowledgements

IT WAS TŁĮCHǪ ELDER THERESE (TERRI) NASKAN WHO TOLD me about the Yabati, the protectors and warriors of the Dogrib—now known as the Tłı̨chǫ Dene—and I am forever grateful to you. Mahsi cho. I would like to thank Chief Fred Sangris for sharing his wisdom and insights with me on how the peace treaty between Edzo and Akaitcho came to be. I am grateful to Henry and Eileen Beaver for their master storytelling and guidance during all these blessed years together. Eileen, mahsi cho for writing out everything I asked you to in the Chipewyan language. Willie Sellars, mahsi cho for being our cultural consultant for grass-dancing regalia information and protocols. I would like to acknowledge Don and Sandra Jaque and the entire team of the *Slave River Journal* for giving us forty years of print and online history of our community: Fort Smith, NWT. Crystal Benwell, mahsi cho for bringing me up to Fort Smith so I could inhale the land I grew up in. I am indebted to the Dragon family in Fort Smith for sharing that fireweed was originally one of the offerings for "paying the land" for a safe journey in the South Slave Region of Denendeh. I am grateful to my wife, Keavy Martin, and our sweet miracle, Edzazii Van Camp, for their faith in me and for all their cheerleading. I am also grateful to Tony Rabesca and Rosa Mantla, my Tłįchǫ Elders, and for my Tłįchǫ language teachers, Georgina Franki and Rosie Benning. As well, I am grateful to my agents, Janine Cheeseman and Tracy Essex-Simpson, for helping me hone this manuscript numerous times. To my publisher, Anna Comfort O'Keeffe, I am so eternally grateful to you for championing this novel and for your editing prowess. To Barbara Pulling, Emma Skagen, Noel Hudson, Alicia Hibbert and Lynn Rafferty, thank you all for helping me to take this story where it deserved to go. To my publicist, Corina Eberle, thank you. A huge mahsi cho to each and every one of you. All of you RULE!! I'd like to also thank Jackie Baker, Susie Moloney, Lianna Ryan, Lara Apps and Scotty Olsen for their encouragement and early readings of this manuscript. I'm grateful to Fort Smith: the land, the people, our ancestors. To my fellow Dene, Métis, Inuit and northerners, may we continue to honour and celebrate our friendship treaties for all future generations to learn from. Mahsi cho.

Oh, by the way, I cranked Courage My Love, all my favourite tunes from the '80s and the Deftones as I worked on this, and I hope you crank them, too. I really want to thank Stephen King, Mike Grell, and Ernest Cline as well, for a lifetime of inspiration and I'd like to thank Chief Lady Bird for a very cool cover.

I acknowledge that we, as Tłįchǫ Dene, were called Dogrib years ago because of our creation story. This novel is set in 1986, and Dogrib is what we were called then.

All mistakes in this novel are my own.

Mahsi cho and with utmost respect,
Richard Van Camp

https://spoti.fi/4bAtPzo

bitly

William Au photo

A recipient of the Order of the Northwest Territories of Canada, **Richard Van Camp** is a proud Tłı̨chǫ Dene from Fort Smith, NWT. He is the author of thirty books. His novel *The Lesser Blessed* (D&M, 1996) was made into a feature film by First Generation Films. His collection of short stories *Moccasin Square Gardens* (D&M, 2019) won both the CODE Burt Award for First Nations, Inuit, and Métis Young Adult Literature and a 2020 Alberta Book Award. You can visit Richard on Facebook, X, Instagram, SoundCloud, YouTube and at his official website, www.richardvancamp.com.